RATED

RATED

MELISSA GREY

SCHOLASTIC PRESS * NEW YORK

Library of Congress Cataloging-in-Publication Data available

ISBN 978-1-338-28357-0

10 9 8 7 6 5 4 3 2 1   19 20 21 22 23

Printed in the U.S.A. 23

First edition, September 2019

Book design by Christopher Stengel

FOR MY DAD—
THANK YOU FOR SUPPORTING
MY WEIRD HOBBIES
AND TEACHING ME RIGHT
FROM WRONG

There is peace in dungeons, but is that enough to make
dungeons desirable?
—Jean-Jacques Rousseau, *The Social Contract*

RATED

PROLOGUE

THE RATINGS ARE NOT REAL.

The words were written across the front doors of Maplethorpe Academy when students arrived on the first day of school. The spray paint was a lurid red against the dark wood, dripping to the white marble steps like freshly spilled blood. Graffiti was a rare sighting in that part of town, but not one that was unheard of altogether. The perpetrators were usually apprehended in short order thanks to the cameras mounted around the property, recording each and every moment that transpired within and directly outside those hallowed halls. The culprits typically belonged to one of a few categories: bored kids with more privilege than sense wanting to rattle their parents'—and their own—sterling ratings, a renegade Unrated who somehow made it past the security guards, a delinquent student on the cusp of losing their own rating and wanting to go out with a bang and not a whimper.

It was almost impossible to escape the notice of those blinking red eyes that never tired, never faltered. The cameras were pointing directly at the spot where the graffiti artist must have stood while he—or she—vandalized the towering mahogany doors. Their lenses should have received a crystal clear portrait of the person who'd defaced the school. If not those cameras, then the others, positioned at regular intervals along the wrought-iron gates circling the school's verdant lawns, should have committed the crime to their digital memories. The case should have been closed within hours, maybe less. Just as long as it took for the headmaster to alert campus security and for them to track down whoever did it. Except for one minor detail.

The stickers.

They were plastered on the lenses of the cameras, obscuring their view. The faces of jesters in garish red-and-white masks, grinning down on the scene as if it were all part of one big joke. And maybe it was. Because if there was one thing everyone at Maplethorpe Academy knew, it was that the ratings were very, very real. And the ratings were everything.

CHAPTER 1
BEX JOHNSON

RATING: 92

It was the first day of school, the glorious start of a new semester, that time of year when the humidity of summer faded to a fond memory and the air held the promise of a brisk autumn chill. For Bex Johnson, it was the beginning of her senior year. She fidgeted in her seat on the bleachers, the energy of a shiny new semester buzzing in her veins, awash in possibility. She watched as students filed through the row of doors on the left side of the gymnasium, each wearing a navy-blue blazer, the rich color accented by the maroon-and-gold crest of Maplethorpe Academy on their chests. They didn't have a uniform so much as a loosely enforced dress code, but the blazer was a tradition. It was a symbol of the school's prestige and long history. Bex loved the feel of hers, the rough texture of the dark wool, the crispness of the lapels, the raised embroidery of the stitched crest. It reminded her of her place in the world, of her ranking at school. She took pride in it, in what it symbolized. Her parents wore the same blazer during their days as students at Maplethorpe, and all she wanted—all she'd ever wanted—was to make them proud.

Pride was sparingly dispensed in the Johnson household. It was treated as a finite resource, something to be distributed only in extraordinary circumstances. Bex had to fight for every scrap of it. Sometimes, doubt niggled at her mind. That she would never live up to her parents' lofty expectations, or that nothing she did would be enough to satisfy them. But it was simply the way things were done in their family. Bex's wildly accomplished parents held themselves to a high standard and expected nothing less from their own flesh and blood. Bex would simply need to work harder this year than she ever had before.

As her father liked to say, *A Johnson can always work more, do more, and be more.*

And so Bex was going to dominate this semester and the next. She would not be stopped or slowed down or distracted.

Her best friend had other ideas.

Melody leaned against Bex's shoulder, her breath warm against Bex's ear as she stage-whispered, "I wonder who did it."

The words were all but lost in the cacophony of morning assembly as students filed into Maplethorpe's gym and tramped up the bleachers to their seats. Freshmen were against the far wall, then sophomores, juniors, and finally seniors closest to the entrance. Bex remembered the giddy feeling of advancement every time she moved along the bleacher seats at the start of each year. Freshman students were ensconced in the deepest part of the gym, while each year saw the classes get closer and closer to the door until they were gone, off to bigger and better things after graduation.

Students flowed around Bex and Melody where they sat, seeking their own seats and shouting to the friends they hadn't seen since the end of spring semester, separated by the long reprieve of summer and whatever activities had dominated those warm, sunny months. Part-time jobs, volunteering gigs, math camp, drama camp, band camp. There was a camp for everything. In Bex's case: space camp. The kind meant to entertain not starry-eyed little kids but the more sophisticated sort that was actually concerned with teaching gifted participants what it took to become scientists exploring the far reaches of space.

Headmaster Wood climbed the steps to the dais upon which he led morning assembly. He cut a striking figure in his tailored cream suit, his bald head gleaming mahogany under the gym's fluorescent lights, his goatee freshly trimmed. He didn't look like a teacher, or at least none that Bex had ever encountered. She wondered if the shaved head and artful facial hair were an attempt to maintain an image of coolness, of approachability. He was young, younger than the school's last headmaster. Bex once caught him sipping coffee from a mug that boasted *You Put the Pal in Principal*, even though he was technically not a principal. He was a headmaster. It was the sort of linguistic detail Bex couldn't *not* notice.

The headmaster waited a moment for the students to settle themselves, but when the soft buzz of conversation failed to die down completely, he held up his hands in the universal gesture for silence. He leaned toward the microphone mounted on the podium and fixed each grouping of students with a hard glare.

"I'm sure that by now you've all either seen or heard of the recent incident of vandalism on campus."

A burst of frenzied whispers erupted from the assembled students, but it faded when Headmaster Wood very pointedly cleared his throat.

"As if anyone could have not seen it," Melody whispered into Bex's ear once everyone else had fallen silent. Bex hushed her, but it was too late. Wood's eyes cut to them, picking the source of the sound out of the crowd with uncanny precision. Without missing a beat, he tapped on the face of the device on his wrist, once, twice, then swiped down on the screen. A subtle vibration against her wrist alerted Bex to a shift in her rating. She looked down at her own smartwatch.

The display lit up. The number had changed. A glowing 91 stared back at her, and her stomach seized at the sight of it. One minute into the semester and she'd already been docked a point because her best friend couldn't keep her mouth shut.

"Oops," Melody murmured, her gaze angled down at her own rating, which Bex assumed reflected a single point loss as well. It wasn't a big deal, not really. Minor disciplinary infractions usually expired by the end of the day. With luck, she would be back at 92 by eighth period, but it still stung. Bex huffed and looked back up to find Headmaster Wood lifting a single eyebrow in her direction. She shifted in her seat. Wood continued with his speech, unperturbed by her discomfort.

"I don't think I need to remind you that the punishment for defacing school property will be harsh and swift. Not only would such a student face immediate expulsion, but a disciplinary infraction of that magnitude would leave a permanent stain on one's rating."

The threat was enough to send a palpable, collective shiver across the student body.

The ratings were not taken lightly, no matter how many stupid stickers were deployed in an effort to make fun of them. Most people hovered in the mid-range for most of their lives—

40s, 50s, 60s—but the expectations for students at Maplethorpe were higher, especially by graduation. The school had boasted a graduation average of 72 for the past couple of years, and Headmaster Wood had seemed determined to raise it even higher since his tenure began when Bex was a freshman.

"And that's all I have to say about that." Wood straightened his already-straight tie. "I see no reason why this one act should cast a pall on the rest of our year." He spread his arms wide and smiled benevolently, but his gaze was still sharp as it raked across the gymnasium. "With that unpleasantness out of the way, we can move on to happier topics, like the upcoming Founder's Day Festival. The planning committee is looking for volunteers for the dance, so all interested students should speak to the committee chair, Summer Rawlins."

A redheaded girl waved from her seat on the dais. A few heads of school clubs sat there during assembly if they had announcements to make. Bex would soon, once it came time to recruit new members for the *Lantern*, the school newspaper.

Founder's Day was the most sacred day on the Maplethorpe calendar. It commemorated the birth of John Maplethorpe, the founding father of both the academy that bore his name and the Rating System that governed seemingly every aspect of life. He'd been a genius, an innovator, and a philanthropist. His brilliance was marked with both an annual festival and a marble bust of his likeness in the school's foyer. It was the first thing every student saw when they entered and the last thing they saw when they left.

"This semester may have had a rocky start," Wood continued, "but I'm sure we can get it back on track in no time. Consider this a very warm welcome back to Maplethorpe

Academy. I look forward to seeing each of you shine brightly over the course of the coming year."

Polite applause shepherded the headmaster away from the podium as he stepped aside. Then the president of the student council skipped forward to make the more mundane announcements.

Bex let the president's voice drone on in the background as she peered down at her smartwatch. It was set to School Mode, which meant all incoming calls would immediately be sent to voicemail and her email notifications would go off only at the end of eighth period, so as not to distract her. The home screen on her device displayed the same thing as everyone else's: her rating. But unlike every other junior in her school last year, Bex had cracked the 90s at the end of last summer. She stared at the number, letting the reality of the 91 sink in. It wouldn't be easy to maintain it over the course of the year, but achieving a number so high in the first place hadn't been easy either. If Bex could keep up the good work, not get distracted, and maybe even add a few points to her score, her future was bound to be the brightest of any student at Maplethorpe Academy.

"You never answered my question."

The words cut through Bex's focus, threatening to interrupt the mantra she liked to repeat in her head every morning before first period.

Good grades mean good ratings. Good ratings mean a good college. A good college means a good life.

Bex's locker door rattled with the force of Melody's shoulder smacking into the one beside hers. Her best friend never did anything quietly. Her arrivals were always marked with forceful nudges, or books jovially slammed onto tables, or her own body falling dramatically against a wall of lockers.

Today, Melody drummed the fingers not holding a half-eaten lollipop against the burgundy metal of Bex's locker door, punctuating her impatience.

"What question?" Bex asked, not lifting her eyes from her tablet's screen. Her schedule—color-coded for easy reading—was filled from end to end with different shades of pastel. Blue for her classes, pink for extracurriculars, yellow for volunteering, green for tutoring at the middle school, and lilac for independent study. In theory, white rectangles meant a free period, but she didn't have one of those this week. Or next week. Or any week in the foreseeable future. The hours stretched out on the screen like a cheerful rainbow of activity. No one hit the 90s halfway through high school by taking a nap between chemistry and comparative literature.

"Are you serious?" Melody pulled the lollipop out of her mouth with an audible pop. Bex met her friend's incredulous stare. Melody's watermelon-pink nail polish perfectly matched the spit-slick lollipop. Bex didn't eat sugar the way Melody did. It rotted the teeth, and Bex hadn't had a cavity since kindergarten. Tooth decay, her father liked to say, was a personal failing.

"The graffiti on the front doors, Re-bec-ca. Who do you think did it?"

Melody stretched out the syllables of Bex's name. She did that whenever she thought Bex was being particularly obtuse. As if Bex had time to keep abreast of every exciting scandal.

"Oh," Bex said, turning her attention back to the tablet. "That." There was a ten-minute gap between morning assembly and first period to give students time to get their books from their lockers and organize themselves for the day ahead. Bex's mind had already course corrected to focus on her next period, though now the headmaster's words came back to her. Wood had made sure to emphasize the seriousness with which violations of the school's honor code were handled. The warning had settled deep in Bex's gut, chilling her to her core. She shuddered at the thought of what getting kicked out of school would do to a person's rating. Wood was right. It was the sort of stain that would never wash clean. "It was probably just someone messing around."

Melody heaved a dramatic sigh and tossed her long black hair into the open door of Bex's locker. She liked flipping her hair; it made a show of how perfectly long and thick and straight it was, like a waterfall of black ink. Bex's own hair never flipped like that. Her curls answered to no master, not even the person to whose head they were attached. Melody stuck the lollipop back in her mouth, obviously disappointed in Bex. Speculation had gripped the rest of the student body, but she just honestly didn't have time.

Bex had more pressing things to think about. Like the fetal pig they were going to dissect in Advanced Placement Biology this semester. The notion made something churn unpleasantly in Bex's stomach, but she did her best to push her unease far, far down. The same way she had last night during dinner. She hadn't been able to touch the pork chop on her plate, knowing that in a few weeks her scalpel would be slicing open a soft pig belly.

When she'd tentatively raised the issue with her mother—a neurosurgeon—Bex had been met with a gentle, condescending pat on her shoulder. If she couldn't handle a fetal pig, then she wouldn't be able to handle an actual human cadaver in medical school. Her parents never chided or berated or yelled. They simply reminded Bex that everything she did was in the service of her future. She could deal with a little discomfort for a good grade.

Good grades mean good ratings. Good ratings mean a good college. A good college means a good life.

"But why write that?" Melody wondered aloud. "'The ratings are not real'?"

She tapped her finger against the screen strapped to her wrist by a rainbow-striped band. It was so vibrant compared to the plain black of Bex's wristband. Melody herself always seemed so vibrant compared to Bex. Her grades might not be better, but her social scores were considerably higher. Bex hoped that some of Melody's affability would rub off on her over the course of the year. Positivity was nearly as important as an impressive academic performance, after all. "The ratings are super real, whether they like it or not. See?"

The small screen came alive under Melody's finger. A number blinked into existence as Bex watched. 76. Not bad.

"You're up two points from last semester," Bex remarked. "Nice work."

Melody rolled her eyes; once again Bex had focused on exactly the wrong thing. Considering how wildly their priorities differed, it was an expression Bex had come to know well. "Thanks. Drama camp was quite the success. The counselors loved me."

11

As if there had ever been any doubt they would. Bex smiled, glad her friend was doing so well. "They'd be idiots not to. Everyone loves you."

Melody waved away the compliment, but Bex noticed a pleased flush rise in her cheeks. Melody wanted to be liked the same way Bex wanted to excel. It was a primal need. A craving that had come to define her personality. "Yeah, yeah. I'm more interested in our resident street artist. You still haven't told me who you think did it."

Bex slipped her tablet into her backpack, along with the books she would need for the first two periods. Literature and history. Nice, easy subjects to start the day. She shrugged. "Who knows? Probably just some dumb kid looking for attention."

Melody leaned closer to whisper her next words. "Or an Unrated. I heard the cops arrested some at the park trying to protest." She leaned back against the lockers and blew an errant lock of her hair off her forehead. "Can you imagine? Standing outside all day like that, advertising how much you've failed at life. I honestly feel kind of bad for them."

"I don't know why they bother," Bex said. "The protesters, not the police. Maybe if they'd spent the amount of time working on their own ratings as they did whining about them, they wouldn't be in that situation to begin with."

Melody raised her eyebrows. "Getting a little frosty there, Ice Queen Rebecca? That's not like you."

Bex zipped up her backpack and hefted it over her shoulder. "I know it sounds unkind." Especially from someone who volunteered every Saturday morning at a soup kitchen for the local Unrated. "I'm just stressed out. School stuff."

"Always, with you," Melody said, but there was no venom in the words. Melody was the fun one. Bex was the smart one. Their relationship had been based on that divide ever since they'd exchanged sloppily made friendship bracelets in first grade. Bex pulled Melody up beside her—getting her to study when she'd rather procrastinate, and dragging her to help out at volunteering opportunities—while Melody softened Bex's harder edges. The arrangement worked for them.

Sometimes, though, Bex envied Melody. Her mother was a sculptor and her father did graphic design. In all the time Bex had spent at Melody's house, she'd never once heard them discuss their daughter's schoolwork or prospective colleges. During one memorable dinner, Melody's mother had described grades as demoralizing. The concept was utterly foreign to Bex, that life could exist without an array of numbers to quantify every facet of it.

The bell rang, signaling the three-minute mark until the beginning of first period. Bex slammed her locker door shut and began striding down the hall. Melody kept pace with a skip in her step.

Bex would have to stop by her locker after second period to pick up her bio textbook. An image flitted through her mind: small unborn pigs, their sightless eyes filmy and half-closed, all packed into a tub. A shiver danced along her spine. Science. It was just science. And science was Bex's thing. She could do it and do it well. She had to do it.

Her rating depended on it.

Her *life* depended on it.

CHAPTER 2

NOAH RAINIER

RATING: 65

There was a certain beauty to being invisible.

Noah found that it was easy to see people—really see them—when they didn't see you back. When you were invisible, you had the luxury of witnessing people in their natural habitats, unguarded and unpolished. When people knew they were being watched, they behaved differently. They performed.

But Noah preferred truth to performance. And he didn't just want to see it. He wanted to record it, to seal that one perfect moment in celluloid and silver. He hefted the camera he never went anywhere without—a vintage Leica gifted to him by his father—and framed the shot.

He stood under the shadow of a copse of trees, within comfortable viewing range of Maplethorpe's front doors, but well outside the *un*comfortable viewing range of the headmaster's office. The windows overlooked the school's entrance, but a towering oak blocked the line of sight at a certain angle. It was within that angle's protection that Noah camped.

THE RATINGS ARE NOT REAL.

The graffiti wouldn't last long. Imperfection had a short shelf life at Maplethorpe. Desks that had been marred by sloppily etched declarations of love (*D ♡ J 4EVER*) were carted out of the building in the dead of night, replaced by brand-new ones come morning. Imperfect students, whose ratings fell below Maplethorpe's bare minimum allowance of 20, were whisked away to reform schools to be melted down and remolded in society's image. In theory. Noah had never seen anyone return from expulsion. He had his own ideas about what happened to those kids. His current favorite was that they were turned into some kind of Soylent Green–type meal replacement drink. It was a little ghoulish, but there was no harm in a good conspiracy theory.

Already, a member of the school's janitorial staff was hurrying to the scene of the crime, arms laden with cleaning supplies. The wooden doors and marble steps would be pristine by the end of first period.

The student body wouldn't be as easily scrubbed of its memory. Several teachers were trying to corral stragglers into the building, reminding them that missing morning assembly was an offense punishable by a full point shaved from their rating. But it was thankless work. This single act of vandalism was probably the most exciting thing to ever happen on a first day at Maplethorpe Academy. People would drink it up, savoring its illicit flavor as long as they could.

And Noah would photograph it, as he did all things worth recording. He would treasure the preserved image, would puzzle over its hidden meaning from the comfort of the darkroom his father had helped him construct in their basement. He'd develop it later, after he visited his little sister in the hospital. She'd never forgive him if he failed to pass on this juicy bit of gossip as soon as possible.

None of the teachers noticed Noah. If they saw him standing by the trunk of the massive oak, their minds erased the image as soon as it developed. Noah had refined the art of casual anonymity over the course of his young life. His invisibility was both a blessing (people didn't see him if he didn't want to be seen) and a curse (people didn't see him when they really ought to).

Noah was about to press down on the camera's shutter release when a much larger, broader body slammed into his shoulder. The camera slipped from his nerveless fingers to land in the grass at his feet.

"Watch where you're going, creeper."

A clump of baseball players passed Noah by, following in the wake of their leader, Reeve or Steve, or whatever his name was. One of them shot Noah an apologetic look over his shoulder as he mouthed the word *sorry*. Noah was pretty sure that one's name was Chad or Chase. The uniforms made them blend together.

Noah watched them walk away, the maroon of their letter jackets bright in the morning sun. Technically, the school had a dress code, not a uniform. Ninety percent of the student body wore blue blazers with a nice pair of trousers or a skirt, and a button-down shirt. The athletes, especially the male ones, opted for their letter jackets. Since they bore the emblem of Maplethorpe on their breasts, this fell within the limits of allowable outerwear. And there was a certain prestige that accompanied a letter jacket. Noah tried not to be jealous of the privileges afforded Maplethorpe's star athletes, but sometimes it wasn't easy. Nobody ever purposefully collided with somebody wearing one of those jackets.

With a sigh, he knelt down to pick up his camera. But a quick pair of hands beat him to it. Hands with long, elegant fingers, like a pianist might have.

"Jocks, am I right?"

Noah's eyes darted up to the owner of those hands.

Javier Lucero.

Those four words were the first Javier had ever spoken to him. Noah's long-standing shyness didn't exactly invite conversation.

"I . . ."

Noah's voice came out in an embarrassing croak, as if it had fled at the sight of this very good-looking human taking notice of Noah when he least expected it.

Javier's hazel eyes danced with commiseration and amusement.

The boy was holding the Leica out to Noah, seemingly unperturbed by the fact that Noah hadn't yet reached out to accept it. He blinked. Noah blinked. After a second that stretched to its fullest capacity, Noah took the camera, giving it a cursory examination for dents or scratches. It *seemed* fine.

Noah cleared his throat before attempting to speak again. "Thanks . . . Javier."

A smile worked its way across Javier's lips, stretching along his bronze skin like a charmed snake. "Call me Javi."

He didn't wait for Noah to call him Javi. Or to call him anything. He winked. He *winked*. And then he left, ambling toward the school with a quick, unselfconscious glance back at Noah.

Without pausing to think about it, Noah raised his camera and snapped a picture of Javi.

Only when Javi smiled at him, raising his hand in a jaunty little salute before turning away, did Noah realize how taking the other boy's picture like that was probably a weird thing to do. Capturing candid photographs of people when they weren't looking was one thing. But this was different.

He hadn't bothered framing a shot. He hadn't worried about lighting or f-stops or apertures. He'd just seen something—someone—beautiful and wanted to remember the moment, even if the picture wasn't perfect.

An unfamiliar sensation marched across Noah's skin.

He hadn't simply observed Javi out in the wild, capturing an image with his subject none the wiser. Noah himself had been *seen*.

And not just seen the way Reeve-or-Steve's eyes had glanced off Noah at the moment of impact. Javier—Javi—Lucero had looked at Noah in a moment when he'd felt thoroughly invisible. And Javi had even engaged him in a brief but meaningful dialogue. It made Noah feel utterly exposed.

For the first time in his life, he wished his camera was digital. Javi was gone. He'd entered the school with a cluster of other students. Noah couldn't look at him anymore. If he had a DSLR camera instead of the Leica, he'd be able to gaze upon the photo he'd just taken. His satisfaction wouldn't be delayed by the need to develop film. He'd probably be able to find Javi again at assembly, but it wouldn't be the same. Noah wanted to relive that exact moment again. Now.

"Are you planning on standing out here all day, Mr. Rainier?"

Noah jumped a little. His eyes had been trained on the figure of Javier—Javi—disappearing into the school. He hadn't heard the soft steps of Ms. Stevens, his chemistry teacher, sneaking up behind him.

"Sorry, Ms. Stevens, I was just . . ."

Staring at a boy who had seen me when I sincerely believed I was invisible seemed like a bad follow-up to those words, but so did *skipping morning assembly so that I could photograph an act of vandalism that'll be hushed up and forgotten come morning.*

He opted for silence.

"Don't much care *why* you're out here, Rainier. I do care that you *are* out here. Instead of"—she dipped her head in the direction of the school—"in there, where all good boys and girls are meant to be. I'm sure Headmaster Wood has a few choice words prepared for"—another inarticulate gesture, this one seeming to encapsulate the graffiti and the jester stickers and the societal discontent that had led to their placement—"all of this."

"Of course, Ms. Stevens." Noah hurried to put his camera in his backpack. He'd gotten some okay shots of the graffiti at least. He wanted one without students, janitors, or teachers blocking any of the letters, but these would have to do.

Ms. Stevens watched him fumble with his bag, tapping her foot against the grass in impatience. "You have thirty seconds before I dock your rating, champ." Her finger was poised for the strike, hovering over the smartwatch at her wrist.

Noah spared a thought for his rating. It wasn't entirely shameful, but it was far from respectable. But so long as he hovered somewhere in the middle of the pack, attracting neither notoriety nor celebrity, he was perfectly content. That didn't mean he wanted to incur a deduction if one could easily be avoided.

"Right, right, sorry." He slung his backpack over his shoulder. The Leica thudded against his spine, a staccato beat that mirrored the hammering of his heart. The hammering had little to do with Ms. Stevens's threat to dock his rating and a lot to do with the memory of hazel eyes and a wink and a smile and a gaze he couldn't escape.

CHAPTER 3
Tamsin Moore

RATING: 37

Maplethorpe Academy prided itself on its ratings. This sense of accomplishment didn't limit itself to the numerical displays on its students' smart devices—mostly watches, but pricier bespoke accessories like rings or necklaces were also available. Rather, it reflected every aspect of academic existence that could be codified and quantified.

The academy boasted a matriculation rate of 100 percent. By the time senior year rolled around, the students Least Likely to Succeed had already been culled, either shipped off to reform schools out west or politely expelled, left to live among the unwashed and Unrated.

The academy also laid claim to an admission rate of less than 5 percent. Students either had to prove themselves as truly exceptional or come from truly exceptional stock, the latter of which was a mixed bag when it came to individual achievement. It was an honor to attend Maplethorpe Academy, which is why their attendance rate was also—almost—100 percent.

Almost, because one student was determined to tank that statistic.

Tamsin Moore popped her artificially sweet bubble gum, the flavor of which could best be described simply as blue. Her hiding spot—a music building that had been out of commission for decades after the new, state-of-the-art facility was constructed—was far enough from the main school building to evade detection; no faculty member could be bothered with the trek to the campus's outer edges. Especially not for one wayward student who'd probably never make it to graduation anyway.

She peered down at her watch, sparing a sliver of a thought for the rating it displayed. If it dipped much lower, her less than esteemed career at Maplethorpe would come to a premature end even sooner than she'd expected.

Once upon a time, Tamsin had been exceptional. So exceptional, perhaps, that it was unsustainable. The novelty of Maplethorpe had worn off a few months into her freshman year, and the school had yet to regain its luster. She scraped along for her mother's sake. Ms. Moore's disappointment was harder to bear than anyone else's, to Tamsin's eternal chagrin.

With a tap, Tamsin switched the watch's display from rating to clock. First period was well underway, and her clients were late.

Clients, she supposed, was a generous term for the bright young things she led off the beaten path, but she liked that it made her business seem official.

Just as she was about to call it a day and depart, a red ponytail emerged from the other side of the ridge between Tamsin and the rest of Maplethorpe.

A smile stretched her Atomic Purple lips.

By the time the red ponytail and the person—people, really—attached to it arrived, the scene was set. Candles sat in puddles of melted wax, as many as Tamsin could salvage from the reject pile at her mother's new age apothecary/general store. A black square of fabric, peppered with golden stars, lay on the floor. On top of it lay a well-worn deck of tarot cards, their edges softened by years of shuffling.

Tamsin watched the trio enter the building from her perch at the window. Their footfalls were loud as they climbed the stairs to the second floor, but their voices were louder. She took her place, sitting cross-legged by the cards, her spine straight, her long black sweater pooling around her like a cloak.

"Who do you think did it?"

"I bet it was the weird kid with the camera. What's his name? Noel?"

"Did you see the way he was creeping in the bushes this morning, taking pictures? Bet he wanted trophies of his handiwork."

The boy's name was Noah, Tamsin knew. She made it her business to know the other outcasts and misfits at Maplethorpe. A small part of her acknowledged that she did this because she was curious if she would develop the type of bond among weirdos she read about in books, where friendships formed between those on the periphery. But so far, she hadn't approached any of them and none had approached her. No one wanted to be associated with the lowest-rated student at the academy. Tamsin was poison. Most of the time, she liked it that way.

But strange as Noah was, Tamsin would have bet her most valuable possession—a pristine limited-edition hand-painted Rider-Waite deck accented with real gold foil—that he was innocent. Tamsin hadn't bothered attending the mandatory school assembly that morning, but even she had seen the graffiti

23

emblazoned on the school's polished doors. It didn't seem like Noah's style. That boy was all crisp edges and clean corners. There was a violence to the way that red paint had been slashed onto the wood. It had dripped onto the pale marble like blood, as if the words were an open wound. They contained a rage Tamsin didn't think Noah possessed. He seemed eccentric but not privately furious at the arbitrary chains that held their society prisoner.

She wished she knew who had done it, even if just so she could shake the perpetrator's hand. Vandalism like that wasn't for the faint of heart. Speaking truth to power took balls.

The ratings *were* a sham. A farce, forced on the masses so that they all danced like obedient little marionettes. Sometimes, Tamsin felt like she was the only soul at Maplethorpe who saw the strings. It gladdened her to know she wasn't alone in her disdain.

The footsteps fell silent when they reached the door to what Tamsin had come to consider her office, though the term didn't seem witchy enough. *Parlor.* Now that was a word with personality.

"I can hear you," Tamsin called. "Come into my parlor. I don't bite."

Three girls entered the room, two flanking the one with the red ponytail. The two other girls had names, but Tamsin couldn't remember them. Sasha and Sarah, maybe. The alliteration sounded vaguely familiar. While she cataloged the weird and the whimsical, she took little stock of the painfully ordinary. Usually, knowing their type was enough. More often than not, they were satisfied with some vaguely mystical reading, paraded with the right amount of ambience. So long as she read the cues people so rarely realized they were broadcasting, Tamsin could spin a yarn worth the price of admission to her candlelit parlor.

"Welcome, Summer," Tamsin said, injecting as much mystique into the words as she could. She motioned to the three flat cushions across from her cards. The bangles on her wrist jingled as her arm moved. "Sit."

The girls hesitated, the two looking to their leader for a sign. After a moment, Summer Rawlins nodded. As one, they sank onto the cushions, tucking their identical pleated skirts around their thighs, as if they were proper ladies visiting Tamsin for tea and cakes.

"Well? Aren't you going to summon the spirits or whatever it is you do?" Summer's disdainful gaze swept across the room. She wrinkled her nose in disgust. It was a little musty but not nearly enough to justify that kind of attitude. She toyed with a pendant hanging from a golden chain around her neck. It was designed to look like a locket, but Tamsin recognized it for what it was. Custom-made wearable tech. Instead of the clunky smartwatches most plebeians like Tamsin wore, Summer donned her rating in style. Those custom jobs didn't come cheap. "I'm surprised you don't have a Ouija board in here. Isn't that, like, your brand?"

Summer was aiming for glib, but Tamsin saw through the girl's artless facade. She was afraid. Not of Tamsin, as much as Tamsin would have loved that to be the case, but of this single act of deviance. For a girl like Summer (rating: 82), one skipped class was a minor snag in a tapestry of perfection. Her rating might take a temporary hit, but even that was unlikely. While the threat of the ratings was ever present in the lives of every

Maplethorpe student, the practice of doling out punishment was anything but equal. No one was truly perfect, even if Summer Rawlins and her ilk thought they were. But the faculty at Maplethorpe tended to overlook the occasional transgressions of the privileged, provided they were anomalous. It was one of the reasons that the private school maintained an average student body rating so much higher than the national mean.

For Tamsin, truancy was just another Monday.

"Payment up front." Tamsin gestured toward a small ceramic dish beside the cloth, as if sullying her fortune-telling hands with something as mundane as money would taint the magic in them. Mystique. It all came down to the tiny details. Summer didn't need to know that the dish was another reject repurposed from Tamsin's mother's shop. Ms. Moore would not be pleased that her daughter was using the wisdom of the ancients to swindle money from her fellow students, but she would at least be happy that Tamsin was recycling.

"How much?" Summer asked. As if it mattered to her. The Rawlins family owned half the town, and that was a conservative estimate.

"Forty for you. Another twenty for Tweedledee and Tweedledumb. Each."

Tweedledee gawked in indignation, but Summer merely nodded and placed two crisp twenties in the ceramic dish.

With a flourish, Tamsin spread the cards across the cloth. "Pick a card. Place it facedown in front of you. Do not turn it over."

She'd had a different spread in mind—the Celtic Cross, for which she charged extra—but tardy clients demanded a little improvisation.

Summer reached out to select a card from the deck, taking an obscene amount of time to decide on just which one was right for her. Silence thickened in the candlelit room. Tamsin waited patiently until her patience ran out.

She popped her gum, and as one, always as one, the three girls jumped.

Tamsin smiled. "Sorry."

She wasn't.

When Summer settled on a card, Tamsin made a show of turning it over. She did it slowly, so as to draw out the dramatic tension of the moment. The girls sitting across from her held their breath in unison. Tamsin wondered if they did everything in unison, even when they weren't dizzying audiences at basketball games with their unerringly coordinated pom-poms.

For forty dollars, Tamsin would shuffle her tarot deck and deal the cards, reading the fortunes of anyone with enough money to pay. If she liked them, she'd make it interesting. If she didn't like them, she'd make it *really* interesting.

Today's customers were people Tamsin really didn't like.

Summer Rawlins was the captain of Maplethorpe's cheerleading squad. Maplethorpe hadn't even had a cheerleading squad—something about it being antithetical to the academy's mission statement to form young minds into contributing members of society. That is, until Summer and her trust fund rolled in freshman year. Daddy Rawlins donated enough money to completely renovate the school's aging library, and Summer got to nurture whatever pet project she wanted. And that project had been building a cheer squad from the ground up.

Summer's two minions watched the cards over Summer's shoulders with rapt attention and too-wide eyes. Their lips glistened with the same shade of lip gloss Summer preferred. Their nails were painted in complementary colors. Coordination. It was their thing.

With a flourish, Tamsin turned over the card. Summer gasped as a prone figure, run through with ten long swords, was revealed on the card's face.

"The Ten of Swords," Tamsin said, injecting every ounce of doom she could muster into her voice. A draft gusted at the candles, making the shadows in the corners of the room jump. Summer jumped with them. Tamsin swallowed a smile. She couldn't have asked for better theatrics.

The Ten of Swords was widely regarded as the most pessimistic card in the deck. It was synonymous with misfortune, defeat, and backstabbing—both literal and figurative. Oftentimes, it symbolized the lowest point in a seeker's life.

For Tamsin, it meant an easy way to scare an extra twenty bucks out of fools with more money than sense.

"That's not good, is it?" Summer's voice was more of a squeak than a question. "What does that mean? Am I gonna die?"

Tamsin shrugged. "We're all gonna die, Summer. The real questions are when and how."

Summer squinted at the cards, then at Tamsin. "Can you tell that?"

"Some mysteries must be left to the universe," said Tamsin. "But we can consult the cards and see if they're in the mood to elaborate."

"Okay, good, so do it," Summer said, with the air of a girl who was accustomed to getting her way.

Tamsin directed a pointed look at the ceramic dish. "The cards tend to be chattier when they've been fairly compensated."

"Fine, whatever." Summer rummaged in her backpack for a moment before yanking out her wallet and dumping another twenty in the dish. "If I didn't know any better, I'd say you were scamming me."

Through sheer force of will, and maybe even a little divine intervention, Tamsin held back the laughter threatening to bubble up her throat. "Then it's a good thing you do know better."

Tamsin said a quick prayer to whatever deity might be listening that the next card at the top of the deck be a nasty one. It would make Tamsin's day to have the distinct pleasure of ruining Summer's.

She turned over the card and bit her lip to hide her smile.

The Lovers, reversed.

Excellent.

The face of the card showed two figures with their arms intertwined. They were gazing, not at each other, but at the ground. Above them floated an ominous face in the clouds, staring down at them, its gaze heavy with judgment. Beneath the image were scrawled two words . . .

"The Lovers," said Summer. "That's good, right?"

Summer's big blue eyes slid to the first card she'd drawn.

The Ten of Swords.

"Or maybe it's not . . . ?"

"It's not," Tamsin confirmed. It took everything she had not to cackle like the witch she knew they liked to say she was.

"So . . . what does it mean, then? I paid you, you can't not tell me now."

And now it took everything Tamsin had not to roll her eyes. The Rawlins family thought that money made the world go around. The truly disappointing thing about it was how often they were right.

But still, Tamsin could have some fun.

"Upright, the Lovers represents unity and balance. Harmony within the self and in relationships. Reversed, well. Reversed, it means just the opposite."

That was actually true.

"And when it follows the Ten of Swords, a card that signifies treachery . . . Well, I hate to be the one to bear such unfortunate tidings . . ." Tamsin knew she was laying it on a bit thick, but sometimes she simply couldn't resist. "But I think your relationship isn't heading in the direction you probably hope it is."

Summer leaned forward, her expertly manicured eyebrows pinching. "Are you saying he's gonna break up with me?"

"*I'm* not saying anything," Tamsin insisted. "I am but a humble messenger through which the arcana speaks."

Definitely too thick.

"So, how do I get him to not break up with me?" Summer pressed. "Nobody breaks up with me."

And now the real fun could begin.

"I might have something to help with that," Tamsin drawled. "A special remedy to keep the heart true. But, as the saying goes, nothing good in life comes free."

A frantic energy had seized Summer, making her nearly quake with its force. "Whatever it is, I'll pay it."

Of course she would. Money was no object to a Rawlins. Tamsin would come up with a suitably absurd price once she decided what innocuous ingredients she was going to toss into a glass vial later. Her mother had started mixing her own essential oil blends to sell in the shop recently. She was bound to have a few extra bottles lying about.

"Tomorrow," Tamsin said. "Meet me here after eighth period."

Summer and her minions pushed themselves to stand on shaky legs. Tamsin bit back a smile. She did so enjoy striking fear into the hearts of Maplethorpe's student body.

"I'll have what you need, but first . . ." Tamsin reached into the velvet pouch beside her and took her sweet time sliding out the most impressive of all her tools. A silver blade set in an ebony handle. Her athame. It had started life as her great-grandmother's letter opener, but a little sharpening had transformed it into something altogether more intimidating. Tamsin relished the way Summer's eyes widened as she took in the blade. "I'll need a little something from you."

She didn't, of course, but Summer didn't need to know that.

CHAPTER 4
HANA SAKAMOTO

RATING: 78

Hana Sakamoto was haunted by numbers.

The sight of the numbers shining on the digital scale in the bathroom that morning buzzed through her mind as she walked through the crowded halls of Maplethorpe Academy. She had missed morning assembly because of figure skating practice, so she headed straight from the front doors to her first-period class—Advanced Placement Biology—without pause. Now she dragged her heels toward the cafeteria, knowing full well she wouldn't be eating anything they served there. She was half a pound heavier than she'd been the day before. Her parents had roped her into an overly filling dinner, insistent in a way they rarely were.

Her mother had gotten it into her head to make *her* mother's okonomiyaki, a dish heavier than anything Hana had eaten in weeks. Months? She'd only consumed half of the layered monstrosity of cabbage, flour, egg, and pork, but the damage was done. It sat like a stone in her stomach, weighing her down, even after the 150 crunches Hana did before bed in a vain attempt to compensate.

The scale wasn't fooled. The scale told the truth.

Numbers never lied.

They couldn't. It simply wasn't in their nature. Numbers were absolute truth, unadorned. They managed to strike a delicate, pristine balance between brutal honesty and elegant simplicity.

And the truth was that she would have to work much harder if she wanted to qualify for nationals this year. She'd missed last season because of a stress fracture in her right foot—her doctor had mentioned something about low bone density and malnutrition, but Hana had tuned him out after he said she would have to skip the season.

The silver medal she'd won at her last competition—junior nationals, two years ago—was still rattling around in the bottom of her skate bag. The display case at the Sakamoto home was reserved strictly for gold. Silver and bronze had no place of honor behind that particular glass exhibit. Those medals were relegated to a box shoved to the back of Hana's closet, alongside her wrinkled ribbons from horse shows of years long past, before she'd settled on figure skating as her sport of choice.

Her parents were both champion equestrians, show-jumping victors in back-to-back Olympics. Her mother still competed, with Hana's father coaching her. They'd made sure she knew how to ride about as soon as she could walk, and hadn't tried to contain their disappointment when Hana hung up her riding boots in exchange for figure skates.

Still, it wasn't long before they'd hired the best coaches and choreographers in the country to mold Hana into a champion.

The molding was not going nearly as well as Hana suspected her parents desired. Oh, she'd started out strong. She'd shown prodigious talent as a child, picking up the fundamentals after mere moments on the ice. Within minutes, she'd learned how to stroke and glide and balance on one foot. After a few sessions, Hana was spinning and performing little bunny hops from one skate to the other. By the time she was eleven, she had all her triple jumps—though the clean edges of some of the takeoffs continued to elude her. She was on the road to Olympic stardom, ready to bring home a gold medal to match those of her parents.

And then, puberty hit. And it hit hard.

When her body changed, her balance changed. Suddenly, she had to learn everything from scratch, but this time with an entirely new center of gravity. On the ice, she grew slow and sluggish, her blades heavy and loud as they scraped the surface, so different from the gentle whispers they'd produced before her body betrayed her.

"It's your curves," her coach, Dmitriev, had informed her after a particularly clumsy practice eight months ago. "They're slowing down your rotations."

"So, what do I do about it?" Hana had asked, winded in a way she never had been before.

"You have two options. You can bulk up and build enough muscle to give yourself more height and distance on your jumps."

Hana had barely even considered it. She'd always wanted to be a Nancy, not a Tonya. What appealed to her about figure skating was its ethereal nature. When she was skating, she felt like a nymph, skimming across a frozen pond. No one wanted to look at a bulky nymph.

"And my second option?"

Dmitriev shrugged and took a sip from the travel mug he carried so often. Hana wouldn't have been surprised if it were soldered on to his hand. "You can become more aerodynamic, but I would not recommend it. Already you are too thin. You need muscle."

She'd tuned him out after *aerodynamic*.

The first ten pounds came off easily. Every time she stepped on the scale in her bathroom, her body sizzled with the thrill of victory. But eventually, she hit a plateau. Hana knew this extreme slimming down wasn't what Dmitriev meant for her to do, but her tangible progress was too seductive to ignore.

Numbers didn't lie, and the scale told her that if she wanted to make progress, to become as aerodynamic as possible, she was going to have to make some sacrifices.

Sacrifices didn't involve okonomiyaki, no matter how delicious it was.

Having arrived at Maplethorpe Academy long after the morning's hubbub died down, Hana hadn't even realized there *was* a hubbub until she overheard two girls discussing it on the line for lunch. A lunch that she had no plans on eating.

"Can you believe it? I mean, I live for start-of-the-year drama, but like . . . what a weird way to go about it," said one girl whose name Hana had probably known at some point in time but had long ago forgotten. She never paid much attention to the other students at Maplethorpe. Her life revolved around the ice. Everything outside that was extraneous. Unnecessary.

Hana turned around, just enough to see the girls behind her.

"Sorry, what drama?"

The two girls slammed the brakes on their conversation, their dual gazes settling on Hana as if she were a bug that had smashed herself on their window.

"Um, the graffiti?" Girl Number One said slowly, as if she were reminding a very stupid child of something exceedingly obvious. "On the front doors?"

"I was late today," Hana said. "I didn't see anything on the doors."

Girl Number Two offered Hana a small, chilly smile. Hana wondered if she knew about the special permission Hana had received to skip morning assembly for the sake of her practices and resented her for it. "Some idiot with a can of spray paint wrote 'The ratings are not real' on the doors this morning. Nobody knows who did it."

"Oh," Hana said, for lack of anything better. The girls were already turning away, bending their heads even closer together to resume the conversation she so rudely interrupted. "Thanks."

They ignored her, picking up again at a much quieter volume so Hana could neither overhear nor be tempted to insert herself into the conversation.

It was such a silly thing for someone to write. The ratings are not real. The ratings were numbers, and numbers never ever lied.

"What'll you have, dear?"

Hana jerked her attention from the frantic buzz of the whispered conversation behind her to the lunch lady across the counter. It was the same woman who had held the position since Hana's freshman year. There was something calming and maternal in the soft lines of her plump figure. Hana loved and loathed her in equal measure. She looked like a woman who found enjoyment in food, a thoroughly foreign concept for Hana. Though Hana wished she understood the comfort other people experienced in eating, all she ever felt was anxiety that gnawed at her gut even more than her hunger did. Her strength of will depended on her rock-solid association with food being detrimental to her physical and mental health. She knew, objectively, that this notion was unsound, but it was best left unanalyzed, lest the entire fragile structure come crashing down around her.

Hana let her eyes rove over the options presented to her. The literature Maplethorpe provided to prospective students and their parents boasted of their nutritious meal options, but everyone knew that teenagers wouldn't sustain themselves on quinoa and kale alone. There were cheeseburgers and fries—with the option to drench them in cheese and gravy should one desire to clog their arteries before they could legally vote—and mozzarella sticks, deep-fried and slathered in marinara sauce.

Her stomach lurched at the sight of all that food, either in protest or trembling desire. Hana was never quite sure these days.

"I'll just have an iced coffee," Hana said. "Large, please."

The lunch lady let loose a soft, discontented hum, as if she found Hana's refusal to partake personally offensive.

"Cream and sugar?"

Hana hated black coffee. She hated the bitter, watery taste of it. She hated the way she could feel it wearing a hole in her stomach. She hated the way it made her fingers tremble and her spine shake.

But cream and sugar were calorie sinks.

"No, thanks. I'll take it black."

That way, her beverage was, at the very least, calorie negligible.

Numbers never lied, and at the end of the day, she would be forced to confront the truth of them in her food journal, a document she treated with the utmost secrecy. She knew it looked bad, obsessively noting every morsel that passed her lips. She wasn't stupid. But she also knew that in order to succeed, sacrifices had to be made.

To Hana, depriving herself of food was no different than depriving herself of a few extra hours of sleep so she could get to the rink before sunrise. And if there was a tiny voice at the back of her head that tried to convince her that it was . . . well, that was something she would just have to ignore.

Hana paid for her iced coffee and sipped at it. The taste made her cringe. Cream and sugar would have made her forget that coffee was, at its core, just bitter bean juice.

She inched away from the line, trying to keep close enough to overhear the conversation still going on behind her. Another student bumped into her shoulder, muttering a quick apology as they left too fast for Hana to catch a face. She sulked away to sip her sad bean juice at the last small table left unoccupied in the cafeteria. It was set in a corner right under an air-conditioning vent. The spot was too cold for mere mortals but not for someone who spent the majority of their time in a freezing ice rink.

It was difficult keeping abreast of the hottest Maplethorpe gossip. Hana was as unplugged from the social systems of the school as one could be, while still maintaining a presence for the sake of her grades and attendance—competitions permitting, of course. Friendship presented an unnecessary and unwanted complication, and Hana had little desire to complicate her life any more than it already was. Friends placed demands on one's time, and time was a precious commodity, of which Hana was in a perpetual deficit. She rose before the sun every morning, groggily bundling herself in as many layers as humanly possible to warm her tired muscles before arriving at the rink. She only ever had a few hours of practice before she had to leave to make it to Maplethorpe's first-period bell. Her special dispensation to skip morning assemblies ended with that chime. Missing it meant the band on her wrist tightened—or perhaps that was just her imagination—and her heart sank as the smartwatch vibrated, alerting her to a dip in her rating.

Numbers never lied, after all.

Hana reached into her backpack to retrieve a little black notebook and the red pen she preferred to write with. It held all her secrets. The jumps she landed in practice. The greater number of jumps she fell on. The foods she ate and their corresponding caloric values. It was a litany of her successes and her failures. She never went anywhere without it.

She chewed the top of the pen as she flipped to the page she'd started that morning. Every day was laid out the same, each page divided into sections to track her progress.

Breakfast
Hard-boiled egg (1)—70 calories
Apple (1/2)—50 calories

Post-practice snack
Celery sticks, small (6)—3 calories

She clicked the pen, switching to green ink, and scribbled her most recent addition to the list.

Lunch
Iced coffee, black (1)—2 calories

The sight of the number two sent a little thrill through her at the same moment her stomach cramped, begging her to put something more substantial in it. Her limbs felt heavy now that she was sitting, but it was nothing she couldn't push through. She had skated on broken bones, trained with torn ligaments. A little discomfort was nothing.

Pain is progress, she reminded herself.

Her coach had said that to her once and she had written it onto the first page of the diary in black marker, stark and permanent.

One hundred twenty-five calories.

Not bad.

But she could do better.

She *would* do better. She would work so the numbers on the page, and on the scale, and on her smartwatch reflected the perfection for which she aimed. Because numbers never lied.

CHAPTER 5
CHASE DONOVAN

RATING: 54

No matter how often or how thoroughly it was cleaned, the boys' locker room at Maplethorpe Academy always smelled the same. The scent was an obnoxious mix of sweat, that vile body spray marketed to men under twenty-five, and the bleach the janitor used to try to keep everything sanitary. Chase's dad liked to call it the smell of victory, but to Chase, it just smelled like body odor combined with humanity's vain attempts to combat it.

He stood before his locker, a speck of silence amid the cacophony of Maplethorpe's varsity baseball team unwinding after practice. Shouts ricocheted off the bank of lockers as players exchanged anecdotes about their summer vacations and plans for the weekend, as if it wasn't only Monday. Locker doors slammed shut, and the old pipes rattled as the showers ran. But all Chase could hear was the ringing in his ears that sounded every time he looked at the letter in his hands, the one that Headmaster Wood had given him at the end of last semester, coaxing a solemn promise from Chase to make sure his father saw it and signed it in acknowledgment of receipt. It was a promise Chase had no intention of keeping. He'd managed to dodge Wood's watchful eyes for the entirety of the day, probably because the headmaster had far bigger fish than Chase to fry, what with a spray-paint-toting vandal loose on campus. Chase sent a silent prayer of thanks to his savior and their graffiti, but he knew it wouldn't last. The headmaster would eventually catch up with him.

Dear Mr. Donovan,

We regret to inform you that your son, Chase Donovan, has failed to maintain the standards expected of scholarship students of Maplethorpe Academy. As a valuable member of the community, Chase occupies a very special place at Maplethorpe, and as such, we would like to provide him with any assistance necessary to rise to the standards that have solidified our school's sterling reputation. The Academy has several options available, from office hours with faculty to peer-to-peer tutoring sessions. As you are aware, the conditions of your son's athletic scholarship require that he maintain a rating of at least 55. We believe that Chase is fully capable of rising to the occasion, and we look forward to working with you and your family to ensure your son's place with us in the year to come. Do not hesitate to call my office if you have any questions or concerns.

Warmest regards,
Dr. Jeremiah Wood
Headmaster, Maplethorpe Academy

Chase's grip tightened, wrinkling the paper. The creases had gone soft after being unfolded and folded countless times over the summer. He'd taken the note with him to summer training camp with the rest of the team. The thought of his father stumbling upon it in one of his rare moments of sobriety was too troubling to contemplate. But avoiding his father wasn't the problem. At least, not the biggest one.

The problem was Chase.

He tried to study, he did. But sometimes the words on the page didn't make sense, no matter how hard his strained eyes tried to puzzle them out. And numbers never appeared to stay in one place, complicating even the most basic arithmetic. He knew there were kids like him who struggled with learning disabilities—such a thing was hardly an academic death knell—but he also knew that the arduous process of learning to live with them took time and discipline, the two most precious commodities in Chase's life. He couldn't imagine trying to find the hours for one-on-one tutoring when every spare moment he wasn't in class was devoted to baseball.

Chase had been Maplethorpe's star pitcher since his freshman year, bypassing the junior varsity team entirely when the coach saw him at tryouts. No one had taken a Maplethorpe team by storm quite like that since Chase's own father twenty years prior. His dad's picture, along with the numerous football trophies he'd won for the school, were still displayed in a place of pride in the corridor outside the gymnasium.

And if Chase was honest with himself, the thought of asking for help made his skin itch. He'd learned to be self-sufficient by middle school. He had also learned that revealing one's weakness was never wise, not at home and not at school. His difficulty embarrassed him, and his embarrassment made him want to set the note, and the numerous report cards he'd never brought home, and the smartwatch constantly reminding him of his failure—his rating one point short of adequate—on fire. And then he wanted to dance on the ashes.

But Chase could do none of those things. He didn't know what to do, and that scared him most of all.

A sharp slap to his back broke Chase's tether to his woes. He turned to find Steve, the team's shortstop, blinking at him with a quizzical expression. An artfully messy lock of hair tumbled across Steve's forehead.

"Hey, buddy, I called your name like five times. What's up?"

Chase hastily shoved the letter to the darkest depths of his backpack.

"Sorry, I was just . . ."

Contemplating the inevitable demise of my athletic career and maybe even the rest of my life, Chase thought, but did not say.

Steve rescued Chase from having to say anything with a flippant wave of his hand. "Yeah, not important. Anyway, a bunch of us are heading to the Lucky Penny. You in?"

The letter prodded at the parts of Chase's brain responsible for actions and reactions, choices and consequences.

"I don't know, I should probably head home . . ." Chase didn't say *to study* because that was unthinkable.

Steve's brows drew together in consternation. "Dude. Burgers. Milkshakes. Cheerleaders. What could beat that?"

Many things, Chase thought. World peace. Saving the whales. Freedom from the Rating System currently grinding his soul to dust. A brain that functioned the way brains were meant to function. Enough money not to need a scholarship. At least one sober parent. Two, ideally, but even fantasizing about that felt greedy.

But home wasn't exactly an optimal location for quiet contemplation or studying. He knew exactly what he would find there. His father, a beer in one hand as he sat in the ancient recliner in their living room, watching old VHS tapes of twenty-year-old football games. He'd be mumbling about the injury to his shoulder cuff that had cut his own career off before it started, whether or not Chase was there to listen.

"Well," Chase said, "when you put it like that."

Steve knocked Chase two inches to the left with a jovial clap to his arm. "Knew you'd see reason. Now hurry up before all the good booths are taken."

"Yeah, yeah," Chase said. "I'll meet you outside. I just need a minute."

"Five minutes!" Steve was already halfway to the door. "Then we're leaving without you."

Chase tossed Steve a loose salute and turned back to his locker. With a sigh, he zipped up his backpack. The letter—and all the trouble that came with it—could wait another day. He slammed the door shut hard enough to knock loose a piece of paper that had been shoved between the little vents at the top. He bent down to pick it up, squinting at it. It was written on red construction paper, the kind he used to draw dinosaurs on as a child. He still liked dinosaurs, albeit in secret.

He didn't bother reading it. It wasn't unheard of for some of the cheerleaders to leave notes in the athletes' lockers, particularly at the beginning of the year when couples started pairing off. A girlfriend was another thing Chase didn't have time for. He shoved the note in the front pocket of his backpack to read later.

Chase left the locker room, injecting pep he didn't much feel into his step. He didn't notice the sticker sealing the note shut, a ghoulish jester.

A jester identical to the ones left on Maplethorpe's security cameras.

The Lucky Penny was one of those diners that promised a retro atmosphere and managed to deliver a sterile, amusement-park version of a past its primary clientele was too young to remember. Red vinyl booths lined windows lit with neon signs, visually screaming about the establishment's "Mega Milkshakes!" Stools upholstered in matching crimson dotted the baby-blue counter, which ran nearly the entire length of the diner. On each table stood a small placard reminding patrons to tip their server, not just in cold, hard cash, but in positive ratings. Those were more valuable than money.

A jukebox tucked in the corner played songs much older than Chase. A dollar got you three songs. Each booth was similarly equipped with its own decorative miniature jukebox; the sides of each held napkins, salt and pepper shakers, and tiny bottles of ketchup. All the table jukeboxes were red with silver trim, except for an odd one in the corner booth that was trimmed in gold.

The team occupied the rounded booth in the corner of the diner, with a small red jukebox at their table. They were being way too loud, but no one complained. Maplethorpe's baseball team was the pride of Jackson Hills, the town adjacent to the school. The team could do no wrong, and that knowledge was intoxicating. Antics that would dock the ratings of any other student were waved away with a wink and a smile when committed by a member of the baseball team.

Chase sat beside Steve and Steve's girlfriend, Summer. They'd gotten together at the end of last year, but Chase wasn't sure the relationship would last much longer. Steve never kept girlfriends for very long, though Summer might prove to be an exception. She had her own power at Maplethorpe, and her family practically owned the town. Steve would be wise to be more careful with her.

Over the summer, Chase had caught Steve making eyes at another of the girls on the cheerleading squad. Sasha, he thought her name was. She'd tried flirting with Chase years ago, when he'd distinguished himself as Maplethorpe's best pitcher, but he hadn't had time for girls then and he didn't now. And there was something uncomfortably incestuous about the dating pool in which his circles swam. It seemed healthier to just stay out of the water altogether.

He nursed the strawberry milkshake before him, not really enjoying it, but not hating it enough to push it aside. It cost eight whole dollars. Chase had left the house with twelve in his wallet, so the damage was too grievous to ignore. He would drink it, whether he liked it or not. His father worked in construction, but he hadn't been to the site in days. Chase wondered if he'd been let go again, or if he'd just been told to go home until he sobered up. The thought of the former incited too much anxiety for Chase to ask. The fewer words he exchanged with his father when he was in one of his moods— which he'd been in for weeks now—the better.

Steve nudged Chase's shoulder with his own. The action

brought Steve's wrist into Chase's line of vision. The rating on Steve's watch flashed, bright and mean.

70.

Must be nice, Chase thought. Not that Steve's rating had much of an impact on his life. He wasn't on scholarship. His father was the CEO or CFO or COO of some company whose name ended in *Industries*.

Chase wondered what it would be like to go through life with a successful, prestigious family to cushion his rating.

"I heard scouts are coming to the game next week."

Chase glanced across the table at Alex. Alex (rating: 64) played various positions in the outfield and was unlikely to ever attract the attention of any scout, much less one diligent enough to go to games this early in the season. But Chase admired the optimism.

Steve nudged Chase with his elbow. "Coach told me they heard about our boy Donovan crushing the competition last year."

Chase forced a smile to his face. The very mention of scouts had sent an agonized sizzle of longing through him. It would be the dream, for one of them to offer him a chance at a college scholarship. The dream wasn't even about baseball, really. Baseball was simply a way out of Jackson Hills and toward a bright, shiny future. He'd never be able to afford out-of-state tuition on his own. An athletic scholarship was his only chance to start a new life far, far away.

"I'm only as good as my team," Chase said, because he knew it was the right thing to say. One could preen in front of girls or civilians, but never in front of teammates. It soured the dynamic. And it was true, mostly.

The rest of the guys accepted his aphorism, however trite it was, with a chorus of agreement. Never mind that Chase worked harder than any of them. He had to. Even without baseball, *they* still had futures. They had well-rated parents, safety nets woven of hereditary cash, and homes that didn't reek like distilleries.

But if Alex was right and there really were scouts coming to the game, Chase had to throw everything into impressing them. It would leave little time for anything else. He spared a thought for the warning letter crumpled at the bottom of his backpack. All he had to do was last the year, get a scholarship, and, with luck on his side, get out of Jackson Hills.

CHAPTER 6
JAVI LUCERO

RATING: 83

"Cover me, I'm going in."

Javi holstered his submachine gun. He sprinted faster when his hands were free.

"Got your back, Vulpes," his sniper, Rouge, assured him. Her voice echoed in Javi's headset. "Try not to make this another suicide run."

"Ha, ha," Javi uttered humorlessly. "More cover fire, less subpar banter."

Armored feet clanging against the naked metal of the ship's hull, Javi powered toward the glowing orb at the center of the space.

"My banter is anything but subpar," the sniper said.

Javi would have chastised her for distracting him from his definitely-not-a-suicide-run, had Rouge not expertly taken out the two sentries lurching for him. The clawed tips of their gauntlets would have taken precious seconds to shake off, seconds the team didn't have if they were going to make it out of that base alive.

"Head shot, baby!"

"Nice," Javi said. A good leader praised his team when they deserved it. "Now keep it up. This is where things get tricky."

Javi grabbed the orb, its purple light casting shadows on the ridges of his plated armor. He tucked it under one arm and bolted, ducking and rolling to the side before a third sentry could sink its talons into him.

"Payload en route," Javi said, mindful not to shout into his mic. He had a bad habit of doing that, to the chagrin of his squad. Sometimes, the excitement was hard to deny, especially when they were all playing their parts, moving together like a well-oiled machine.

"Clock's a-ticking, Vulpes," the medic, Domino, warned. He hung back while Javi and the others did their thing.

"Yeah, I know, dude." Javi gnawed on his lower lip as he pressed on. This was the part that had tripped them up the past three times they'd attempted this mission. He had to time his jump just right. A millisecond too early or too late and the entire team would wipe. And he didn't have time to stand and wait for the platforms to align perfectly. The orb was a ticking bomb. If he held it for too long, it would explode. Then jumping on five consecutive moving platforms would be the least of Javi's worries.

"I hate this level," Domino muttered. "Have I mentioned how much I hate this level?"

"Yes, multiple times," Rouge replied. "And we're all super sick of hearing you say it."

Javi's guild—the Marvelous Cosmic Assassins, or Team MCA for short—was the first in the world to make it to this level of the cooperative play mode in *Polaris*, the world's largest space-faring, alien-shooting MMO game. But unless they completed it soon, they wouldn't be the first to finish.

And that, Javi knew, was unacceptable. For his team, and more importantly for his sponsors.

Nobody got endorsement deals for coming in second place. Victory paid the bills. Victory put food on the table, tuition checks in the mail, and fresh school uniforms on his siblings. Victory slapped a coat of polish on his rating, keeping it high enough to rake in the big bucks.

"Come on," Javi whispered to no one. His team usually ignored him when he started talking to himself with the mic on. It was one of Vulpes's eccentricities. Part of his charm. "Come on, come on, come on."

It was all in the thumbs.

Javi's flew over the buttons, angling the thumbstick and lightly tapping on the X button at just the right times. He played that controller like Franz Liszt played his trusty Bösendorfer piano.

He was almost there, almost at the nexus of energy in which he had to deposit the orb. One more leap and—

"OH, COME ON."

And, a millisecond too late, he watched as his toon plummeted to an ignominious end, mulched to a bloody pulp by the ship's engines.

"Told you it was a suicide run." The sniper's voice was laden with equal parts disappointment and smug satisfaction. She liked being proved right almost as much as she liked winning.

Javi let the controller slip from his hands. His palms had gone clammy on the approach. It made his thumb slip at precisely the wrong moment. He wiped at his brow, mopping away at the sweat that had begun to bead there. His room was sweltering. The attic of their old house wasn't properly insulated. It boiled in the summer and froze in the winter, but it was quiet. Javi needed solitude when he gamed. He had a tendency to get a little too intense when he was six hours into a campaign. Even his little sister Eva said he looked scary.

But Eva didn't know that it was that intensity that put food on their table and new sneakers on her feet.

"Better luck next time, Vulpes," came the medic's decidedly less smug voice. Domino took every loss to heart.

"Yeah, sorry, guys." Javi rubbed at his eyes. They'd gone dry staring at the glowing monitor. "I'll try soloing this part later to practice. We've got the keys for the checkpoint so I can try again tonight."

Rouge chuckled, the sound tinny in Javi's ear. "No way you can solo this, Vulpes."

"Maybe *you* can't." Javi flexed his hands, cracking his knuckles and stretching his fingers. His carpal tunnel would act up later if he didn't go through his wrist exercises before bed. Gaming took a physical toll, even if it was an almost entirely stationary activity. His hands were his moneymakers. Without them, he was nothing.

And without him, his family would lose their house. It may have had shoddy insulation, cramped bedrooms, and a rickety boiler, but it was still home.

The rest of the team recapped the day's work with varying degrees of grumbling. Cooperative play was low on their list of preferred activities. They excelled at PvP combat, but co-op was the game's hot ticket item at the moment. The developers had offered a special sponsorship package to the first team to complete all *Polaris*'s punishing stages, seven unique levels culminating in the hardest boss battle any of them had yet to encounter.

He extended his arms out in front of him to stretch his wrists. He half listened to the guild chatter as he gently pulled back on the fingers of one hand, then the other. Javi's mind wandered to that morning. He used to love the first day of school, but now class represented little more than hours spent not gaming. But today had provided enough amusement to forget his resentment. Like the cute boy with the camera and his dark wavy hair and his equally dark eyes and the freckles that dusted the bridge of his nose.

And like the graffiti.

"Hey, guys?" Javi formed fists with both hands and angled them down, lengthening the stretch across the top side of his wrists. It felt nice. "Have any of you heard about weird graffiti recently? Something about the ratings?"

"Nope."

"Non."

"Nyet."

"No, why?" Rouge asked.

Javi shrugged before remembering they couldn't see him do it. "Just something strange at school. I noticed it wasn't popping up online and wanted to ask."

It was curious that there had been no mention of the graffiti on the doors of Maplethorpe Academy on social media. A few posts had popped up that morning in its immediate wake, but by lunchtime they'd been thoroughly scrubbed, leaving not so much as a digital footprint.

Javi felt a part of his brain perk up. The part that liked to devote itself to wildly unfounded theories about aliens building the pyramids in Giza or constructing the Nazca Lines in Peru. He loved a good conspiracy theory, and the graffiti felt like it had the makings of one.

Rouge hummed in his ear. "Can't say I've noticed anything, but I'll keep my eyes peeled."

"Thanks, Rouge. You always do." Javi flexed his fingers and shook out his hands. That would have to do for now. "All right, I'm out. See you guys later."

He didn't wait for their muffled goodbyes. He slid his headset off. His ears ached in relief. They weren't a perfect fit, but they'd come as part of his latest sponsorship package, along with a customized lumbar support and gaming mouse. Each item was emblazoned with the Panthera logo, a leaping jungle cat, claws bared and mouth open in a silent roar. Panthera was the leading manufacturer of gaming peripherals and Javi's primary sponsor.

Or at least they would be, so long as he and his team stayed on top of their game.

And so long as Javi's rating hovered in the eighties, a rare feat for a seventeen-year-old orphan.

His grandmother would slap him across the back of his skull if she heard him refer to himself as such. He might have lost his parents seven and a half years ago, but his grandmother had been the one to raise them even before their parents had died in a car crash, their tires skidding off an icy road in the dead of a night Javi desperately wished he could forget.

"Javi!"

His grandmother's voice rang with the resonance of a church bell from three floors down.

"Come down for dinner before your brothers and sisters eat it all!"

55

It was not an empty threat.

"Abuela, I'm coming!" Javi shouted, loud enough for even her failing hearing to catch.

Javi pushed away from his desk, delighting in the satisfying pops and cracks sounding from his joints as he stood and stretched. His back ached and his left leg had lost feeling below the knee, but the discomfort was the sign of a job well done.

Even if he had borked the gauntlet.

But tomorrow was, as they said, a new day.

The Lucero children were already crowded around the table by the time Javi made it down to the dining room. He squeezed into his seat between Eva (tall for a twelve-year-old) and the twins, Daniela and Dario (short for ten-year-olds).

"How was school?" Abuela asked as she piled heaping servings of arroz con gandules onto their plates.

"Oh, you know, fine."

"That's all you ever say: fine," grumbled his grandmother. She waved one hand in disdain as the other removed the bowl of rice from Eva's clutches. "Everything is always just fine. Considering the tuition at that fancy school, they should be expanding your vocabulary, not shrinking it."

The truth was Javi paid very little attention to school, a fact he kept to himself. It wasn't very difficult, coasting in the top 15 percent of his class. His grades were good enough to be moderately distinguished without being spectacular enough to draw his attention away from more lucrative pursuits.

Javi rarely studied. He didn't have to. His memory, a child psychologist had told his parents when they'd brought him in for evaluations at the age of eight, was nearly photographic.

His mind was a vault. Once something was in there, it was in there forever.

Most lectures he listened to with only one ear. He had a true gift for multitasking, an ability that contributed to what he seriously—and his siblings derisively—called his gaming prowess.

"My friend Sandra said someone spray-painted bad words on the side of the building," Eva announced.

"Qué?" Abuela stretched that single syllable to three times its natural length. "Vandals? At *that* school?"

"It wasn't a big deal," Javi said, even though it was very much a big deal. A big deal that curiously hadn't made the news, local or otherwise. People and events critical of the Rating System rarely did. "It was probably just some dumb start-of-the-year prank."

"I don't want you getting involved with any of those people causing trouble, Javi. You're a good boy and you better stay that way."

"I'm not involved!" But all his protest earned him was a pointed glare. So he added, "Yes, Abuela."

A squawk from one of the twins was enough to change the subject. Dario had stolen Daniela's pork chop or she had stolen his. The details didn't matter. They did this every night. It was comforting in its familiarity.

Javi let the sound of their squabbling wash over him as his mind wandered. What occupied his thoughts wasn't the high drama of the vandalism or the simmering tension that had grasped the student body the entire day in its wake, but one student in particular.

A boy with a camera, standing off to the side, watching a world that didn't seem particularly interested in watching him.

Javi had always been told he had a nice smile. A powerful smile. And it wasn't just his grandmother who said so. His was the smile that launched a thousand Panthera headsets—and that was in preorders alone. He had smiled at Noah, and Noah had stumbled over his words, and the sound of it had sent a frisson of pleasure through Javi's body. It was one thing to know his smile was appreciated by thousands of people he would likely never meet, but it was a whole other thing entirely to know that it was appreciated by one person in particular.

That morning on the lawn wasn't the first time Javi had noticed Noah. He'd been noticing him since freshman year. The boy was quiet and more often than not kept to himself. He was usually the last to be picked for team sports in phys ed. He was so easy to miss. Noah had a tendency to fade into the background. It was almost an art form. He faded with as much virtuosity as Javi shined.

It was his silence that appealed to Javi. His solitude. Noah was good-looking in a frustratingly effortless way, but that appreciation had come later. Javi surrounded himself with friends, with fans, with his guild. He was never alone, not at home, not at school, not even in the game. He didn't know what to do with himself during instances of unexpected isolation. He couldn't help but admire the way Noah took to it as if it were his natural state. Being alone seemed so hard, so alien. But Noah never looked lonely. And that, Javi thought, required a strength of character that he didn't think he possessed. Javi always appeared confident, even—especially—when he wasn't. He wrapped his confidence around himself the way Noah did his solitude. It was familiar, well worn. It was, in its way, armor.

He'd wanted to ask Noah how he did it. How he managed to move through the world without allowing it to touch him. But the words never left his lips. Talking came easy to Javi. Most of the time. It was like performing. From reading his siblings stories at bedtime to entertaining the followers of his Twitch stream while he played, he'd become comfortable with speaking. But speaking to Noah felt as if it would be different, more demanding somehow. Noah didn't waste words, and Javi rarely ever had to think about his own. He wasn't sure how to go about navigating a person like that.

But he very much wanted to find out.

You're obsessing, he told himself.

Acknowledging it didn't seem to help.

He finished his dinner and trudged upstairs. Maybe *Polaris* would distract him. As soon as he booted up the game, a small red badge appeared on the upper right corner of the message icon. In-game mail was notoriously unwieldy. It was poorly maintained. Messages had a habit of disappearing from one's inbox of their own volition. The anonymity of the game encouraged the sort of failure of humanity common on social media platforms. But every now and then, a fan reached out to Javi to express their delight at encountering him in-game, and those were always nice messages to receive.

Javi clicked the message icon, drumming his fingers on his desk as he waited for his overtaxed broadband to connect. He'd need to upgrade again, to ensure his connection remained stable and strong while gaming, but upgrades cost money and tuition was due in a week, for him *and* his siblings.

His fingers stilled as the message loaded. It wasn't text, but an image.

A jester, exactly like the stickers affixed to the security cameras at the front entrance of Maplethorpe Academy. Beneath the jester's painted face, four lines of text stood out, written in the same lurid red as the jester's makeup.

On the day of the prophet false
One mustn't dance a forbidden waltz
A copper found and a fortune told
All beside a box of gold

"What the fish sticks?" Javi said softly. His abuela would whip him upside the head with her *chancla* if she caught him swearing under her roof.

He grabbed the nearest scrap of paper he could find amid the disorganized clutter on his desk. It was a poster featuring Javi wearing the very Panthera headset he'd just removed, with a mustache drawn on his face in Sharpie, courtesy of one of his siblings. They thought his endorsement deals were hilarious.

With the same Sharpie that had probably been used to deface his own image, Javi scribbled down the message before the game's unreliable inbox had the chance to devour it whole. He snapped a picture with his phone, too, just in case.

He leaned back in his chair, huffing out a heavy breath.

It was a troll. It had to be. He was being trolled by someone with too much time on their hands. And since *he* had too much time on his hands, he'd fallen right into their trap. The urge to reply to the initial message was too powerful to ignore. He always told his guild not to feed the trolls, but it was late and he was tired and his eyes were straining from staring at a glowing screen for too long. And making sound decisions was for chumps.

He wiggled his fingers over the keyboard, puzzling over how to respond. Then the Polaris client crashed. Javi blinked at the screen.

That was weird.

He clicked the icon to boot the game up again. It took longer than usual.

Also weird.

When he got back to his inbox, he found it empty.

The message was gone. The jester had vanished.

"Trolls," he whispered up at the glow-in-the-dark stars on his ceiling. He'd stuck them up there when he was nine and never got around to removing them. "It's just a troll."

But no matter how many times he silently repeated the words as he got ready for bed, he couldn't shake the sight of that jester's uncanny, knowing smile.

The Jester smiles as the message disappears from the boy's Polaris inbox.

Their smile widens as they think of the name they've adopted. It's fitting, considering the role they mean to play.

A jester.

A figure who speaks truth to power, who holds a mirror up to society. A person who can laugh in the face of kings and live to see another day.

They are, of course, one of many.

The Jester is not an individual. The Jester is an idea. A movement.

Right now, this particular Jester is also a gardener.

Planting the first two seeds is easy.

One is analog, the other digital. The latter is far easier for the Jester to track, though there is a certain pleasure in the physicality of the former. It's the same pleasure that came with the feel of aluminum in their hand as they left their first message, the resistance of the can's trigger as they pressed down on the nozzle. The hiss of paint as it slashed across the doors.

They know that sowing the harvest will be much more difficult, but nothing worth doing is ever easy. Young minds are fertile, though the conditions for growth are hardly ideal. But still, like any patient gardener, the Jester will do the work.

Now all that's left is to see how those seeds blossom. Whether the fruit will ripen or wither on the vine.

CHAPTER 7
BEX JOHNSON

RATING: 91

At Maplethorpe Academy, pupils lacked for nothing. The school boasted state-of-the-art laboratories, fully equipped athletic facilities, and a library large enough to satisfy the needs of the most curious scholars. But it wasn't simply enriching minds that Maplethorpe offered prospective students. The school's ethos promised a range of benefits for attendees: a stellar education, yes, but also a promising future, a healthy boost to the ratings of its graduates, and, most importantly, student *wellness*.

The wellness quota was served by offering the entirety of the student body a free period in the middle of the day, during which no classes were scheduled. It was officially called the Rest Period and unofficially called Siesta, but few actually rested during it. True, *some* distressed students might grab quick naps on any soft, quiet spot they could find, but Bex Johnson was not one of those students.

Not a day went by without at least one scheduled activity taking place during her Rest Period.

Monday: Flute lessons in the new music hall.

Tuesday: Planning meeting for the *Lantern*, Maplethorpe's student-run newspaper, of which Bex was the editor in chief. (She'd held this role since her sophomore year, an unprecedented move for an underclassman, but she'd refused to settle for any lesser position.)

Wednesday: Mathletes practice.

Thursday: Speech and debate team.

Friday: Linguistics club. (Bex was merely treasurer of the club, a fact that made her mother frown whenever she remembered that there were two offices—president and vice president—ranked above her daughter's post.)

After Maplethorpe was stricken by a vandal armed with a can of bloodred spray paint, Bex spent her Tuesday Siesta calling to order the year's first meeting of the *Lantern*.

All anyone could talk about was the graffiti. It had been wiped from the doors, but not from the minds of Maplethorpe students. Talk of it was quickly shushed by teachers in classrooms and hallways, but there was no way to truly silence several hundred teenagers who had just witnessed the juiciest bit of gossip to hit the academy since Elizabeth Reynolds, student council vice president, had a nervous breakdown two years ago and attempted to blow up her smartwatch in the chem lab using a highly combustible potassium chlorate solution.

Melody bumped Bex's shoulder as they sat at two desks they'd pushed together to bend their heads over Bex's tablet. Melody's position at the *Lantern* wasn't exactly editorial in nature—she wrote the weekly horoscopes—but she attended meetings with Bex when her schedule allowed.

"Looks good, Bex," said Melody.

Bex put the finishing touches on the mock-up of Friday's front page. There was only one event that was newsworthy enough for a full-page splash, and everyone knew it.

Bex stared at the blank space over the article she'd written up in the stolen snatches of time between classes. "We need a photo."

"Oh!" Melody slapped her hand against the desk, jolting Bex's carefully arrayed set of colored pens off the surface. Bex frowned at her as she bent down to pick them up, but like all her frowns, it had minimal effect on Melody.

"I forgot to tell you; I saw that kid taking photos of the graffiti, the one with that hipster camera. I told him to come in today to let us take a look at his pictures. Thought we could use one."

"Good thinking." Bex once again lined up her pens in a neat row, assorted by hue. "Which kid?"

"The weird one. You know. With the floppy hair and the long blank stare and the benign antisocial tendencies."

As if summoned by the incomplete (but, Bex noted, not wholly inaccurate) description, a student Bex had never encountered before appeared in the doorway. His hair was indeed floppy and he did hunch his shoulders slightly, as if engaging in even this minor social interaction caused him physical pain. But his stare wasn't blank so much as guarded.

"Hey!" Melody hopped out of her seat and twirled, arms extended. "Welcome to the illustrious offices of the *Lantern*." She gestured to Bex with a grand sweep of her arm. "And this is our benevolent dictator, Bex Johnson."

"Hey," the boy said, hoisting the camera strap higher on his shoulder. The device was distinctly vintage. "I'm Noah."

"Hi, Noah."

"Um, Melody said you wanted photos? Of the graffiti?"

"Yeah," Bex said. "If you have some high-res ones, that would be great."

He swung his backpack off and pulled a thick folder from it. "I developed some last night, actually. I couldn't wait."

Noah grew slightly more animated as he spoke about his work, flipping through each photograph as Melody and Bex admired them.

They were good. Very good.

Bex pointed to one that caught her eye. The framing was perfect. Students milled about the vandalized doors, their faces all pointed to the scene of the crime. A teacher stood off to the side, hands on her hips, brow pinched in consternation. "Do you mind if we use this one?"

"Yeah . . . I mean, no. I don't mind," Noah said. "It might be kind of cool actually. I never really show these to anyone."

"Never?" Melody asked. "That's a crime. You have talent. And I almost never admit when anyone else does."

A modest smile worked its way onto Noah's face. It softened the sharpness of his bone structure, making him look even younger. "Thanks."

Before Melody could flirt with him further, the door opened. Bex turned to see Mr. Donahue, the *Lantern*'s faculty advisor, enter the room. Normally, his hands were full of professional newspapers from across the country he liked to share with his students as examples of the type of journalism they should aim for. But today, his hands were empty and his expression tight.

"Ah, Rebecca. You're here already. Good. Good, good, good," Mr. Donahue said. "Oh, and we even have a new face. Always nice to see."

He didn't sit down at the large desk at the front of the room like normal. He stood, hands hanging awkwardly at his sides.

"Is something wrong, Mr. Donahue?" Bex asked.

"No, no. Well. Yes, I suppose. But nothing truly terrible, I promise."

"Then," Melody prodded, "what is it?"

"Here's the thing," Mr. Donahue said.

Bex steeled herself. A *thing*, when delivered in that tone of voice, was rarely "nothing truly terrible." Donahue looked like he was about to reveal their ratings had dipped by five points each.

"The school's administration has decided to suspend publication of the *Lantern* for the time being."

Melody jerked back as if struck. Ever the dramatist. "What?"

"Mind you, the hiatus won't affect the titles you include on your college résumés. The *Lantern* will be lit once more, don't you worry." He smiled at his own turn of phrase.

"Why?" Bex asked. She hadn't displayed the immediate, knee-jerk reaction Melody did. It simply wasn't in her nature. But something cold and hard had formed in her gut at the news, and it worked its way up her throat and out of her mouth in the stoniest single-word inquiry she had ever uttered.

"Well, you see, it's due to the rather unfortunate incident that happened this week. Certain extracurricular activities will be suspended until the school can conclude its formal investigation into the crime."

It was *technically* a crime, Bex supposed, but it had seemed like a relatively harmless one. Just a senior having a bit of ill-advised fun. There was at least one every year.

"But that isn't fair," Bex said.

Donahue blinked at her, surprised. She had never talked back to a teacher before. Not once, in all her years of grueling education.

"I understand that you work very hard here, Rebecca," said Mr. Donahue, "but this isn't about you."

The words stung. She wasn't being selfish. She wasn't. She simply didn't understand why they were being penalized for a crime *they* hadn't committed.

Donahue was already inching toward the door, his reluctance to answer any more of Bex's questions written in the stiff lines of his posture.

"I'll be sure to let you know when the suspension has been lifted. Until then, consider yourselves free to rest." The cheer in Donahue's voice was so obviously forced, Bex had to suppress the urge to roll her eyes at him. Eye-rolling a teacher was a quick way to take a small hit to one's rating. "It *is* Rest Period after all."

With that, he was gone, leaving Bex, Melody, and Noah to stare at the door slowly swinging shut behind him.

"Well, that was amazingly weird." Melody did always have a penchant for stating the obvious.

"They don't want us talking about it," Bex said. It was the conspicuous subtext of Donahue's announcement. Maplethorpe wanted to make sure it controlled the narrative surrounding the unprecedented act of vandalism. Perhaps they wanted to erase it altogether.

"But why?" Noah asked.

"That," Bex said, "is the question."

CHAPTER 8
Noah Rainier

RATING: 64

Noah had always been a healthy child. He was small for his age and prone to injury because of an innate clumsiness he never seemed able to shake, but otherwise healthy. The only time he'd ever been admitted to a hospital was when he had fallen out of a tree at the age of twelve and broken his leg. He'd climbed it to hide from a group of kids who used to call him Nerdy Noah, because kids were clever like that. Unfortunately for Noah, they'd decided that his small stature and thick-framed glasses (which he'd since replaced with contacts) made him the perfect punching bag. *Fortunately* for Noah, they hadn't bothered to look up as they'd passed under the tree's branches, hunting their prey. Finding no one to torment, they'd settled under the tree, backs against the trunk, and played an interminably long game on their phones. From what Noah could hear from fifteen feet above their heads, it was some kind of multiplayer fighting game and none of them were particularly good at it.

Eventually, the kids grew bored and left, but by that point Noah had been in the tree for two hours and his muscles were stiff and unresponsive. Shimmying down proved a significantly greater challenge than climbing up. One wrong step and he plummeted to the ground, breaking his fall with the tibia of his left leg. His phone was smashed on impact, rendering it useless.

So he lay on the ground for fifteen excruciating minutes until his little sister, Cecelia, found him. Cece was only seven at the time. He was supposed to have been watching her as she cavorted in the nearby playground, but he'd failed in his most fundamental duty as a brother. Cece, on the other hand, proved herself the better sibling. Not only had she summoned a passing adult to call their mother, but she hadn't even tattled about Noah's negligence. Ever since then, they'd been ride or die.

Despite the five-year gap in their ages, Noah often felt that Cece was his best friend. He took her to the movies, even if the animated fare she preferred made Noah want to drown himself in the jumbo popcorn they always ordered. He saved up his allowance so they could eat like kings at the pick-and-mix candy station at the mall. They'd even created their own shared language—a sloppy combination of pig Latin and the rudimentary Spanish Noah learned in middle school. And she'd held his hand at the hospital when he cried as they were applying the cast to his broken leg.

Noah had worn that cast for weeks. The most popular he'd ever been in school was the Monday after the fall. All the girls in class wanted to sign his cast. One of the boys (of the same group who had driven him up the tree to begin with) gifted Noah with a crudely drawn example of the male anatomy. One of the girls in his class (Melody or Melanie, Noah was as terrible with names as he was good with faces) had thoughtfully covered it up with a large, rainbow unicorn.

But despite a relatively healthy youth, Noah was far more familiar with hospitals than most people his age. His little sister hadn't shared Noah's genetic fortune. Cece had been diagnosed with acute lymphoblastic leukemia at the age of eight and spent her childhood in and out of hospitals. These days, it was mostly in. He was thirteen when he first asked his parents if he could give Cece his own bone marrow. They'd shared a look that seemed to say a great deal of things, but all they'd told Noah was that one had to be eighteen in order to donate.

And so he waited. Until today. The day after his eighteenth birthday, he went to the hospital—without his parents, who were both at work—to discuss donation with Cece's primary oncologist, Dr. Reginald Lowe. Dr. Lowe offered Noah a smile and a consent form for the blood test, to see if Noah was a match.

He sat in the stiff-backed chair in Dr. Lowe's office, the buzzing in his ears overpowering the sound of Dr. Lowe's calm, steady voice. It was a good voice for a doctor who worked with terminally ill children. It was smooth and deep and Noah was sure people found it reassuring.

In that moment, he didn't feel reassured. He was unmoored.

"Noah?" Dr. Lowe's brow furrowed in what looked like concern, but his brow was almost always furrowed, so it was hard to tell. "Are you listening to me?"

"Yes," Noah lied.

Well, it wasn't entirely a lie. He had been listening, at the start of the conversation. Only he'd stopped a few sentences in.

He wasn't a match.

Cece needed a donor, and Noah was not a match.

Dr. Lowe folded his hands over the papers on his desk, the ones that had declared Noah unfit to be Cece's donor. "I know this must be hard to hear, and I commend you for trying, but it was always a long shot."

Noah blinked. "A long shot?"

Dr. Lowe nodded. It was a good, sage nod that went with his deep, soothing voice. Noah wondered if the doctor practiced these incredibly soothing expressions in the mirror before he left for the hospital in the morning. Or perhaps the repeated work of delivering the worst possible news to families with sick children was practice enough.

"Matches are more likely to be found within families, for the most part. Siblings are usually most likely to match."

"One in four," Noah said. His voice sounded distant, as if it was echoing around in his skull after someone else had spoken.

"Excuse me?"

"There's a one-in-four chance of siblings being a bone marrow match," Noah said, though why he was explaining this to an oncologist of all things seemed the height of absurdity. "I looked it up. I did all the research."

One in four was a good chance, but it left a 75 percent chance that Noah wouldn't be a match. Still, he'd felt so certain.

Dr. Lowe nodded again, even more slowly this time. "For *biological* siblings, yes."

The buzzing in Noah's ears swelled to a feverish concerto. *Biological siblings.*

"But I'm her brother," Noah said, though the truth was already poking holes in the shield of Noah's certainty.

Biological, biological, biological.

The word felt damning.

Dr. Lowe's hands unfolded. Folded again. Unfolded once more. He pressed his palms flat to the papers on his desk.

"Noah, have your parents discussed your adopt—" He didn't finish this question. He didn't have to. "I apologize. I assumed you knew."

"I'm her brother." Noah was speaking only to himself now, not to Dr. Lowe. Repeating it wouldn't change a thing, but his mind was clinging desperately to the lie he'd believed his entire life.

"You *are* her brother," Dr. Lowe said softly, insistently. "Cecelia is your sister, and she loves you very much. Nothing will change that."

Noah blinked again. He must have looked so slow and stupid and dumbstruck.

"Blood doesn't make a family," Dr. Lowe said. And then, sensing perhaps that he had wildly overstepped his bounds, he added, "You should speak to your parents, Noah."

Noah nodded. It was not a good, sage nod like the doctor's. It was shallow and too quick, and it made him feel slightly nauseated.

Noah's hands tightened on the stuffed animal in his lap. It was bright green and looked like a cross between a chinchilla and a cat. He'd picked it up on his way to the hospital after spotting it in a shopwindow. It was an alien companion from some video game Cece liked, cute in a weird, extraterrestrial sort of way. Cece lived for stuff like that. He'd brought it with him to Dr. Lowe's office, hoping that he would be able to visit Cece afterward to convey the good news.

But he didn't have any good news. He hadn't told her he was testing his bone marrow. He hadn't even told his parents. Maybe if he had, this whole conversation with Dr. Lowe would have been avoided. Maybe they would have told him themselves. Or maybe they had never planned on doing so. Maybe they'd intended for Noah to live his life without this vital piece of information about his own biology.

His biology wasn't their biology.

His blood was not their blood.

Blood doesn't make a family. And it didn't. Noah knew that family was about a lot more than the womb in which one had been carried. But the information sat in his stomach like a hard and indigestible lump.

It remained hard and indigestible the entire bus ride home, the dumb green space chinchilla thing still in his hands. He hadn't gone to see Cece. He wasn't sure how to face her, if he'd be able to school his expression into something normal and comforting for her sake. She never wanted to be treated like she was sick, and Noah mostly excelled at that, but he didn't trust his own shifting emotions. He wasn't angry. He wasn't even particularly sad, beyond the sadness that had come with knowing he couldn't help Cece. He wasn't sure what he was feeling, but he was sure that he was feeling a great deal of it.

His parents were still at work by the time he arrived home. Noah didn't bother going upstairs to his bedroom to change out of his blazer and slacks, despite the fact that it was one of the greatest pleasures in his life. The fabric of the blazer itched and the slacks made him feel like the dweeb he probably was. He didn't even stop to grab a snack from the kitchen as he did every day after school, despite the fact that he'd skipped lunch in favor of snapping candids of the students of Maplethorpe around campus. He was afraid that if he put anything in his stomach, it would rebel against the great, unnameable feeling and be expelled from his body immediately.

Noah made straight for the darkroom he and his dad had built in the basement two summers ago. Cece had just been admitted for another lengthy stay at Magnolia Children's Hospital, and having an activity to occupy them had benefited both Noah and his father.

His father, who wasn't his father. Except for all the ways in which he was.

The darkroom felt more personal to Noah than his own bedroom. The walls of Noah's room were decorated with posters of bands he'd long ago stopped following. His bed was still covered in dinosaur sheets, because Cece liked them and he was loath to remove anything that gave her even the smallest amount of joy.

The darkroom was *his*, in a way nothing else in the world was. No one was allowed to enter, not since the time his mother had thrown on the lights and ruined the photos he'd been developing of Cece's birthday. Her face had been smeared with rainbow frosting from the Funfetti cake Noah had baked for her. They'd eaten it by the handful because doing so was disgusting and made Cece laugh so hard she snorted. But those pictures had been destroyed, inspiring the strict entry policy for Noah's darkroom. The Rainier family respected this, and when he was in there, no one bothered him.

Today Noah didn't want to be bothered. He wanted—needed—to be alone.

Solitude made processing information easier, and he had a lot of processing to do.

The red light of the darkroom soothed the ragged edges of Noah's thoughts. Hours passed as he sat on the floor, backpack tossed to one side carelessly, his camera placed on the ground beside him with much more care.

He hadn't realized how long he'd been sitting there until a knock sounded at the door.

"You in there, Noah?"

It was his father. The man who raised him and whose blood he didn't share.

"Yeah." The word came out of Noah in a croak, his voice shaky and disused.

"Well, dinner's ready. Your mom made lasagna."

His mother had *reheated* lasagna. She made a big batch on Sundays, and they lived on it until the large glass dish was empty.

"I'm not hungry."

His father was silent on the other side of the door for the span of a few breaths, which Noah dutifully counted. Then, eventually, "Suit yourself."

Noah listened to his father's footsteps as he climbed the stairs. The hard, indigestible lump in his gut grew with every retreating footfall.

CHAPTER 9

TAMSIN MOORE

RATING: 32

Standing at her locker between periods, Tamsin grimaced as the device on her wrist buzzed. Again. It was the fifth time that day, and while she often took pleasure in flouting the rules of Maplethorpe (and society as a whole), she was certain that she hadn't earned five separate rating reductions. Yet.

Maybe she'd pissed someone off on the bus ride to school? Or her chem teacher was feeling less generous than usual about her slight tardiness. She actually enjoyed her science classes, so she went to most of those. Ms. Stevens was normally more lenient than the rest of the faculty, especially with her sentimental favorites. Maybe Maplethorpe teachers had been instructed to bring down the hammer in light of the vandalism.

"Ms. Moore, may I have a word with you?"

The voice came from the other side of Tamsin's open locker door. She couldn't see the face of the speaker, but she didn't need to. That voice belonged to the man who delivered the news at morning assembly every day in authoritative tones. And even though Tamsin's attendance at such assemblies was sporadic at best, she still knew the stern disapproval of that voice like she knew the back of her own hand. She didn't think she'd ever heard anything but stern disapproval from it, come to think of it.

With the slow, deliberate speed of a death row inmate walking to her execution, Tamsin closed the locker door and turned to face Headmaster Wood.

He was tall, far taller than a school administrator had any right to be, and Tamsin had to look up to meet his gaze. She hated looking up at people. She was far more comfortable looking down on them.

"Sure, Dr. Wood. I don't have anything important on the old agenda."

Wood pursed his lips in a distinctly unamused fashion. "As a matter of fact, you have chemistry this period."

Tamsin offered him her best artful shrug. "Wasn't like I was planning on going anyway."

"Ah, there's that blatant disregard for authority I've come to know and love," Wood said. "Come with me."

He turned and used his unreasonably long legs to stride down the hallway, not even looking back to see if she was following.

For a few seconds, Tamsin considered *not* following him, just to spite the unwavering confidence Wood had in his own authority. But she didn't. For starters, she had a feeling that was exactly what he was expecting of her, and she so hated to be predictable. And there was the minor fact of her rating. The system was a sham, a disgrace, an arbitrary algorithm designed to maintain the status quo of privilege and prestige, but the thought of flouting it to the point where she was expelled gave her pause. Not that she cared about the consequences for her own life, but her mother ran a tiny apothecary in a gentrified part of town, catering to far-wealthier people. They barely scraped by as it was. Despite her bravado, Tamsin didn't truly want to hurt the one person in her life whose opinion actually mattered.

Her mother wanted her to graduate. Maybe she should try.

Tamsin trudged after Wood, the heels of her heavy block boots dragging on the polished wooden floors. The halls had quieted, with most students sitting dutifully in class, where Tamsin was supposed to be. A not insignificant part of Tamsin was curious about Wood requesting her presence during a class period. He could have intercepted her after school—provided she didn't cut, which would have honestly been a bit of a gamble—or during her designated lunch period. He'd waited until most of the student body and staff were preoccupied.

Interesting.

And so, she followed him all the way to his office. The room was set in one of the towers overlooking the main quad on campus. It reminded Tamsin of the diagrams of old prisons she'd seen in a textbook in the library's recycling pile. (The school sent outdated or otherwise undesirable books to be turned into mulch and made into new books, but Tamsin enjoyed a spot of literary dumpster diving the way she suspected other girls like shopping for prom dresses.)

From the bank of large windows set into the curving walls of the room, Wood had a view of practically the entire campus. It wasn't her first time in the office. That was how she knew the abandoned music building was just out of his line of sight. It made her business dealings safe from his prying eyes.

"Take a seat, Tamsin." Wood gestured to one of the leather chairs before his desk. They were far less grand than the one he lowered himself into.

An obvious power move, Tamsin thought. Reminding one's opponent of their place. Making them feel smaller.

The joke was on him. Tamsin was so accustomed to the disdain directed at her from her fellow Maplethorpe students that she hardly felt Wood's intimidation tactic.

"I won't beat around the bush." Wood set his elbows on his desk, resting his chin against his loosely clasped hands. She wondered if he'd seen the pose in a manual designed to teach school officials how to look relaxed and casual while still projecting an air of foreboding. "We need to talk about your rating."

Tamsin held up her wrist, beaming with something a lot like pride. "Yeah, it's abysmal, right?"

Wood managed to look even less amused. "It is. You're on the cusp of expulsion."

Tamsin nodded. None of this was news. She was only surprised it had taken Wood this long to say what they both knew out loud.

"I don't want to expel you, Tamsin."

She rolled her eyes, exaggerating the move to make sure he knew she *really* meant it. "Right. Let me guess. You think I could be a valuable asset to the Maplethorpe community. You see a great potential in me to be a productive member of society. Yada yada. I've heard the spiel before."

Wood cocked his head to the side, as if studying a dog that had just learned how to ride a bike. "Hardly."

Tamsin blinked at him. "Pardon?"

"I don't think you'll ever be a valuable asset to the Maplethorpe community, Tamsin. Nor do I think you have much interest in productivity to society as a whole."

This wasn't how she'd been expecting the conversation to go. "So, why did you call me into your office if you're not going to try to convince me to get my act together?" She motioned between them, hoping her loose hand gestures succinctly conveyed the disparity of their positions, life philosophies, and regard for the rule of law and order. "What's the point of this?"

"Here's the thing. I don't want you to get your act together to please me or your teachers or anyone else."

"Um, is that not how society operates?"

He ignored her, plowing toward his point. "I want you to get your act together for yourself. You're smart. Smart enough to skirt the rules without falling so far afoul of them that you lose your place here. Smart enough to get decent-enough grades to pass while putting in the absolute minimum effort. Smart enough to spearhead your own flourishing underground business."

So he knew about her tarot card hustle. *Interesting*, Tamsin thought, *that he didn't put a stop to it.*

"I do see potential in you and I do believe that you're capable of great things, but one thing I don't want to see you nurture is your own stupidity."

Tamsin had been accused of a lot of things by her various teachers throughout the years. Stupidity had never been one of them. "Excuse me?"

"Whatever you want to do in this life, you won't be able to if you shoot yourself in the foot before you even get it in the door."

"Maybe I don't want to get my foot in the door. Maybe I want to stay outside and light the whole house on fire."

She wished she had the lighter she used for her candles in the music building. Flicking it right then would have been the height of self-indulgent drama.

With a swift twitch of his fingers, Wood tapped something on the face of his own smartwatch. Half a second later, her own buzzed against her skin. She glanced down at the screen, not surprised to see it flash an even more abysmal 31 back at her.

"Here at Maplethorpe, we have a zero tolerance policy for arson. You'll remember that in the future."

"But I wasn't . . ." Tamsin swallowed her protest. It was a power move, like the disparate seating arrangements and the Orwellian view of the campus behind him. George Orwell, the author of another book she'd found in the library's mulch pile. *1984*. She'd tried to find any of his other works in circulation, but her search of the library system's catalog hadn't returned a single title.

"Your position here is a precarious one. I want to make sure you understand it."

Tamsin bit down on the tender flesh on the inside of her cheek before giving her answer through clenched teeth. "Trust me, I do."

Wood straightened up, relinquishing the pretense of being relaxed and approachable. "Good. See that you remember it. When I read the names of this year's seniors at graduation in the spring, I expect to see your name on it. Not for my sake. But for yours."

He reached for a stack of papers in a chrome tray on his desk, before flicking his gaze to her. "That'll be all, Ms. Moore. I've already told Ms. Stevens you'll be late for class, so you needn't worry about a rating deduction for being tardy. I hope that you take the time to think about what I've said."

Tamsin grumbled out an extremely insincere thank-you and goodbye and trudged out of his office with double the speed she'd entered. The halls were empty as she made her way back to her locker. The thick soles of her boots thudded dully against the wooden floor with no other sound to cushion their fall.

She *could* go to class. She probably wouldn't. Maybe she would. Maybe sitting through the drudgery of a lecture would be worth not subjecting herself to another one of Wood's.

He wasn't wrong about her. Not really. She was smart. She was probably the smartest person she knew. Not only had she managed to disable a number of fire exits in the school to enable her numerous escapes, but she'd figured out how to confuse the motion sensors installed in the derelict music building. Simply turning them off triggered an alarm in the facilities office, but redirecting them to a patch of grass near the back . . . now, that took skill.

But Tamsin didn't know what she wanted to do with all that genius. She knew what she *didn't* want to do. That was easy. She didn't want to be a doctor or a lawyer or a hedge fund manager—or whatever career Maplethorpe's best and brightest were funneled into after graduating from college. And while she admired her mother's work ethic and her ability to keep a small business afloat in a place like Jackson Hills, she wasn't sure the life of a humble shopkeeper was for her either. So far, the only vocations in life that gave her pleasure were hoodwinking the rich and gullible and inspiring a vague sense of unease in everyone around her.

Tamsin's boots skidded to a stop when she reached her locker.

There was a card taped to it.

She approached cautiously. It wasn't the first time someone had messed with her locker. There had been an unfortunate incident her freshman year when a group of girls—she'd always suspected Summer Rawlins had been involved—scribbled a slew of unkind messages on it. The nicest of them was a simple *freak*.

But this wasn't the vengeful scrawl of mean-spirited fourteen-year-olds.

This was a single tarot card. The nondescript blue-and-white pattern on the back was marred by a sticker of a smiling jester.

Tamsin plucked it off the door and turned it over, expecting something uninspired like Death or any of the more violent-looking sword cards. Maybe an angry client was seeking revenge for a negative reading. But the face of the card presented none of those. She blinked at it, puzzled.

The Hanged Man.

It wasn't a bad card, despite the connotations of the name. It could be interpreted to mean letting go of negative patterns of behavior or shedding bad habits holding you back. It could also symbolize surrender. Sacrifice. Martyrdom. There were a number of ways to read the card, just as there were a number of ways to read almost any card, especially those in the Major

Arcana. But there was something about the card that felt sinister to Tamsin.

She looked at it more closely. What had initially looked like a design on the white border of the card was actually text. Each letter had been surgically cut out from what Tamsin could only assume was a book with a vintage typesetting and precisely glued to the card.

On the day of the prophet false
One mustn't dance a forbidden waltz
A copper found and a fortune told
All beside a box of gold

She looked to her right. Then her left. The corridors were as empty as they'd been when she'd left Wood's office. Whoever had left the card had likely done so in the sliver of time between the bell ringing and her arrival. She didn't imagine someone would have done it with an audience of dozens of students milling about the halls.

Tamsin slipped the card into her pocket and made for the stairwell nearest her locker. She made sure the door didn't slam behind her. The hinges were temperamental on that one. The old music building waited for her, and hopefully, there she would be able to solve the riddle of the hanged man and the jester.

Her feet had barely touched the grass outside the fire exit when a voice broke her stride.

"Going somewhere, Ms. Moore?"

Tamsin bit back a groan. She pivoted in place. Leaning against the wall was the physical education teacher, Ms. Lynch.

Her cropped red hair fluttered in the gentle, early autumn breeze. She flicked the ash off her cigarette as she regarded Tamsin with an ambiguous expression.

"As a matter of fact, I thought I could use some fresh air," Tamsin said. "It gets real stuffy in there."

Lynch barked out a laugh. If she hadn't been a phys ed teacher, Tamsin probably would have liked her. She'd always seemed different from other faculty members at Maplethorpe. Not more relaxed—her personality skewed a little too close to drill sergeant for Tamsin's liking—but less conservative perhaps.

"You're telling me." Lynch took a slow drag of her cigarette. It was rare to see a teacher smoking at Maplethorpe. Tamsin wondered if Headmaster Wood would dock Lynch's rating for it if he caught her. "You supposed to be in class?"

Tamsin considered lying. But it would take naught but a few taps on her watch for Lynch to pull up Tamsin's schedule and catch her in the lie. It wasn't worth risking an even greater deduction for dishonesty.

"Would you believe me if I said no?"

"Nope."

Tamsin sighed. "Fine. What's it gonna be?"

Lynch regarded Tamsin thoughtfully for a moment before speaking. "Nothing, so long as you don't tell anyone you saw me out here."

"Deal."

Lynch nodded. Tamsin remained there for a second or two longer than necessary. She couldn't go to the music building now. Not with Lynch watching.

"You waiting for an engraved invitation?"

Tamsin shrugged. "Bum a smoke?"

It seemed like a reason to justify her presence outside. It fit with the whole persona she'd spent years crafting. Even though cigarettes were disgusting cancer sticks and she wouldn't smoke one if paid.

Lynch tossed back her head and laughed. With the hand holding the cigarette, she tapped at her own smartwatch with her ring finger. A second later, Tamsin's device buzzed against her skin in a sensation so familiar she often felt it in her sleep.

She didn't need to look down to see what had been done. Her rating. One point lower. One inch deeper into her own grave.

"You could've gotten away clean, Moore, but you just can't help yourself, can you?"

Tamsin bit back all the responses that would result in the same thing—even more points shaved off her rating. "Guess not, Ms. Lynch. But thankfully, I've got you to keep me on the straight and narrow."

She didn't wait for Lynch to respond. The door was still unlocked, and so she went through it, back into the belly of a beast that was liable to chew her up and spit her out before the year was through. Maplethorpe would have its pound of flesh from Tamsin, one way or another. And it felt like there was nothing—absolutely *nothing*—she could do about it.

CHAPTER 10
HANA SAKAMOTO

RATING: 76

Speed had always been Hana's greatest strength as a skater. Today she'd pulled her hair back from her face into a ponytail, as she always did before practice. She was skating so fast across the nearly empty rink that the end of her ponytail lashed against her cheeks like a whip. Her coach, an imperious Russian veteran of the sport and former Olympic champion, watched her fly by from the boards. Maxim Dmitriev was ancient, but his advanced age did nothing to reduce his demand as a coach. A scowl marred the lines of his weathered skin, but since Hana had never seen him without it, she was pretty sure that his face just looked that way even when he was happy.

He wasn't happy now.

She'd removed her smartwatch for practice—she never wore it while she was skating—but was sure that if it had been strapped on her wrist, she would have felt it buzz with Dmitriev's displeasure. He wasn't afraid to dock her rating if he felt like she wasn't trying hard enough. Hana's rating depended not just on the judges she faced in competition. Her own coach's approval was paramount. And Dmitriev was unforgiving, which was precisely why Hana's parents paid him an absurd amount of money to turn her into a champion.

She shot by him and his scowling face, her blades scratching against the ice as she set up the jump that had eluded her all afternoon.

The triple Axel. The crown jewel of ladies' figure skating. An element so difficult that only a handful of women had ever successfully completed it in international competition. A few girls around Hana's age had tried their hands at quadruple jumps—a mainstay of men's skating—but none had managed to work up enough consistency to incorporate them into their programs. The elusive triple Axel was fiendishly difficult, but Hana *knew* she could land it. Deep in her heart, she knew.

Unfortunately, her body wasn't nearly as sure.

The jump had a longer lead-in than the others in her short program. She needed to build up enough speed to launch herself from a forward outside edge—it was the only jump with a forward takeoff—and spin three and a half times before landing in a backward glide. In skating's code of points, falling on a fully rotated triple Axel was still worth more than cleanly landing a double. It was a risk, but one worth taking.

Hana squared her shoulders, bent her knee, and skidded the blade of her working leg into the ice, pushing into the air. The world whizzed by in a blur as she pulled her arms into her chest to speed her rotations. One and a half turns, two, three—

Pain shot up Hana's hips as she slammed into the ice. Again.

"That's enough." Dmitriev's thick accent was as icy as the Siberian lakes on which he'd learned to skate. He hailed from the city of Novosibirsk, and any time Hana grumbled about the cold, he was quick to remind her that she was soft and spoiled. Had she grown up in a place like Novosibirsk, she'd be as hard and cold as he was.

Hana pushed herself up, brushing the snow off her leggings. She shuddered to think what her legs must look like under the stretchy black fabric. A symphony of black and blue and that disgusting mustard yellow.

"I can do it," Hana said, though her voice quavered in a way she knew Dmitriev wouldn't miss. She'd started their session so sure that a clean landing was just within her reach, but with every fall her certainty crumbled, bit by bit. What had felt strong and light as air had grown heavier and heavier as the hours wore on. Her limbs weighed her down in every jump and spin.

"Not today." Dmitriev beckoned her to the boards and like an obedient soldier she followed. She skidded to a stop in front of him, the pain settling deeper into her sore muscles and bruised bones. "You are too slow. Like slug."

Sluggish, Hana thought. It was one of her least favorite words, climbing up the ranks every time her coach slung it at her like a sharp rock. He'd been saying it more and more lately.

The worst part was that Hana knew why.

She had ingested six hundred calories all day, each one meticulously tracked in the little black notebook tucked into the side pocket of her backpack. Not enough even for a person leading a sedentary lifestyle. And most assuredly not enough for an elite athlete of Hana's caliber. But the thinner she was, the faster she would spin, the higher she would fly. It was a double-edged sword, and every day she buried that blade deeper and deeper into her bruised and battered body.

Dmitriev's frown deepened as he looked down at her. He wasn't very tall—few male singles skaters were—but Hana was petite, even for a skater.

"Your conditioning is no good. We have to build up stamina and strength."

Hana nodded, trying to mask how winded she truly was. She doubted that Dmitriev would be fooled, but she had to try anyway. If he didn't think she was mentally strong enough to compete at the highest level of her sport, she knew he would not hesitate to move on to a new pupil, abandoning her without a coach.

"I think I'm coming down with something." She sniffled for good measure. Her nose was usually runny at the rink anyway, so she had that working in her favor. "I've been feeling off all day."

An understatement, to be sure.

Dmitriev hummed thoughtfully. From the depths of his coat, he produced a small beat-up wire-ruled notebook and a pen. He scribbled a few lines on a piece of paper and ripped it from the notebook.

"We will end here today. Now you will go to this shop. Ask for these herbs. They are the best for what ails you."

Hana looked at the list. His handwriting was, as always, utterly illegible. She could just make out the name and address of the shop, but the identities of whatever herbs he'd written down were beyond her. That he hadn't specified what it was he thought ailed her wasn't lost on her.

"Okay," she said, slipping the scrap of paper into the pocket of her snugly fitted fleece. Normally, she warmed up enough during her after-school practice sessions to eventually shed the fleece, but today she'd remained chilled no matter how hard she worked. Maybe a nice herbal tea was exactly what she needed. It wouldn't fix what was truly wrong with her—too many things to count—but maybe, for just a few minutes, it would make her forget about them.

She wanted to tell Dmitriev that she could keep going, that she could fight through whatever was ailing her, but when her coach made up his mind, it was made up. Nothing she could say or do would change it. And even if she *did* manage to convince him, she wasn't entirely sure she'd be able to live up to the promise. She ached in places she hadn't known a body could ache. Lately, it felt as though she wasn't recovering the way she used to, despite the ice baths and the anti-inflammatories and the cortisone injections. A skater's body had to be accustomed to a baseline state of discomfort, but she felt like she was slipping deeper and deeper into a quagmire of her own invention.

She stepped off the ice and slipped on her blade guards. They were gold, like the blades on her skates.

"Wishful thinking," Dmitriev had called it when he'd supervised her selection.

"*Positive* thinking," Hanna had replied, but his words had stuck in her mind, surfacing whenever she was alone with nothing but silence and her own fear to keep her company.

She was afraid almost constantly. Afraid that he was right, that she would never capture the most elusive medal in the world, an Olympic gold. That her rating would hover at good without ever reaching truly great. That all her hard work and sacrifice would amount to nothing.

Positive thinking, she reminded herself, even though she was starting to forget what such thinking felt like. She wondered if she had ever really known at all.

Hana took the bus to the shop, tucked away on a small side street near the downtown area. Dusk had fallen when she'd been on the ice, and shadows lengthened in the spaces streetlights couldn't touch. Hana's experience of sunlight was limited to a few snatches on Maplethorpe's campus between classes. She rose before dawn to get to practice and arrived home well after dark. Her parents were home maybe half the year. The other half, they were traveling for her mother's competitions or attending conferences or seminars or whatever it was they did with their time. Hana honestly didn't know. She didn't much care either. She loved them, and in their way they loved her, but that love was best served at a comfortable distance.

Hana alighted from the bus, squinting into the evening gloom to find the sign for the apothecary. The fact that an apothecary existed in this corner of the world, in this century, was something of a curiosity to Hana. She hoisted her skate bag higher on her shoulder and walked toward an awning flanked by two crescent moons. A bell rung as she pushed the door open, an antiquated little sound that matched the antiquated little shop.

A wild barrage of scents assaulted her the moment she crossed the threshold. Incense hung thick in the air, cloying in its intensity. The power of it made Hana sway on her feet. She had to close her eyes and grope for a nearby surface—a tall mahogany bookshelf that matched nothing else in the room—

to keep herself upright. The hollow pit in her stomach widened, like a chasm torn by a glacier. She'd been light-headed all day. Practice, and now the strange and potent scents of what surely had to be some kind of witch's brew, was not helping.

She opened her eyes to see a black cat, heavily pregnant, sauntering across her path. It gazed at her with deeply un-impressed amber eyes.

"Don't mind Sprinkles," came a voice from the back of the shop. "She's in a mood."

The voice sounded vaguely familiar, but the speaker was kneeling as she unpacked a box of candles to stack on a lower shelf. The girl stood and turned around. She was wearing a bulky black cardigan, the sleeves of which swallowed her hands, and an aubergine top that matched the purple gloss on her lips. Her hair was mostly dark blond with a hint of laven-der coloring the ends. Hana recognized her immediately.

The Witch of Maplethorpe.

The girl's actual name—it would probably be impolite to refer to her as a witch—eluded Hana. Thankfully, the girl didn't seem much interested in exchanging pleasantries.

"Can I help you with something?" Her tone implied that she would rather not, but it wasn't belligerent enough to put Hana off her task. When her coach told her to do something, she did it.

"Yes, actually." She groped in her pocket for Dmitriev's hastily scribbled note. "I'm looking for some herbs." She handed the Witch of Maplethorpe the note.

"Looks like somebody slept through penmanship class," the girl said as she squinted at Dmitriev's illegible scrawl.

"I don't know if they had those back in the Bronze Age."

The Witch of Maplethorpe cracked an actual smile. It softened her face significantly.

"I think I can just about make these out." The girl squinted at the paper, as if urging it to relinquish its secrets. "Might have to go to the back to find some of these, though. Herbal remedies that taste like butt aren't exactly flying off the shelf."

Hana nodded and immediately wished she hadn't. The room swayed on its axis. Or maybe she was the one swaying. She reached out to place a steadying hand on the countertop. The sensation reminded her of the head rush she got when she came out of a scratch spin. She squeezed her eyes shut, willing her equilibrium to find itself.

"Hey."

Hana blinked her eyes open. The Witch of Maplethorpe was looking at her expectantly, as if she'd been speaking to Hana for some time. But her eyes couldn't have been closed for more than a second. Probably. Possibly? Hana wasn't so sure.

"You okay?"

Hana nodded again, because apparently she was a fool. Her grip on the counter tightened, the skin across her knuckles turning white, then pink. "I'm fine."

"Uh-huh." The girl held Dmitriev's note aloft. "I'm gonna go find the rest of these."

The rest . . . ?

Hana looked down at the counter to find two little baggies full of dried herbs sitting on top of it. Those hadn't been there before. Time had gone weird and elastic, and Hana didn't like it one bit.

The beaded curtain that separated the front of the shop from the back tinkled like chimes as the other girl went through it. Hana watched the long strands sway in her wake.

The world tilted the way it did when she was off her axis in a jump. Sometimes, even the jumps with wonky takeoffs could be saved with a hand down or a two-footed landing or sheer determination. But some couldn't, no matter how hard she tried. Those were the times she knew she was going to fall.

And fall she did.

The curtain swayed again as the other girl emerged, just in time to watch Hana sink to the ground, her fingers sliding down the glass display case as she went.

"Holy crap. Wake up. Wake. Up."

Hana woke up and immediately wished she hadn't.

A light was shining in her eyes and she tried to bat it away, before realizing it was a lamp on the table beside her. Hana squinted at it from her position on the couch.

Wait a minute.

How did she get on a couch?

The last thing she remembered was gawking at the Witch of Maplethorpe.

"Oh, thank the goddess."

Hana blinked at the voice. As her eyes adjusted to the light, the girl resolved from a blur into a person. She was kneeling next to the sagging, well-worn couch. She stared down at Hana, her heavily lined eyes wide and worried.

"I thought you were dead."

It was a minor struggle, reaching for words, but Hana found them all the same. "That seems . . . dramatic."

"You went down like a marionette that just had its strings cut. *That* was dramatic." The girl reached for something on the table and held it out to Hana.

It was a glass of water. The sight of it made her realize just how parched her throat was.

She accepted it with as much grace as her shaking hands could muster—not very much—and sipped. Her stomach roiled in revolt, displeased at being so assaulted after a day of deprivation.

"Are you okay?"

Hana sipped her water again so she wouldn't have to answer. They didn't have the time to discuss all the ways in which she wasn't okay.

The girl sighed. "Okay, fine. Do you have a name?"

"Everyone has a name," Hana mumbled into her glass. Realizing how rude it sounded, she added, "Hana."

The other girl nodded. "I'm Tamsin Moore. Is there someone you want me to call?"

Tamsin. It was an odd name. It suited her, this Witch of Maplethorpe. Maybe more so than her reputation. Tamsin didn't seem nearly as misanthropic as Hana had been led to believe.

Hana shook her head too fast. A surge of nausea threatened to erupt, even though she knew there was nothing in her stomach to expel.

"No, no," Hana said in a rush. "It's okay. It was just a dizzy spell. Not a big deal."

Tamsin's eyebrows inched upward. "Really? Because you were pretty much out cold."

"Pretty much isn't entirely."

"There was a vague attempt at shuffling your feet as I carried you to the couch, but okay. Have it your way."

"Thanks," Hana said quietly. She looked at her surroundings. They were in an office, from the looks of it. A large desk sat under the oppressive weight of several sloppy stacks of papers. The faint scent of incense hung in the air. There was a small altar in the corner covered with a dozen partially melted candles, a statue of a wide-hipped female figure, and what looked like an honest-to-god crystal ball.

"Are you really a witch?" Hana asked.

Tamsin blinked at her for a moment before a laugh bubbled from her lips.

"No, but my mom is."

Hana didn't know what to do with that information, so she just stored it away to mull over later.

"I'm sorry for passing out in your shop." It seemed like the right thing to say.

"Don't sweat it. It was the most exciting thing to happen here all day. Oh! Before I forget." Tamsin held up a little black notebook, its corners soft and round from use. "This fell out of your backpack."

Hana's hand shot out and snatched the notebook from Tamsin's grasp. Nausea rolled in her gut. Her body wasn't ready to move quite so abruptly just yet, but the thought of someone flipping through her deepest, darkest secrets made Hana want to hurl and then die.

"Whoa, there." Tamsin held out her hands in a placating gesture, as if she expected Hana to lash out like a wounded beast. In fairness, that was exactly what Hana had done. "I didn't read your diary, weirdo. I wasn't raised by a pack of socially inept wolves."

Hana cycled through a number of possible responses, the book clutched tightly to her chest. She settled on the most basic. "I'm sorry. I just . . . I write dumb, embarrassing things in here sometimes."

"No worries. Girl's gotta have her secrets. I respect that," Tamsin said. "Besides, not like I'd let you read my grimoire."

"Is that, like, a spell book?"

"Yeah."

"Do you really have one?"

"No."

"Oh."

A smirk ticked at the corner of Tamsin's lips. "You sound disappointed."

"I'm not," Hana said, even though she kind of was.

"Does the infamous Witch of Maplethorpe fail to live up to your expectations?"

Hana shrugged. It felt nice, this casual banter. She couldn't remember the last time she'd shared anything of the sort with someone her own age.

Tamsin sat back on her heels, casting an appraising eye over Hana. "You sure you're okay?"

A door slammed in the front of the shop, saving Hana from having to answer.

"Tamsin! Sunshine, I'm home!"

"Sunshine?" Hana asked. Tamsin didn't seem like a *sunshine*.

"Ugh, gross." Tamsin pushed herself to stand, brushing

her hands on the thighs of her artfully torn black jeans. "In the office, Mom!"

All the shouting was making Hana's skull pulsate as if it were trying to liquefy her brain.

An older woman entered the room, and Hana did a double take. If one were to scrape off the layers of dark eye makeup from around Tamsin's blue eyes, she and her mother would be nearly identical. Mrs. Moore had aged astonishingly well. She didn't look old enough to have borne a child Tamsin's age. And there was a way to how she carried herself that seemed utterly foreign to Hana. Her limbs were loose and her steps assured. In contrast, Hana's mother had a gait that was as clipped and precise as everything else about her. Tamsin's looked like she would be equally at home fronting for a gently alternative rock band or telling fortunes in a tent at a Renaissance festival.

Hana loved her at once.

Upon seeing the strange girl half lying on her couch, Mrs. Moore dropped the bags she was carrying and rushed to Hana's side. She must have looked even worse than she felt.

"Oh, honey. What happened to you?" She looked at Tamsin as she said it, as if some mystical maternal intuition told her Hana's word on the situation was not to be trusted.

"She just sort of fainted," Tamsin said. "This is Hana, by the way."

"Hello, Hana."

Hana stilled as Mrs. Moore's hand settled on her forehead to check her temperature. Hana couldn't remember the last time she'd been touched like that. Illnesses were like injuries. Obstacles on the path to perfection. Hurdles to be leaped without a second glance.

"It's okay," Hana said. "I just got a little dizzy. I worked out hard at skating practice today."

Mrs. Moore popped up to stand. "Aha! Did you eat after this skating practice?"

Hana blinked, perplexed at both the woman's casual acceptance of teenage girls fainting in her shop and her quick leap to a solution. She was stunned enough to admit, "Um, no."

"Well, that's something we can fix. I picked up some incredible cheese at the Public Market. I was thinking of using it to make some pasta." She was already bustling back to her bags, ordering Tamsin to carry the rest to the kitchen. "Hana, you're staying for dinner. Not negotiable."

The Public Market was one of the main grocery stores in Jackson Hills, but not the nice one Hana's parents shopped at. It was open to anyone, regardless of their rating. The supermarket Hana's mother preferred required scanning in with a minimum rating of 80.

But that wasn't what made Hana swallow the rising tide of her nausea as she swung her legs off the side of the couch and forced herself to stand. Her equilibrium hadn't fully recovered, but years of spinning on a steel blade only four millimeters wide made her excellent at faking balance when she had none.

"No, that's really okay, Mrs. Moore," Hana said, biting the inside of her cheek to distract from her clamoring stomach.

Tamsin's mother looked at Hana over an armful of brown bags, bursting with groceries. "It's Ms. Moore. There's no mister in this picture. And are you sure? It's no trouble at all. You really should eat something, sweetheart."

This woman didn't even know her and she was calling

her sweetheart. Hana blinked back the sudden moisture in her eyes.

"I'm okay." She scooped up her backpack and her skate bag, settling them on opposite shoulders.

She couldn't bear it. The thought of these kind, generous people watching her pretend to eat. Hana had the feeling that it would be harder to trick Tamsin's mother than her own.

"Thank you," she said to them both. "I . . . thanks."

She ducked behind the beaded curtain before either could respond. Over her shoulder, Hana caught a glimpse of Tamsin's expression as she made her escape. Tamsin's brow was pinched and her mouth set into a stern line. Ms. Moore just looked confused.

Hana pushed herself home despite the lingering weakness of her muscles and the persistent pounding in her head. The journey went by in a blur. Neither of her parents was home. That made things easier. Though the sense memory of Ms. Moore's soft hand on her forehead made something inside her clench that wasn't hunger.

It wasn't until Hana had changed into a nice, warm pair of sweats and sat down to record her afternoon practice in her little black notebook that she noticed the note stuck between the pages, sealed with the face of a smiling jester.

CHAPTER 11
CHASE DONOVAN

RATING: 56

Chase's luck ran out sooner than he thought it would. He'd done well in practice that week. Really well. His rating had crawled up two whole points, but it was still hovering on the cusp of disaster.

Not even a week into the school year and he found himself cornered by the man he'd been studiously avoiding for days.

Headmaster Wood smiled benevolently at Chase. They were almost the same height, but somehow Wood still gave off an air of smiling *down* instead of *at*.

"Ah, Chase. Just the man I've been waiting to see."

"Hi, Dr. Wood." Chase swallowed thickly, his hand tightening on the strap of his backpack. "What's up?"

Wood's eyes softened, either in sympathy or condescension. It was a fine line between the two and Chase had never been much good at telling the difference.

"We both know what's up, Mr. Donovan. The letter."

The letter.

The one still lurking in the bottom of Chase's backpack.

Chase didn't know what to say, so he didn't say anything at all.

"Look, Chase," Wood began.

Somehow, being called Mr. Donovan was less excruciating than being called Chase by the headmaster. First names felt too intimate, especially when said with such oozing pity.

"I understand that this isn't something you want to talk about, but we're going to. Rest assured, this won't be a long, painful conversation."

Wood smiled. Something like hope fluttered in Chase's chest. He knew it wasn't fair, technically, to grant athletes special status, to let them get away with things other students might not, but perhaps there was hope that a societal imbalance would work in his favor this time.

"I've already spoken to your coach, to let him know you'll be missing a few practices to make room for tutoring."

And just like that, Chase's fragile, half-formed hope shriveled into nothingness.

"But, Dr. Wood—"

"But nothing." Wood spoke with such authority that Chase's teeth clacked shut. There was absolutely no way Coach was on board with that plan. The fact that Wood had likely pulled rank on him to get Chase time off—if it could be called that—had probably only irritated Coach even more. Chase knew *he* would be the one to pay for it when he returned to practice. "I've arranged for you to meet with one of our best peer tutors this afternoon. I thought you'd be more comfortable with someone your own age."

He said this as if he'd just performed an act of supreme magnanimity, instead of broadcasting Chase's shame. Embarrassing himself in front of a teacher was one thing. Chase had plenty of experience in that arena. But another student? Someone smarter and more accomplished and probably far higher-rated than himself?

"Dr. Wood, if I could just—"

"This isn't a negotiation, Mr. Donovan. You *will* report to your tutor and you *will* pull up your grades. Failure to do so will result in your immediate expulsion from the baseball team and the loss of your scholarship. Any questions?"

"No, sir."

"Very good. Rebecca Johnson is a great tutor. You'll see."

With that, Wood sauntered away, off to torment the next poor soul on his list of underperforming elites.

And that was how Chase Donovan, star pitcher of the Maplethorpe Academy baseball team, regional champions for seven years running, found himself standing before the future valedictorian of his senior class, Bex Johnson. They stared at each other for a frozen moment, the three feet between them feeling miles wide. He'd never spoken to her before, despite the fact that they'd been in school together for years. It wasn't that he didn't like Bex. It's just that he had nothing in common with her. She was everything he wasn't. Academically gifted. Multitalented. Well-rounded.

A girl like Bex didn't bother with guys like him. And if he was honest, guys like him didn't often bother with girls like her. They were too smart. Too unpredictable. Most of the guys on the team didn't like it when girls were better than them at things, and Bex was good at pretty much everything.

Chase did one thing extremely well. And if he wasn't allowed to do that one thing anymore, he had nothing else to fall back on.

"Hi," he said, because she seemed perfectly content to let him stew in the roaring silence of his own inadequacy.

"Hi," she replied. "I'm supposed to tutor you."

She said it like she wasn't quite sure she wanted to be there. Chase definitely didn't want to be there, so that was one thing they had in common.

Progress.

"Listen, you don't have to," Chase said. "Tutor me, I mean."

Bex furrowed her brow. "But Headmaster Wood said you needed help . . ."

"I don't." That was too much of a lie, even for Chase's wounded pride. "I mean, I do, obviously, or we wouldn't be having this conversation."

"So you need it," Bex said, "but you don't want it."

It sounded so petty when phrased that way. She wasn't wrong, not really.

"I . . . yeah." Chase hefted his backpack higher on his shoulder. "That about sums it up."

Bex nodded thoughtfully. She looked down the hallway, at the swirl of students around them, each of them off to practice, or rehearsal, or whatever it was other overachieving Maplethorpe students did once the last bell rang.

"I was thinking we'd use the library," she said, "but we can go someplace else if you'd like."

The thought of libraries made Chase itch all over. He never felt quite welcome in them, like a weed growing in a garden.

"How about the Lucky Penny?" Chase offered.

Bex smiled.

It's a nice smile, Chase thought. Not an ounce of judgment in it.

Maybe this won't be so awful after all.

The diner was as packed as it was after any school day, but the vibe was different this afternoon. Chase rarely went without the rest of the team in tow. In a large group, as a star athlete, he almost never paid for his own food or drinks. Somebody else with less social—but more financial—capital usually did.

Today Chase stared at the large laminated menu, pondering how many singles he could find crammed into his backpack or smushed into the pockets of his Maplethorpe letter jacket. A signature Lucky Penny milkshake cost eight dollars. He might be able to get a plain vanilla one if luck was on his side.

"So," Bex said, her eyes on her own menu. Her gaze was still, not tracking lines from side to side, so Chase was pretty sure she wasn't really reading it. "Tutoring."

He put down his menu and folded his hands on top of it. Maybe he wouldn't need to order anything at all.

Bex followed Chase's lead and set her own menu down on the table. She took out a notebook and a pen with those multi-colored tips, so you could switch between hues with minimal effort. As she flipped to a clean page, he couldn't help but notice that her handwriting was the neatest he'd ever seen. The letters were arrayed on the page with military precision. And they were small. So ridiculously small. His eyes trembled, ready to cross at the thought of attempting to read any of it.

"Any subject in particular?" Bex asked. "Dr. Wood didn't get into specifics."

All of them.

"Math, I guess." Numbers were a safer bet for him, but only just slightly. He didn't want to look stupid in front of Bex. Technically, she already knew he was stupid, or they wouldn't be sitting in the Lucky Penny talking about tutoring, but he wanted to hide the depths of his stupidity from her as long as possible. He wasn't used to being bad at things—not publicly, anyway. And being bad at academics stung much more than being bad at, say, skiing, which he'd tried once on a school trip and vowed never to attempt again.

Bex's pen paused over her notebook. The purple ink seemed to yearn for the page just out of reach. "You guess?"

Her tone wasn't unkind. That small shred of softness was perhaps what made it easier for him to say what he desperately did not want to admit.

He drew in a breath, steeling himself as he loosened the white-knuckled grip he had on his pride.

"I need help . . . with everything."

Gently, Bex placed the pen down on the open notebook without writing anything. "It sounds like that was hard for you to admit. Am I right?"

Chase nodded. Gestures were easier than words.

Bex's face softened. She offered him a soft smile. There was no pity in her expression . . . just simple understanding. "I'm not here to make you feel bad, Chase. You have nothing to feel bad about anyway. I'm here to help. We can tackle everything."

"Everything seems like a lot."

"Yes, by definition."

"But aren't you, like, super busy taking over the world?"

"Huh?"

"You're a super genius."

Bex shrugged and took a sip of her water. "I set a few hours aside on the weekends for world domination. I'm free after school Tuesdays now that the school newspaper is on hiatus."

"Is it?" Chase asked. "Why's that?"

Bex shrugged, but there was tension in her shoulders that made the gesture far less casual than she probably intended. "Something to do with the graffiti the other day. I don't think they want anybody talking about it."

"That's weird," Chase commented.

"Yup. And you're changing the subject."

Now it was Chase's turn to shrug, shoulders stiff.

"Why would I change the subject? It's so much fun to talk about how stupid I am."

Bex narrowed her eyes. "You're not stupid."

"Okay, but I am, though."

"No, you're not."

"Yes, I am."

"You're not."

"I am."

Bex threw herself back against the booth, her arms crossing over her chest in defiance. "I can sit here all day, if that's what it takes to convince you that you're not stupid."

"Then why can't I do simple things like everybody else?" Chase hadn't planned to ask that question out loud, but now that the ball was rolling, he found it difficult to stop. There was a catharsis in saying these things out loud. He hadn't realized how rancid his thoughts had become, left to fester. "How come basic stuff makes my head hurt?"

"Because education isn't one size fits all," Bex said. "What works for me doesn't work for you, and that's okay. We just have to find what works for you."

"If education isn't one size fits all, then why does our school act like it is?"

Bex picked at the skin around her nails. Her cuticles were disastrous—shredded and red with inflammation. The picking must be an anxious tic. "I don't know. I think that's just the way most schools work, I guess."

"Well, *that's* stupid."

"Finally. We agree on something."

Being around Bex wasn't what Chase thought it would be. He'd assumed it would be awkward and uncomfortable, but now they'd slipped into something that was starting to feel like camaraderie. Chase had been on teams before. He knew what it was like to bond with people because of circumstance. This was different. They had nothing in common that he could identify, but that didn't feel like much of a problem. He talked and she listened. It was . . . nice. Really nice. It stilled the restless anxiety that had plagued him since Wood stopped by his locker.

Bex picked up her menu to scan it, just as Chase's stomach growled loud enough to be heard several counties over.

She lifted an eyebrow at him. "Are you hungry?"

He shrugged. There might be a few dollar bills squished into his backpack, but he didn't want to look and come up empty. That would be far too embarrassing.

"Well, I am," Bex said. "And my mom and dad never let me eat fun stuff."

"Fun stuff?"

"Grease. Refined sugars. Processed foods. Pretty much anything that doesn't occur in nature."

She had just described approximately 90 percent of Chase's diet. "Ah, they must not have heard of the fabled milkshake tree."

Bex stared at him dumbly for a moment. Then the edges of her lips twitched minutely, a tentative smile crawling across them. "A rare species, I'm sure."

Chase flipped the menu closed. "Well, I don't think I have any money on me, so get whatever you want."

He said it casually, hopeful that she wouldn't read too much into it. Plenty of people walked around without cash. Most restaurants had gone paperless, allowing customers to pay with a scan of their smartwatches—with prices adjusted for ratings, naturally. But not Lucky's. She was an analog girl in a digital world, the Lucky Penny.

Bex shrugged. "My parents never give me cash either. I have a credit card for emergencies, but if I used it for a jumbo strawberry milkshake, I don't know that I'd live long enough to enjoy it."

She extricated a well-worn twenty-dollar bill from the rear pocket of her planner and held it gingerly, as if it were some great treasure she'd unearthed on an archeological dig. "But I've been saving this for a special occasion."

Something in Chase's gut gave a peculiar little twist, for reasons he couldn't explain. "Is this a special occasion?"

She placed the bill on the table so it was ready to go at a moment's notice. "I can't remember the last time I actually went someplace that wasn't school or flute lessons or the soup kitchen or Mathletes practice or—"

"Do you actually do all that stuff?" Chase asked. He had to stop her before she went on, further reminding him of his own inadequacy. He was beginning to think her ambition for world domination wasn't actually a joke. She was operating on a plane beyond mere mortals like himself. "Like, it's not just application padding for college?"

Bex nodded. "Yup."

Chase let out a low, deeply impressed whistle. "When do you find time to breathe?"

"Oh, I don't. My plan is to slowly suffocate and then take a break when I'm dead."

"That . . . doesn't sound healthy, Bex."

"It's not," she agreed, a little too readily.

"Okay, so long as you're aware."

She shrugged, like she hadn't just confessed to being on the brink of a nervous breakdown. He wondered if she realized how close to the edge she sounded. Perhaps she'd been hovering on that precipice for so long that she didn't even notice the drop. Bex reached into her backpack to pull out her tablet. She flipped open the case and swiped at the screen. It lit up, displaying a calendar packed with a dazzling array of colors.

"Okay, so how about we order some milkshakes and make a plan to get you back on track. Might have to rearrange a few things, but I think I can make it work." She gnawed on her bottom lip in a way that looked like habit, as her fingers flew across the screen. Her bottom lip, Chase noticed, was noticeably more chapped than the top.

The waitress chose that moment to appear. She was new. Chase knew the staff of the Lucky Penny fairly well, but he didn't recognize her. Her blond hair was piled in a sloppy bun and blunt bangs framed her face. The retro yellow uniform of the Lucky Penny clashed with her natural coloring. She popped a mouthful of gum as she approached their table, notepad at the ready.

"What can I get for you lovebirds?"

Bex was so engrossed in whatever she was doing on her tablet that she didn't notice Chase sputtering at the word *lovebirds*. Or at least he hoped she didn't notice.

"Uh, two milkshakes, please? One black and white and one . . ."

"Strawberry," Bex supplied.

"Comin' right up." The waitress sauntered away, but not before winking at Chase.

He wasn't sure what to make of that.

"Do you have a notebook?" Bex looked up from her tablet, and Chase had a fleeting glimpse of what her future might look like. She already had the air of a professor about her. He wondered if that was where her life would take her, or if her regimented path led toward even greater things. Like maybe the presidency.

"Uh, yeah." The only one he really carried home with him contained notes about baseball and stats and training schedules, but she didn't need to know that.

He went digging into his backpack to find it, bypassing the still-crumpled letter lying at the bottom. If an inanimate object could express disappointment, the sad creases in that letter would be radiating with it.

With a flourish, he yanked the beaten-up marble notebook from the depths of the bag. A red envelope fluttered out with it, landing at the center of the table like a splash of blood on the speckled Formica surface.

He picked it up, looking for a name, but the only one on it was his own.

The letter that had been stuffed into his locker. He'd all but forgotten about it, what with the threat of losing his scholarship and lifelong disgrace looming in his near future.

"Two milkshakes! One black and white, one strawberry."

Chase jumped in his seat and blinked up at the waitress, who apparently traveled on silent cat feet and had the ability to make milkshakes appear in half the usual time.

Bex pushed her tablet to the side so the waitress could deposit a tall, unnaturally pink concoction in front of her. Chase accepted his milkshake with a mumbled thanks and was almost relieved not to receive another wink in response, even if it did feel like the waitress's eyes were lingering a little too long.

His smartwatch buzzed. He glanced down at it to find that his rating had gone up a point. When he looked up, the waitress caught his eye and winked.

Weird.

Bex peered over the rim of her milkshake as she swirled the thick straw around the viscous deliciousness. She jerked her chin in the direction of the red envelope.

"What's that?"

"I don't know," Chase said. "Probably some secret admirer nonsense."

"I don't think so," said Bex, her voice a little strained.

He glanced up at her. Her brows were drawn close together and her hand had gone still on the straw.

"What is it? What's wrong?"

"Look at the back."

Chase picked up the envelope. A sticker held it closed. A smiling jester grinned up at him, as if mocking his inattentiveness.

It took him a moment to recall where he'd seen it before. "Holy crap."

"The stickers on the cameras at school," Bex said.

They leaned over their respective sides of the table, tutoring forgotten.

"Open it," Bex hissed at him. It was as close to a yell as a whisper could be. "What does it say?"

Chase lifted the flap of the envelope, tearing the jester's uncanny smile in half. He read the message out loud, his voice a low whisper. "'On the day of the prophet false, one mustn't dance a forbidden waltz. A copper found and a fortune told, all beside a box of gold.'"

"Does that mean anything to you?" Bex asked.

Chase shook his head. "No. Not at all." He flipped the envelope over to look at the sticker once more. The jester leered at him, as if it knew the punch line to a joke Chase wasn't clever enough to follow.

"Any idea why they would send this to you?"

That seemed like an awfully polite way to ask if he was somehow connected to the vandals who'd defaced the school.

"No," Chase said. "No idea. I had nothing to do with"—another glance at the jester—"whatever that is."

He turned the envelope back over so the sticker was face-down on the table. Chase didn't want anyone walking by to notice it and jump to conclusions. That, and he was sick of looking at those creepy blank eyes.

The shrill ring of Bex's phone made them both jump.

"Sorry," she said, fumbling for it in her jacket pocket.

"I didn't know anyone under sixty used an audible ringtone anymore," Chase said.

"I'm an old soul," Bex said. She swiped to answer the call. "Hey, Mom. I mean, hello."

Hey was too casual for her own mother? Now that was weird. While she spoke, he covered the cryptic letter with his palm. It seemed like the kind of thing best kept secret. He savored his milkshake, knowing it tasted better because he wasn't paying for it, though for once he'd wanted to. He'd pick up the next one . . . somehow. Even if he had to wait for his dad to pass out so he could pull some cash from his wallet. Often the only money Chase's father spent on his son was what Chase took for himself. It was messed up, and he'd probably need a lot more money to pay for the therapy he'd require in the future, but he didn't want to think about it too hard in the present.

Bex ended her call with a bitten-back curse. "I have to go. I'm supposed to be having dinner with my parents and I completely forgot."

A sudden, sharp sadness cut through Chase. "Oh. It's okay. Don't worry about it."

Bex put away her things, leaving her phone for last. "Can I text you? After dinner, I mean?"

It was hard to tell if she was blushing, with the neon lights in the window skimming across her dark skin, but he thought she might be.

"Sure," he said. He took out his own phone—a clunkier model than the sleek one Bex held. It was the best he could get with his father's rating. Access to the best phones was determined by ratings, and Chase's father was in one of the lower brackets. Chase was glad they qualified for mobile phones at all, even if his wasn't anything fancy.

They exchanged numbers, ostensibly to set up a plan for Chase's tutoring, but he had a feeling the mysterious letter was going to dominate their next conversation.

CHAPTER 12

JAVI LUCERO

Javi's phone vibrated in his pocket. Phones weren't technically allowed on campus. Students could carry them into the building, but they were to be left in lockers at all times. Javi had never once followed this rule. It was probably his agent, the same woman who managed both Team MCA and Javi as an individual. The newest Panthera peripherals bearing Javi's likeness on their packaging had been flying off the shelves. The headset was the hottest-selling item, but the gaming mouse and keyboard weren't far behind. The company had kicked him a nice two-part bonus: a check that went straight to new clothes for the twins (who stubbornly refused to stop growing) and four extra points to his rating.

The buzzing was loud enough to be overheard, but the librarian was busy shelving books on the other side of the room. Javi slipped his phone from his pocket and glanced at the screen.

There was a new message in the chat server his guild used to keep in touch outside *Polaris*. A private message.

DMs usually meant one guild member gossiping about another, but there were seven in a row from Rouge, which seemed unusual. Javi swiped the chat window open. Rouge rarely ever indulged in idle gossip.

Dude.

Vulpes.

Ping me.

There's some weird stuff going down and I think it would be relevant to your interests.

Vulpes.

V U L P E S

Vuuuuuulpes

With one eye on the librarian, Javi typed out a reply.

What do you want, Rouge? I'm at school.
The other day, you asked about weird graffiti.

Javi glanced up from his phone. The librarian was still reading the spines of books and slowly placing them on the shelves where they belonged. Still, sitting at one of the computer terminals in the center of the room seemed like too much of a risk. It wouldn't do to have his phone confiscated just when things were getting juicy.

Javi stood and, as nonchalantly as possible, made his way to one of the stacks at the far wall of the room, near the end of the aisle. Maplethorpe was kept obsessively clean by a dedicated janitorial staff, but there was a musty smell about the shelves Javi had ducked between. There wasn't noticeable dust on the books, but the smell seemed to come from the books themselves. A cursory glance at the spines revealed a few titles Javi recognized—*The Scarlet Letter, The Catcher in the Rye*—but even more that he didn't. They were old books, rarely assigned anymore in the school's curriculum. Holdovers from before his time.

If he bent down a few inches, he could see the librarian through the stacks, over the uneven spines of rows and rows of books. So long as he kept one eye on her progress, he'd be safe.

He pulled his phone out and tapped out a reply to Rouge. *Have you heard anything? More graffiti?*

. . .

Javi jiggled his foot at the ankle as he stared at the blinking dots, which meant Rouge was taking her sweet time typing.

His phone vibrated with the incoming message, but it wasn't a text.

Rouge had sent a picture.

A redbrick wall, thick with ivy. The vines had been pushed aside just enough to reveal a line of text, painted in vivid red. THE RATINGS ARE NOT REAL.

"What the banana bread?" Javi whispered before biting his lip to prevent any other renegade sounds from escaping. He'd developed a habit of replacing profane words with the names of various foods. His abuela had washed his mouth out with soap the last time he'd cursed in front of his younger siblings.

Where was this?

University campus, came Rouge's reply. **It was there for a few minutes before it was literally whitewashed away. Went into the student union to pick up some study snacks—ok, gaming snacks, but whatever—and when I came back out, it was there. Couldn't have been inside for more than five minutes. I barely managed to snap a pic before they swooped in to cover it up.**

Any idea who did it?

No, but I'm gonna poke around. See if I can dig
something up.
Let me know what you find. And be careful.

Javi leaned against the wall and sank slowly to the floor,
phone held tightly in both hands.

It wasn't an isolated incident. Whatever was happening at
Maplethorpe was happening elsewhere. The Jester didn't need
to be a Maplethorpe student—or teacher, the thought *had*
crossed Javi's mind. It could be anyone. It could be numerous
people, acting in unison.

But why?

"Are you quite all right, Javier?"

Javi's head jerked up to find the bespectacled—and
judgmental—gaze of the librarian staring down at him.

"Oh." Almost as a reflex, Javi's lips spread into the dazzling grin that paid his tuition and put food on his table. "Hi,
Mrs. Russo. You look nice today. Are those new glasses?"

"Nice try," said Mrs. Russo. "I'm sure you know phones
are not to be used on campus during school hours."

"I do, but . . ."

Javi pressed the button on the side of the phone, locking it.
He was 95 percent sure he could talk his way out of this.

Mrs. Russo arched one thin eyebrow behind her horn-
rimmed glasses.

Okay, maybe 90 percent.

"It's my abuela," he said. "She had a doctor's appointment
today. I was just texting her to see if everything's okay and if she
needs a ride home from the clinic. She always loses the number
for the car service."

The librarian's face softened, but not enough.

"I usually go with her. It's her hearing, you know. She doesn't feel safe on the train these days, but the only appointment she could get was when I was in school and—"

Mrs. Russo held up a hand, stemming the flow of his words. "I get it, Javier."

Almost no one called him Javier, but he let it slide.

He held out the phone in a hand that trembled just enough.

"I'm sorry. I know I'm not supposed to use this at school, but I'm the oldest sibling and it's just my abuela at home. There isn't anybody else . . ."

It was low. He wasn't proud. But he went there anyway.

After a moment of excruciating, silent deliberation, the librarian heaved a sigh. "You're a good kid, Javier. But rules are rules."

She tapped at her smartwatch and a second later, his vibrated. His eyes darted to the small display on his wrist. A red −1 hovered next to his rating.

A provisional deduction. Removed at the end of a twenty-four period, provided there were no other behavioral infractions.

He fought the urge to grin in triumph. The grandma stories did it, every time. No one could resist a quivering chin and an ailing abuelita. No one was that strong.

"Don't let me catch you with that again," said the librarian. "It goes back in your locker, or the deduction sticks."

"Aye, aye, Captain." Javi offered Mrs. Russo a jaunty salute, which made her smile. A little charm to seal the deal.

With a good-natured roll of her eyes, the librarian left, returning to her cart of unshelved books.

He shoved the phone back in his pocket. He couldn't stay in the stacks much longer, not without truly incurring Russo's wrath. It wouldn't do him any good to have the phone confiscated now.

Thankfully, his phone wasn't the only way to access the chat server. The school's computers were layered with firewalls to prevent students from looking at things they shouldn't, but Javi had yet to meet an institutional firewall he couldn't hop. It would take some finessing, but he could massage one of the school's computers into giving him free rein of the internet without leaving a single shred of evidence that he'd done it. There was a computer lab on the fourth floor that would do nicely.

He exited the stacks, sharing a small, sympathetic smile with Mrs. Russo before grabbing his backpack and leaving the library. He'd said he would deposit the phone back in his locker, and she'd watch him like a hawk to make sure he did so right away—or at least appeared to do so.

But first, a pit stop. He'd had a large iced coffee that morning, and now it was yearning to be free.

The door to the boys' bathroom had barely swung shut behind Javi when he skidded to a stop.

Standing at the sink farthest from the door was the boy with the camera. The one he'd noticed that first day of school, taking pictures of the graffiti and getting hassled by jocks. The boy who'd blushed so prettily when Javi had carelessly tossed him one of his trademark smiles.

Noah Rainier.

Not that he'd dipped into the school records to learn his name—also hidden behind a firewall too short to stop Javi.

That would be super weird. Not the sort of thing a normal, sane person would do.

But something he *absolutely* would do.

Noah's eyes were red rimmed, the skin around them puffy, like he'd been scrubbing at it too vigorously. Like he'd been crying.

Their reflected gazes met briefly in the mirror.

Noah sniffed, rubbing at his nose with the navy sleeve of his Maplethorpe blazer.

"Sorry," he said, fumbling for the backpack he'd dropped on the floor by the sink. "I'll get out of your way."

"Are you okay?" Javi asked, despite the fact that the other boy was very obviously not okay.

Noah paused, his hand on one of his backpack's straps. When he looked at Javi, there was something in his expression that made Javi reach behind him to flip the lock on the bathroom door. Someone pounded on the other side.

"Hey, come on. Open up!"

Javi rolled his eyes and shouted, "Ocupado, you soggy walnut!"

Mumbled groaning faded away as the unfortunate soul left in search of more accessible facilities. Javi's smartwatch buzzed against his wrist.

Crud.

Another infraction, even a peer-to-peer one, while he had a provisional deduction pending was sure to make the first one stick.

But misery radiated off Noah in waves. Maybe there were bigger problems in that bathroom at the moment.

"I'm fine," Noah said. Obviously, a lie. "You didn't have to do that."

Javi shrugged. "I'll jump at any excuse to call someone a soggy walnut." He took a few tentative steps toward the other boy, unsure of his welcome. But Noah didn't back away.

"What happened?" Javi asked.

They weren't friends. They'd never really spoken before that first day of school, and in the week since, their interactions had consisted almost entirely of stolen glances and averted gazes.

"Nothing," Noah replied. Another lie.

"Sure, sure." Javi leaned his hip against a sink, aiming for casual curiosity. "I find myself crying in bathrooms for no reason all the time."

"I'm not crying." Noah undermined himself by punctuating the words with a well-timed sniff.

"Of course not. You're just leaking out of your eyes."

"Exactly."

Javi huffed out a small laugh. His smile widened when Noah did the same.

"Look," Javi said, "I don't know you very well, but you seem nice."

"You don't know me at all."

Javi shrugged. "I'm good at reading people. Now are you gonna tell me what's bothering you, or do I have to keep peppering you with increasingly intrusive questions? Because I don't think we've got the time for that."

Noah's smile was a little wobbly, but it was better than crying, so Javi would take it.

Noah drummed his fingers against the sink, the sound echoing dully across the porcelain. "Just family stuff. It's stupid."

"If it's bothering you, it isn't stupid."

Now they were getting somewhere. But before Noah could say anything more, the bell outside shrieked, punctuating the little bubble of semi-privacy Javi had carved for them.

"I've gotta get to class," Noah said, though his tone implied he had little desire to do so. He bent down to pick up his backpack, swinging it up onto his shoulder in one fluid move. Something fell out of a side pocket and drifted to the ground.

"Okay. Yeah, me too," Javi said, bending down to pick up the paper. It looked like a photograph of Maplethorpe, taken from a distance. Javi didn't have to get to class. He had a free period he'd planned on using to commit several school code violations. He didn't know why he said that. He held the photo out to Noah, who accepted it with mumbled thanks. "But if you wanna talk, I'm—"

The rest of Javi's offering went unspoken when Noah turned the photograph over in his hand, revealing the back. Text, written in neat block letters, like they were cut from a stencil. And a sticker.

A macabre jester smiled at them as they both stared at it in stunned silence.

"What the garbanzo beans?" Javi asked the universe. The universe did not respond.

It's difficult, watching from a distance. Viewing the players, anticipating their decisions. It's frustrating, infuriating, satisfying, thrilling. It's all those things and more. But it's not enough.

The pieces are moving together, but they need to move faster. They need to move with purpose.

It's a delicate game, knowing when to apply pressure and when to pull back. When to orchestrate and when to observe.

They need to see the threads woven through each missive, to understand the ties that bind them.

They need a focal point. A thing around which they can rally. A magnet to draw them all in. And then, they will need something to keep them there. A glue to seal them together. A test, to try the strength of their connection.

It's not kind, that which must be done. Unpleasant deeds are, after all, bred by an unpleasant world.

A sacrifice will have to be made. But that is expected.

Success, after all, requires sacrifice.

CHAPTER 13
CHASE DONOVAN

RATING: 57

The front door of Chase's house had been painted a happy sunshine yellow ten years ago. He remembered helping his father complete the job, taping the sides of the door so the paint wouldn't run, dabbing the sharp edges with a small foam brush. He remembered the pride he'd felt gazing upon their finished project, the warmth of his father's hand on his shoulder as they stood on the porch together.

Pride wasn't something he'd felt in his father in many, many years.

The first sign Chase had that tonight would be one of the bad nights was that the front door—now the bruised yellow of an overripe banana—was unlocked.

The hinges creaked as he pushed the door open. He'd have to grease them up soon. Years ago, his father would have handled that sort of thing, but recently basic home maintenance had proved less interesting to the elder Donovan than a six-pack. Or two.

The interior of the house was as sad as their once-proud front door. Stains speckled the beige carpet, no matter how vigorously Chase had tried to scrub the evidence of spilled whiskey away. Cigarette burns gathered in halos around the arms of the couch. In addition to brushing his teeth and at least attempting his homework, part of Chase's nightly ritual was making sure his father hadn't fallen asleep with a cigarette in hand. The couch—a hideous patterned affair that had probably been in style decades before Chase's birth—had the look of something extremely flammable. Every night, he half expected to wake up to the shrill screech of the smoke alarms he kept faithfully stocked with fresh batteries. He couldn't stop his father from lighting himself or the house on fire, but he could take as many preventive measures as possible to keep them both alive.

Sounds drifted from the TV room to where Chase stood just inside the door. He recognized the voice of the announcer and the rise and fall of the crowd's cheers. He'd seen that video dozens, maybe hundreds of times. It was one of his dad's old games, before the rotator cuff injury.

Chase knew what that video meant. His father was in one of his moods. He had an array of them and none were good. A quick and quiet escape was Chase's best option. He made his way to the stairs. He'd lock himself in his bedroom and text Bex and puzzle over the weird, cryptic letter he'd received. He'd think about a future that was—that had to be—better than his present.

The first step groaned under his weight.

"That you, son?" His father's voice boomed from the TV room, loud enough to be heard over the sounds of a game played long before Chase's birth.

Chase bit back a curse.

So much for sneaking by undetected.

"Yeah, Dad," Chase called. "Just got home. Gotta get cracking on my homework."

"Come here for a sec."

Chase contemplated ignoring him, but he knew doing so would only make things worse.

He went to the living room, where he was greeted by a familiar sight. His father, seated in the large recliner, the TV remote in one hand and a beer bottle in the other. His eyes were glued to the screen, where a much younger version of himself, clad in the familiar maroon of Maplethorpe, carried a football to a game-winning touchdown. A plate sat on the table, empty save for a stale pizza crust. Dinners at the Donovan household consisted primarily of pizza and boxed pasta. Tonight was a pizza night, then. Again.

"The scouts wanted me, you know." Chase's father jerked his chin at the TV screen. "I was the best on that team and everybody knew it."

"Yeah," Chase sighed. "I know, Dad."

His father took another swig of his beer. The stubble on his chin was a good two days' worth of growth, the hair speckled a salt-and-pepper gray.

"Grab me another beer, will you?"

With a sigh, Chase went to the small kitchenette squished into the corner of their house. He had vague memories of the pale yellow fridge covered with crayon drawings and report cards, all from a time before his mother walked out. She'd been fed up with his father's drinking and overall lack of ambition. She used to call Chase on his birthday, but the older he got, the more infrequent the calls became. Eventually, they stopped altogether. He hadn't heard from her in almost two years. Sometimes, he wondered if she was happy, wherever she was. Usually, he tried not to think about it.

Four empty beer bottles sat in an uneven row on the counter. The one left in the fridge still had the plastic ring around it. It looked a little like a noose. Chase always tried to cut them up before his father threw them out. He didn't want his dad's bad habits taking the life of an innocent fish in whatever body of water their trash wound up.

The bottle was cold against his palm. He rested his forehead against the closed refrigerator door. That was cold, too. If he closed his eyes, he could imagine that the kitchen looked the way it did years ago, before his mom left. Then, there had always been a vase of freshly cut flowers on the kitchenette table, cut from the small garden in the backyard. There was always a bowl of fruit on the counter and a freshly baked loaf of bread on Sunday mornings, filling the house with a warm, welcoming aroma.

When he opened his eyes, the kitchen remained as it always was. No flowers. No fruit. No bread. The garden out back had succumbed to the wild growth of weeds.

There was a metaphor for the life of the Donovan family in that garden. Chase wasn't particularly poetic, but the metaphor was obvious enough even for him.

Beer in hand, he returned to the living room. His father was rewinding the tape to replay his touchdown.

Chase handed the beer to his father, who twisted it open with a muttered "Thanks, kid."

"Did you go to work today?" Chase didn't want to ask, but he had to. He had to know how deep his father had dug them into this hole.

His father answered by knocking back his beer. His eyes remained glued on the screen. Eventually, he spoke.

"For a while. Came home early."

That wasn't good. His father's many infractions at work had seen their family's average rating go from minimally respectable to nearly the bottom of the societal barrel. They were lucky to have the house, but Chase knew that if his father's rating fell any lower, they would lose it. His scholarship was blessedly independent of his dad's rating, but it would be hard to maintain his standing at Maplethorpe—tenuous as it was—if they were forced out of their home. He'd heard stories about the shelters for the poorly rated; he didn't want to consider living in one.

Chase didn't want to ask, but he felt like he had to.

"Did they fire you, Dad?"

His father merely grunted in response.

"Dad?"

"What?" Only then did his father look away from the screen. He looked older than his thirty-nine years. He'd been young when Chase was born. Both of his parents were. That was why they didn't last. His mother had been kind enough to tell him that before she left. What she didn't say was that she blamed Chase and his father for her stolen youth. He'd managed to deduce that much all on his own.

He didn't repeat his question. It wasn't safe. Not when his father had that look in his eyes. A wild glint, like an animal backed into a corner, ready to defend itself from attack, even if that attack was only a cold and ugly truth. The black eye left behind from the last truthful conversation he'd had with his father had faded just a few days before the start of school.

"Nothing, Dad. It's nothing."

"Watch your attitude, Chase."

"I don't have an attitude, Dad. I just—"

Chase ducked just in time to dodge the empty beer bottle his father threw at him.

The bottle shattered as it hit the wall. A shard of broken glass caught his cheek. Chase gingerly touched his broken skin. His fingertips came away red with blood.

Droplets of beer trickled down the wall to rain on the carpet. Chase stayed down, half kneeling, his heart hammering in his chest. The back of his neck was sticky with beer.

"What did I tell you about talking back?"

To this, Chase said nothing. The question was rhetorical. Silence was the safer option.

After a long moment, his father looked away, turning his attention back to the game.

There, on the coffee table, sat his father's smartwatch. Chase wanted to look at it, to see just how far the rating had fallen since that morning.

Sometimes, all it took was one bad day to make the difference between treading water and drowning.

Icy tendrils of fear snaked their way through Chase's veins. His future had always been uncertain, but at least he thought he'd have one. With his own rating dropping below acceptable levels and his father out of a job, he wasn't sure what he was going to do. He wasn't sure what he could do. They couldn't lose the house. They couldn't go homeless. Once a family's collective rating dropped below a certain point, it was almost impossible for them to claw their way back up.

The construction crew was always looking for new blood. Chase could drop out of school, get a job with them. They could keep their home. But then the house would be all he ever had. No more baseball. No scouts. Nothing beyond those four sad walls, filled with memories Chase would rather forget.

When it felt safe to move, Chase stood, brushing off his knees. He'd clean up the glass later, when his father was asleep.

"I'm gonna go do my homework," said Chase, though his father's attention had drifted away from him. If he heard Chase speak, he gave no sign of it.

It took everything Chase had not to stomp up the stairs and slam his bedroom door shut behind him. A curious heat stung at his eyes. He scrubbed at them, ashamed even though there was no one around to see him do it.

He grabbed a handful of tissues from the box on his bedside table and pressed the wad to his cheek. The cut wasn't bleeding too badly, at least. It probably wouldn't scar, though it would be noticeable until it healed. If anyone asked about it, he'd do what he always did and come up with an excuse to explain the wound. But cuts and scrapes were so commonplace on athletes—and Chase in particular—that no one ever really asked.

With a weary sigh, Chase toed off his sneakers and dropped his backpack on the floor by his bed. He sank into it, ignoring the lumpy springs and the scratchy blankets. The bedroom hadn't changed much since Chase had started attending Maplethorpe, after his athletic scholarship had lifted him from his public school—open to all, regardless of rating—to the ivory tower of private education. The last time Chase had given much thought to interior decor, he'd been deep into superhero comics. The evidence lingered on his walls in the form of posters and wall scrolls of heroes he'd long since outgrown. The only sign that he'd changed was the navy-blue blazer slung across the back of his desk chair.

His phone buzzed. A text alert. He thought about ignoring it, but then he remembered Lucky's. Milkshakes. An exchange of numbers. A mysterious letter. Maybe it was Bex. He rolled over, fumbling for his phone. It took a few moments of rummaging for him to unearth it from the pile of his belongings.

It wasn't Bex. It was Steve, sending some dumb meme to the team's group chat.

It wasn't Bex . . . but he wanted it to be. That was a new and interesting feeling. Closing out of the chat app, he pulled up his contacts, scrolling until he found the list's latest addition.

He stared at the number on his phone. Bex Johnson. Who knew he'd ever exchange phone numbers with Bex freakin' Johnson?

He wanted to text her. Badly. He wanted to call her, to hear the sound of her voice through the phone, to tell her how the quality of his day had drastically plummeted since leaving the Lucky Penny. Talking about his feelings wasn't something he did. Talking about feelings was something people did on daytime talk shows and reality TV confessionals.

He'd never really had anyone to talk to before. He wasn't particularly close to any of the guys on the team. They were friendly with one another; they shared a sort of fraternity. But their brotherhood was too marked by competition to allow for true friendships. The more games they each played in, the higher their ratings. And ratings were everything.

He clicked on Bex's name, then pulled up a new text window. He typed out a single word, hoping it was enough.

Hey.

It wasn't particularly clever, but it was a start.

CHAPTER 14

BEX JOHNSON

Bex pushed a single pea across her plate to join the small mound at the other end. Her parents' voices washed over her as they discussed the events of the day. Her mother was the chief neurosurgeon at Magnolia Children's Hospital, and her day had consisted of digging around in people's brains, rooting out malignant tumors and repairing damaged spines. Her father was an aerospace engineer, working on a government contract wrapped up in so many layers of top secret clearances that listening to him sometimes involved more redactions than information. Bex had no idea what it was he did at work, or the nature of his project. All she knew about her dad—all she'd ever known, really—was that he was a rocket scientist with so many degrees that the string of letters after his name on academic papers was longer than the name itself.

Bex hated peas. She'd always hated peas. She wasn't sure if either of her parents had the slightest idea, though. Her mother had never, in Bex's lifetime, so much as boiled an egg in their spacious kitchen, with its white granite island and gleaming chrome appliances. A housekeeper, replaced every few years because of her father's impossibly exacting standards, prepared the family's meals. The new one, Marta, had not yet discovered that Bex hated peas, so they'd appeared on her plate for the first time in years. Helena, the previous holder of the post, had discerned Bex's distaste after a single meal. Bex had never complained about the peas, of course; Helena had simply observed that more had been pushed around the plate than delivered to Bex's mouth.

"And how was your day, Rebecca?"

Bex jerked her head up at the sound of her mother's voice. It lilted up at the end of her question in a way that implied she knew Bex hadn't been paying attention to the conversation and didn't appreciate it one bit.

Her parents were looking at her, her mother with a sharp gaze, her father with an expression that verged on boredom. He'd suggested on more than one occasion that family dinner was a waste of time, but Bex's mother insisted on the once-a-week tradition. Bex supposed it made her mother feel better about her otherwise absentee style of parenting. Being a neuro-surgeon was a time-consuming endeavor, after all. Bex didn't resent her for it. She had once, when she was too young to understand the rigors of her mother's profession. But the years had gently abraded the rough edges of Bex's abandonment, and now she barely felt the sting of her parents' absence. It tingled a bit when she prodded the old wound, so she avoided prodding it whenever she could.

"My day was fine," Bex said, the same way she'd said it every night since family dinner had become a tradition in the fifth grade.

Usually, that one pithy sentence was good enough. But today there was something different about her mother's inquiring gaze.

"Did anything interesting happen at school this week?"

She had never asked Bex a follow-up question. Not once. Not even when Bex was twelve and had come home with an unfortunately uneven chin-length haircut, performed by Melody in the bathroom of Jackson Hills Middle School.

Bex considered her answer. She remembered the garish letters emblazoned on the doors, the worrisome content of the graffitied message. The taut line of Donahue's lips after he told her the *Lantern* had been suspended until further notice.

"No ma'am," Bex said. She shoveled a spoonful of peas into her mouth, forgetting for one brief moment of insanity how much she hated them. But if she was chewing peas, then she wasn't talking, and she wasn't sure what she would say to her parents about the graffiti. As Maplethorpe alumni, they both held the school in high esteem, and Bex knew they entertained no criticisms of things of which they approved. Things of which they didn't approve were rarely, if ever, discussed within the walls of their home. On the rare occasions when protestors made the evening news, her father would grab the remote with a wordless utterance of disgust to change the channel. The Rating System had served the Johnson family well, and both her parents were staunch supporters.

Difficult conversations were never on the menu for family dinner. They picked up topics that could be carried and discarded with ease. The weather. Award-winning period films. The latest innovations in medical technology. What absurd modernist reimagining of classical operas were to be staged at the theater of which they were valued patrons.

An act of vandalism, particularly one that bled revolutionary sensibility, was hardly the sort of thing the Johnson family discussed.

Bex's mother hummed thoughtfully. Bex had learned to hate that sound. It always meant her mother was about to make a comment that would grate at Bex's nerves.

"Dr. Rawlins mentioned an unfortunate incident that occurred on the first day of school. Apparently some young delinquents saw fit to deface school property with spray paint."

Bex blinked, chewing her peas extra slowly.

"I find it interesting that you didn't mention this to us earlier."

Bex shrugged, though she knew her mother despised shrugging. "I didn't think it was that important."

Her father made that same disgusted snort he normally reserved for people with political views that failed to align with his own. "You'd think someone would be teaching these kids respect. Especially with what we pay in tuition."

Bex's mother tsked. "One would think, darling." Her eyes, the same dark brown as her daughter's, bore into Bex's own. All their features were similar. The same high cheekbones. The same dark brown skin. The same thick curls, although her mother's were perpetually tamed in a tight bun. Bex could probably count on one hand the number of times she'd seen her mother's hair loose and free. "I'm sure you wouldn't know a thing about it, but if you do hear something, I hope you'll remember your responsibility to report it."

"I don't know anything about it," Bex insisted, which was true.

Her mother hummed around a dainty mouthful of steak so raw it might still be breathing. She always did like her steak bloody. Bex couldn't understand how, since her mother spent much of her day looking at the raw red goop of the human body.

"Perhaps that artist friend of yours knows something." The tone of her mother's voice implied much even when her words relayed so little.

"Her name's Melody, Mom," Bex said, more to her peas than to anyone at the table. They didn't approve of artists or actors or anyone who made their career in anything that couldn't be as neatly quantified as medicine, science, or law. Those were the only respectable areas of expertise as far as Mr. and Mrs. Johnson were concerned. Like many of their social rank, being seen to show an appreciation for the arts was no impediment to looking down on actual artists. Under her breath, Bex added, "You've known her since we were, like, six. And she doesn't know anything either."

"Don't say 'like,'" her father interjected. "It makes you sound hesitant."

"Can't have that," Bex muttered, once more to her peas.

"What was that?"

"Nothing."

Her mother's knife scraped against her plate. "Well, enough of that unpleasantness. Have I mentioned the new internship opening up at the hospital?"

Bex moved on to smushing her mashed potatoes with her fork. She actually did like mashed potatoes, but every time her parents brought up a new extracurricular opportunity to add to her résumé, her stomach felt as though it were calcifying into stone. She thought back to the schedule she'd made, her crowded symphony of color coding. She'd even colored in the hours she'd marked off for sleeping, a necessity for humans but a weakness among the Johnsons.

"No," Bex replied. "You haven't mentioned it."

"The internship could be a great opportunity for you," Bex's mother said, her gaze already back on her steak. Bex's agency in decisions like these was nominal at best. "Normally, it's only open to college students, but I'm sure I can put a good word in for you when you submit your application."

Not *if* Bex submitted her application, but *when*. Her participation was a foregone conclusion as far as her parents were concerned.

The calendar flashed through her mind again, with its paucity of empty blank spaces. Every moment of her day was already accounted for.

"I don't know, Mom . . ."

"What's there to know? It's a great opportunity, Rebecca. Your classmates would kill for a chance like this. Think of what it would do for your rating."

"College applications are due in a few months," her father added, as if Bex could forget. The prospect of those applications had been hanging over her like a dark cloud since the first day of her freshman year at Maplethorpe.

"It's just . . ."

"Don't say 'just.' It makes you sound unsure."

Bex fought not to roll her eyes, but her father's eyebrow—the thickness of which was one of his few facial features Bex had inherited—twitched as if he could see the desire to do so written across her skin.

She had to say something. To outright refuse without a solid reason would be to invite more of their persistent pushing, until she found herself shoved right to the edge of her sanity.

"I don't think I have the time. I started tutoring a new kid at school." And before they could protest, she added, "The headmaster asked for me specifically."

"Oh?" her mother said. "And who is the lucky student who gets to occupy your time?"

"His name is Chase. He plays baseball."

Her parents shared a jovial laugh.

"An athlete." Her mother chuckled. "No wonder he needs the extra help. More brawn than brains, I take it?"

The question made Bex bristle, and the intensity of her annoyance took her by surprise. Hearing her parents say less-than-generous things about people they deemed intellectually inferior wasn't anything new, but hearing them say something like that about Chase, who clearly wanted help but didn't know how to ask for it, felt particularly cruel.

"He's not . . . he's a good guy, Mom." She wasn't sure if this was definitely true, but it *felt* true. "He just struggles a little, that's all."

Her father pointed his fork at her. "Keep it professional, Bex. Now's hardly the time to let yourself get distracted by boys."

"Dad! I'm just tutoring him."

"Be that as it may," her mother said, "I don't see why you can't both tutor him and take on the internship."

"Sure, Mom. It's *just* that I don't think I have the time to add another extracurricular to my schedule. There are only so many hours in the day, you know."

The sound of utensils on china came to a very delicate halt.

"Honey," her mother began, blinking at her daughter like she'd sprouted a second head. "Don't sound so defeatist. It's meant for full-time students, so it's only an hour or two a day, once a week. If something's worth doing, you'll find the time."

"How?"

"Excuse me?"

Bex let her fork fall to her plate, the clatter loud in the silence of their elegantly appointed dining room. The decor was the work of an interior designer who had decided that a cold, modernist style had suited the collective disposition of the Johnson family.

"How do I find the time?" The words were out of Bex's mouth before she could swallow them back. "How do I add another two hours to the day? Who do I talk to about making it an even twenty-six?"

It was the most she had ever talked back to her parents in seventeen years.

She didn't know where the capacity to do so had come from. Every day, she bottled up her frustrations, her exhaustion, her fears that nothing she did would ever be good enough. Every day, she tried valiantly to ignore how awful the weight of their expectations made her feel. And now that bottle was spilling over, too full to contain one drop more.

"Rebecca Lee Johnson." Her mother bit out each word with razor-sharp precision. "I don't think I appreciate your tone."

From the corner of her eye, Bex noticed her father's hand flying to his own wrist. He tapped his screen a few times, and Bex's watch buzzed. He'd docked her. Her own dad had sent her a negative.

"Don't talk to your mother like that," he said, his tone inviting no further rebellions, however minor.

And just like that, the indignation that had bubbled to the surface of Bex's being like a shaken can of soda fizzled out of existence. She slouched in her seat, feeling dwarfed by the high-backed leather chair and the table that was just a touch too large for three people to comfortably eat around.

"I'm sorry, Mom. I didn't mean it. It was a long day at school and I'm just kind of tired."

Tired didn't quite cover it.

"Don't say 'kind of,'" her father chided around a generous mouthful of steak.

"Not now, Albert," Bex's mother snapped.

Bex stared at the disaster zone on her plate. It looked like a hurricane had assaulted the mountain of potatoes and peas, leaving naught but devastation in its wake. "May I please be excused?"

Her mother remained silent for a moment, as if considering withholding her permission. Eventually, she relented. "Yes, you may."

Difficult conversations were, after all, hardly appropriate for their weekly family dinners.

Bex pushed away from the table, leaving two-thirds of her meal uneaten, if not untouched. The hunger would hit her later, when she was lying in bed, rearranging the colorful rectangles of her schedule to do the impossible.

Bex's room was a testament to her achievement. Or over-achievement, as Melody liked to say. Ribbons dominated the wall above her desk, an array of mostly blue that told of her multiple victories in science fairs over the years. Trophies weighed down her bookshelves, blocking her view of most of the spines behind them. Every time she wanted to pull a book off the shelf, Bex had to rearrange the entire display. The desk itself was hidden under piles of textbooks and binders and notebooks. Most of her work at school was done digitally, on her tablet, or at the computer consoles provided by the school, but she found studying to be more effective when she opted for good old-fashioned pen and paper.

Normally, she would have gone straight to the desk to get started on her piles and piles of homework, but the sick feeling she'd had all through dinner had yet to abate. She bypassed the desk and belly flopped onto her bed. Burying her face in the pillow, Bex screamed. Just a little scream. Not enough to be overheard by her mother's eagle ears, but enough to dissipate the growing length of anxiety coiling itself around her organs.

A vibration sounded from her nightstand. She angled her face just in time to see the screen of her phone light up through a curtain of her curls.

The only person who ever texted her was Melody, and Bex wasn't quite sure she was in the mood to deal with the girl's incessant optimism.

But Bex was nothing if not a good friend. She snaked out a hand to grab the phone. Her fingers paused in sliding open the lock screen when she saw the sender.

Chase Donovan.

A boy was texting her. Chase Donovan—who was, in fact, a boy—was texting her. At night.

Such a thing seemed so ludicrous that she hadn't really thought it would ever happen. She had given him her number at Lucky's, but the logistics of planning a strenuous academic regimen had distracted her enough from the implications.

And now, a boy was texting her.

Bex pressed the phone to her chest and made a sound that was somewhere between a wheeze and a giggle. After a moment's indulgence—she was allowed that much, surely—she bit the inside of her cheek hard enough to kill any future wheeze-giggles.

"Get it together, Johnson."

She got it together. Then she swiped his message open.

Hey.

"That's it?" Bex asked the silence of her bedroom. The silence did not respond.

Melody had always told Bex that boys were *like that*. As someone with her fair share of suitors—a fact Bex's mother heartily disapproved of—Melody would know what boys were like far better than Bex. But knowing they were *like that* and experiencing just how *like that* they were felt like two entirely different things.

What did one say to a simple, singular *Hey*?

A greeting like that placed the burden of conversational direction on the recipient, and that was incredibly unfair. But responding with another *Hey* felt uninspired at best and passive aggressive at worst.

Bex stared at the screen, wishing she'd listened to Melody's blathering about her romantic escapades instead of tuning her out with well-timed *hmm*s and *you-don't-say*s. If she had, maybe she'd know what to do. She thought of texting Melody to ask for advice, but in doing so, she would have to explain how she came to have Chase Donovan's number in the first place. And if she was just tutoring him, then maybe there was no reason to be nervous. They had to communicate to coordinate said tutoring, and there was nothing untoward in that.

But it wasn't *just* tutoring, Bex suspected. She thought back to the letter and the smiling jester and the immediate sense of camaraderie the discovery had caused. They shared a secret. And Bex wasn't about to invite a third party into that. Not yet. Not when it had the potential to be so volatile.

She typed out and then deleted a series of greetings, each one less satisfactory than the last.

Hi there.

Heya.

Salutations.

Sup?

"Ugh." Bex was disgusted with herself. She could solve theorems that brought mathematics professors to tears, but she couldn't figure out what to say to a guy.

It hadn't occurred to her that Chase could see the blinking dots of her aborted typing adventures until he sent a follow-up to his absolutely incorrigible *Hey*.

Any thoughts on what that letter meant?

"Oh, thank god." Bex breathed a sigh of relief. He'd offered her an actual conversational thread to follow. She could work with that.

Bex pulled her laptop over and launched her browser. The computer was usually on the bed since she fell asleep with it every night. That habit probably said something utterly damning about her psychological state, but it was also probably best left unexamined.

Let me do a search, see if I can figure something out, she typed back.

Do u want me to send u a pic?

"No," Bex said aloud. She knew enough about cell phones to know that nothing that was stored on them or transmitted with them was ever truly private. That he typed *u* instead of *you* should have bothered her, but it didn't. It bugged her so much when Melody did it that she'd spent an entire summer breaking her best friend of the habit. Another thing best left unexamined.

I think I remember what it said.

I can call u . . .

Bex wondered briefly if this was what a heart attack felt like. Sitting with him at Lucky's had been different. They'd gone there under authentic school-related reasons. But the letter had nothing to do with school. And the thought of talking, on the phone, with a real live human boy, while her parents watched the evening news downstairs felt unspeakably illicit. She found that she quite liked the feeling.

Okay, she replied. One word. A multitude of feelings.

Less than a minute later, her phone rang.

She let it ring two times before answering. She remembered that much from Melody's lessons in how to be a normal teenage girl who did normal teenage things.

Keep 'em wanting more, Melody had said. *Never answer before the third ring.*

Bex tried, but she could only make it so far.

"Hello?" It came out as both a question and a squeak. Bex wanted to sink into her mattress and die, suffocated by memory foam.

"Hey." Chase's voice sounded different on the phone. Deeper, like maybe he was lying down. "So, any strokes of genius?"

Bex leaned against her pillows and propped her laptop on her thighs. She typed the words of the rhyme into Google, but none of the hits looked promising. "Nope. I don't know if the internet is gonna help us out on this one."

Chase hummed in Bex's ear. It sent an electric current of delight down her spine.

"Weird," Chase said.

"Super weird," Bex agreed.

"Maybe we just need to sleep on it." There was a rustling against his phone, like he was changing positions.

Don't think about him wiggling around on his bed, Bex thought. *Do not.*

"Yeah," she said. "Maybe."

"You okay?" he asked. "You sound a little, I don't know, strained."

"I'm fine," Bex said, even though she wasn't. Not really. "It's just . . . my parents are driving me nuts."

Chase puffed a little laugh against the phone. "I know that feeling. We can talk about something else if you want."

The floorboards in the hall outside Bex's room creaked.

"Bex, honey? Are you talking to someone?"

"No, Mom!" Bex called. Much quieter she added, "I've gotta go. I'm really sorry."

"Hey, no worries." Bex was probably imagining it, but she thought he sounded a little sad. "Talk tomorrow?"

"Yeah," Bex whispered into her phone. "Talk tomorrow."

She hung up. The rest of the night, the sound of Chase Donovan's soft, secret laugh into the phone echoed in her mind.

CHAPTER 15
JAVI LUCERO

RATING: 88

The boy with the camera had become the boy with the note.

"Noah," Javi whispered to himself as he sunned on a large slab of a rock outside Maplethorpe. Eighth period had just let out, and students spilled out of the doors as he watched them from a comfortable distance. The lingering warmth of summer had fled, but the afternoon sun was persistent enough to warm the stone. He understood why cats fell asleep in sunbeams. Even if everything outside that small speck of light was cold, at least his one spot was warm.

They hadn't talked about the note. The bell had rung, signaling the end of the period. Noah had shoved it back into his bag and vacated the bathroom as fast as his legs could carry him. Javi followed him out, but by then, Noah had been swallowed by the crowd of students heading to their next class.

Javi hadn't had much luck tracking Noah down after that. They shared no classes, and more often than not, the boy left school the second the eighth-period bell rang. He didn't linger to hang out with friends—as far as Javi could tell, Noah didn't have any at Maplethorpe—and he didn't stick around for extracurriculars. Javi wasn't sure where Noah went every day in such a rush, but he wanted to learn. There was so much Javi wanted to learn. Like why Noah had received a message signed by a jester.

His obsession was so intense that he hadn't even felt the wonderful thrill he normally did when his rating crawled upward. The Panthera headsets had proven so popular they had to go into another production run to meet consumer demand. But it was hard to focus on that when his brain was so determined to look elsewhere.

Javi watched groups form and disperse as students left for whatever activities they had planned for the afternoon. Some went straight home. The underachievers. Children of highly rated individuals who didn't need to boost their own ratings with every activity Maplethorpe had to offer. On the steps, Summer Rawlins held court, flanked by two strapping young men in maroon letter jackets. She looked genuinely regal, as if they were her honor guard. It wasn't lost on Javi that she sat on the top step, her minions all at least one step below. He bet it wasn't lost on them either.

His eyes roved over the crowd, until they found the mop of dark brown hair he was looking for.

"Noah," he said again, the name carried away by the wind. He stretched his legs and stood. Reluctant as he was to relinquish the spot of warmth he'd claimed, he had business to attend to.

Making his way through the crowd of departing students took a little finessing. Javi had a reputation as someone who was both highly rated and highly approachable. He dispensed a few smiles, a wink here or there, and a pat on a shoulder or two. And then he reached Noah.

The other boy was standing on the fringes of the lawn, close to the parking lot, his head bent over his phone. He was frowning. A small line had formed between his brows, and

Javi had to tuck his hands into the pockets of his Panthera track jacket to still the urge to reach out and smooth out that little wrinkle.

"Got a hot date?" Javi asked.

Noah jumped, his phone slipping through his grasp. Javi darted out a hand to catch it before it smashed against the pavement.

"What? No. Hi. What?"

Noah was cute when he was flustered. Javi found he rather liked flustering him.

"Hi," Javi said. "You busy?"

The boy's eyes—a nice, soft brown—widened. "Why?"

Javi couldn't help but laugh. "No need to sound so suspicious. I was thinking about going to Lucky's and I hate drinking alone. You want to come?"

"Drinking?"

"Milkshakes, duh. Come on. My treat."

"Are you asking me on a date?" Noah asked. His perplexed face was almost as good as his flustered face. "Is this a date?"

Javi offered him a one-shouldered shrug. "Do you want it to be?"

"I don't know," Noah replied, a little too honestly.

"Okay, well, how about we start walking over to Lucky's, and you can figure it out on the way?"

Noah remained standing there, brow furrowed. For a horrible moment, Javi thought the boy would say no, that he would prove himself one of the few people at Maplethorpe immune to Javi's charm.

"I was supposed to go see my sister," Noah began. "But she's . . . busy."

That sounded odd, but Javi didn't press. And he wouldn't, not until he had a satisfactory answer to his question. "So how about them milkshakes?"

A prolonged silence and then . . .

"Okay," Noah said. "But . . . why?"

"Why what?"

"Why are you asking me to go get milkshakes with you?"

Javi tugged on Noah's sleeve as he steered them toward the gates. Lucky's wasn't far, but it was far enough to have a considerable chat before getting there. And along the way, there would be nothing but tree-lined streets to bracket them in, no one but squirrels hoarding nuts for the coming winter to overhear them.

"Because you seem cool," Javi said. He was keenly aware of the whispers following them off campus. They must have made an odd couple to see. Lonely loner Noah and garrulous gamer Javi, walking off, almost arm in arm.

"I don't think anyone's ever referred to me as cool before," Noah said, his steps falling into sync with Javi's.

"Stop, you're gonna make me cry."

Noah chuckled a little, some of the heaviness evaporating from him as Javi tugged him along, toward Lucky's and milkshakes too thick to suck through a straw and, most importantly, answers.

The Lucky Penny was as packed as it was whenever school let out. A handful of townies sat at the long counter, but most inhabitants of Jackson Hills knew to give the place a wide berth between the hours of three and five. Maplethorpe students, once let off their leashes, were boisterous at best and

extremely obnoxious at worst. Finding a table in the late afternoon required either murder or a bribe.

Fortune, though, had decided to smile on them that day. A
small booth in the corner—barely large enough for two fully
grown young men—was unoccupied. Javi tossed a smile at the
waitress, who followed them to the table with two glossy
menus. They both ordered the milkshake of the day—Orange
Creamsicle—and Javi added a side of fries for good measure.
Noah still hadn't come to a decision on the dateness of their
outing, but if it *was* a date, Javi didn't want Noah to think he
was too cheap to buy him solid food.

"So," Javi began. "I have questions."

Noah's eyebrows inched upward. "Is this some kind of
interrogation? I thought it was a date."

Javi bit his lip to prevent himself from shouting in
triumph.

Good thing he got the fries.

"The photograph," Javi said, leaning over the table. "The
note. The jester. What did it say?"

"Oh. That." Noah fished around in his backpack until
he found the photograph. It was crumpled from having been
unceremoniously stuffed into his bag, and he had to smooth it
out on the table to flatten it.

"It's a picture I took freshman year, on the first day of
school," Noah said. "I don't know how somebody could have
gotten their hands on it, though."

"'On the day of the prophet false,'" Javi read, "'one mustn't
dance a forbidden waltz. A copper found and a fortune told,
all beside a box of gold.'"

Noah looked down at the words, as if he could coax a greater, clearer meaning from them if he stared hard enough. It didn't seem to work. "I have no clue what this is about."

"You don't know why someone would have sent it to you?" Javi asked.

Noah shrugged and shook his head. "No idea." He cocked his head to the side, as if studying Javi. "Is that why you asked me to come here?"

"One of the reasons, yeah." Javi slipped his phone from his pocket and pulled up the camera roll. "Because someone sent me this online."

He held out the phone. Noah's eyes widened as he accepted it. The picture wasn't great. Faint, fuzzy lines cut across the image, the type of distortion that occurred when you took a picture of a picture on another glowing screen. But the image of the jester was clear enough. The text was a little hard to read, but it was legible enough.

"Wait . . . what?" Noah's eyes darted from the screen to Javi and back again. "Do you know who sent this to you?"

Javi shook his head. "Not the faintest."

"That's weird," said Noah.

"Incredibly so," Javi agreed. "I was hoping maybe you'd have some answers, but I guess the search continues."

The waitress returned, her tray laden with two large milkshakes and an obscenely generous serving of fries. They waited in silence as she laid them on the table. When she was gone, Noah picked up a fry, but didn't eat it.

"You said there were other reasons," Noah began. "Why you asked me here."

Javi also took a fry, and he wasted no time popping it into his mouth. He chewed, mulling over how he wanted to play this. It wasn't a game, but there was strategy involved. One had to know when to advance and when to hold the line. He hadn't even been certain that Noah liked guys, but judging from the other boy's casual acceptance of the maybe-date, that didn't seem to be a problem. Still, Noah was a skittish creature. Javi didn't want to scare him off.

"I just wanted to hang out," Javi said.

"With me?" Noah asked.

"Yes, with you," Javi replied with a small laugh. "Is that so hard to believe?"

Noah shrugged. "Kind of." He finally raised the fry to his lips and nibbled on the end. "But I'm not complaining."

A smile stretched its way across Javi's lips. Not a planned one. Not the trademark grin that adorned posters selling Panthera gaming peripherals, but a genuine one. The rarest kind.

"I've been trying to track you down for ages, but you were slippery. Like an eel. Hard to catch." Javi dipped a fry into his milkshake. His siblings claimed dipping fries in anything other than ketchup was a disgusting habit, but Javi thought it made a good food great. "It was starting to feel like you were avoiding me."

"I wasn't," Noah said. And then, immediately, "Okay, I kind of was."

The milkshake-dipped fry was far too sweet on Javi's tongue. "Oh?"

"It wasn't personal," Noah said in a rush. "It was just me being . . . forget it. It's dumb."

Curiosity was one of Javi's greatest sins. Sometimes he couldn't help but poke at things, the more stubborn his target the better. "If it wasn't about me, then what was it?"

"It's stupid," Noah insisted.

"Great. I love stupid."

That got a little smile out of Noah, which, in turn, got a smile out of Javi.

"I was embarrassed," Noah mumbled. "I hated that you saw me crying. I don't like crying in front of people."

"No shame in tears," Javi said. It was what he told his younger siblings whenever they cried, because it was what his parents had told him when he'd cried. "Can I ask what happened?"

The breath left Noah in a sad, shallow sigh.

"My sister's sick."

"Oh," Javi said. "I'm sorry to hear that."

He wasn't good at knowing what to say in situations like this. He felt like he was parroting the words of an older, wiser adult more accustomed to these sorts of conversations.

"Like, really sick," Noah went on. "She's been in the hospital for a while now. She, um . . . she needs a donor."

"For what?" Javi asked.

"Bone marrow," Noah replied.

"Oh."

"Yup."

Javi didn't know much about terminal illnesses, but he knew enough. He knew that finding donors for kids was hard, and finding bone marrow for *anyone* was *really* hard. People stayed on the registry for years, some until they died and it was too late.

"I went to get tested to see if I was a match." Noah paused. He swirled the straw around in his milkshake, once, twice. But his hand fell away before taking a sip.

Javi hazarded a guess. "And you weren't?"

A thin, bitter laugh escaped from Noah. "Nope. Not only was I not a match, I wasn't even . . ."

He let the sentence linger without finishing it.

"You weren't even what?" Javi asked.

"Related. We're not even related."

Javi blinked. "What?"

"I'm adopted," Noah said. "We don't even have the same blood type."

"Jeez," Javi said. That didn't seem like the ideal way for someone to find out.

"So, yeah. Not only am I not a donor, I'm not even her brother."

Javi shook his head. "Hey, being adopted doesn't mean you're not her brother."

"I know." Noah took a sip of his milkshake and then cringed. "That is a crap ton of sugar."

"Yeah, that's the beauty of it," Javi said. "Listen, have you talked to your parents about this?"

Noah shook his head. "No. We don't really talk about stuff. Not deep stuff like that anyway. When we do, it's usually about Cece. I don't want to burden them any more."

"But they're your parents. You wouldn't be burdening them. And if you are, well, then bearing your burdens is sort of their duty. It's in the job description. Trust me, I checked."

The corners of Noah's lips twitched. It didn't evolve into a fully developed smile, but it was a good start.

"I just . . ." Noah leaned back against the booth seat. The red vinyl creaked as he moved against it. "I don't know what to say. Hey, Mom. Hey, Dad. Were you ever planning on telling me I was adopted? Or were you just hoping I'd never find out?"

"I think it's probably worth bringing up."

"How do you talk to your parents about stuff like this?"

"Well, two things. One, I wasn't adopted," Javi said. "My parents had me the old-fashioned way. By accident." Noah smiled at that. "And two, both of my parents are dead."

And just like that, the smile was wiped off Noah's face, like someone had pulled an eraser across it. "Crap. I'm sorry. *Crap.*"

Javi held up a hand to still the apologies he could sense were ready to pour out of Noah's mouth on a wave of regret. "It's fine. Don't worry about it, really. Look . . . I don't know what your relationship with your parents is like, but maybe it's worth trying to talk to them about all this."

"Maybe . . ." Noah stared into the swirling froth of his milkshake as if it had all the answers. If only.

"There's nothing I wouldn't give to be able to talk to my mom and dad just one more time." Javi felt himself going too deep, getting too real, but there was something about Noah that made him want to dive in. There was an incredible sense of catharsis that came from sharing these things. "Sometimes, I worry that I'll forget what their voices sound like. That the voices I think I remember are actually just my imagination. Something my brain made up to fill in the blanks."

It was the first time Javi had ever said that to another human being. He'd never dared talk like this with his siblings. As the eldest, it was his duty to bear the burden of remembrance. And his grandmother . . . losing her son and daughter-in-law had affected her in ways Javi knew he couldn't ever fully fathom.

Noah's hand relinquished the straw. His palm hovered over the table, as if he was reaching out to touch Javi's. But he dropped it before making contact. "Well, that makes my dumb issues sound small and insignificant."

"What? No, that's not what I . . ." Javi ran a hand through his hair. "I wasn't trying to say my problems were bigger than yours. I just meant . . ." He heaved a sigh. "I don't know. Your parents are human. Sometimes humans mess up. But they're still your parents, you know? No matter what."

"I know that," Noah said. His eyes drifted away from Javi, wandering to the rest of the diner. Javi followed his gaze.

It felt as though their table had been carved out of the room. Like they'd made a pocket dimension for themselves amid the afternoon chaos. In a booth by the front windows, a table full of what looked like Mathletes hunched over books and calculators. A clutch of freshman girls broke into a riot of giggles when a couple of sophomore boys walked past their table and smiled at one of them.

"I don't think I'm angry at them," said Noah. "Not really."

Javi turned back to him. Noah's gaze was still off to the side, but Javi had the feeling that Noah wasn't really looking at the other denizens of the diner. "You aren't angry that they didn't tell you?"

"Yeah, but . . ." Noah scrubbed a hand over his face. In that moment, he looked older than his years. "I'm not angry at *them*. I'm just . . . angry. I'm angry because my little sister is sick and I can't help her. I'm her brother. It's supposed to be my job to protect her and I can't protect her from this. I'm angry and I don't know who to be angry at. It's easier to be angry about this."

"I get that," Javi said. "And can I just say, this got way more cathartic than I planned?"

Noah's lips trembled, and then he laughed. A nice, full-bodied sound. It softened the lines of his face and made the golden flecks in his eyes sparkle.

The last bit may have been inventions of Javi's imagination, but that was neither here nor there.

"You mean you don't spill your guts to everyone you take out for fries and a shake?" Noah asked. "And get them to do the same?"

"Not really, no. Might add it to the repertoire, though, seeing as how it's worked so well."

Javi smiled at Noah over the rim of his glass as he lifted the straw to his lips.

"Thanks," Noah said. "I don't think I realized how much I needed to talk about this."

"Yeah," Javi agreed. "Me too."

"But what I really want to know," Noah said, leaning over the table, "is who sent us those notes?"

They had no idea who sent the notes. They racked their brains, demolished a second round of shakes that Javi was beginning to deeply regret, and still, they hadn't the faintest idea of who would send them the letters.

The bigger question also remained unanswered.

Why?

By the time the waitress hustled them out of Lucky's, claiming they needed the table, they were no closer to the answers than when they'd sat down. Javi walked Noah to the bus stop, where they were forced to go their separate ways.

As Noah's bus pulled up, Javi grabbed his arm to stop him. "Wait a second." Javi tapped on his smartwatch, pulling up Noah's rating page. He tapped the little plus sign next to Noah's name.

Almost immediately, Noah's own watch vibrated. He smiled when he looked down at the notification of a positive peer-to-peer rating.

"What's this for?" Noah asked.

Javi pushed Noah toward his bus. If he didn't get on soon, it would leave without him. "I like you. That's what it's for."

Javi skipped away from Noah, so he would have the last word. There was nothing more satisfying than that.

He was walking toward his own bus stop, when a buzz against his wrist not two minutes later made him stop in his tracks.

A peer-to-peer rating notification from one Noah Rainier. A positive one.

Javi smiled the entire ride home.

.

CHAPTER 16

TAMSIN MOORE

RATING: 26

Headmaster Wood's lecture echoed in Tamsin's mind, even with the weirdness of the tarot card crowding out most of her other thoughts. She'd been so distracted by both events, she'd nearly brushed her teeth with zit cream that morning. That she had actually woken up early enough to get to school on time—before the morning assembly, even—might have also contributed to her wandering thoughts. But it was morning, and school was in session, and she was actually, seriously, legitimately considering attending her classes. Most of them anyway.

Her smartwatch buzzed as she reached her locker. It felt like it had been buzzing all morning. She bit back a curse, glancing down at her wrist.

Her rating had slid again. Precipitously. And for no reason Tamsin could discern. She was trying to be good. Honestly. But the number kept falling and falling, the device buzzing on her nightstand even in the middle of the night. And she had no idea why.

Tamsin had barely opened her locker before it was slammed shut again. She yanked her hand out of the way before it could meet an unfortunate end.

"What the—?"

"Why did you put this in my notebook?"

Tamsin turned to see a very angry Hana waving a folded note in her face. A torn sticker marked the place where it had been held closed. Her hair was mussed in a way that seemed unusual for the normally so put together Hana Sakamoto. Her ponytail was slightly askew. Shadows smudged the skin under her eyes, making her look more tired than a seventeen-year-old had any right to look. She had a heavy duffel bag slung over her shoulder, in addition to her backpack. Skates, most likely.

"You look terrible," Tamsin said. "Also, hi. Also, why are you angrily wielding a piece of paper at me?"

Hana waved the note with renewed fervor. "You put this creepy note in my notebook!"

"What are you talking about?"

"This!" Hana thrust the note into Tamsin's face, a hair's breadth away from her nose. "I'm talking about this."

Tamsin placed a hand on Hana's wrist and gently—but insistently—pushed the other girl's arm down. "I have no idea what you're talking about."

The bell rang. They both jumped. Tamsin hadn't even noticed the halls around them emptying. The moments just before the bell were usually a cacophony of frenzied footsteps, as students rushed to their classes, lest their ratings reflect their tardiness.

"Ugh," Tamsin said. "Class."

Hana frowned. "I thought you didn't go to class."

Tamsin shrugged. Her book bag was a lot heavier now that she was putting actual books in it. "I'm turning over a new leaf."

And just like that, the indignant steam that had powered Hana up to that point vacated her body. She deflated, in slow motion. "So . . . you didn't put this in my notebook?"

"No," Tamsin said. "I told you, I didn't read your diary."

"It's not a diary," Hana said defensively.

"Okay, whatever, I didn't read your not-a-diary."

A vibration against her wrist summoned a swear to Tamsin's lips. Hana's device must have buzzed as well because she glared down at her wrist with what looked like betrayal.

Hana swore, then slapped a hand to her mouth as Tamsin's eyebrows arched in pleased disbelief.

"The ice princess curses," said Tamsin. "Who knew?"

"I don't," Hana protested.

"But you just did, and not gonna lie, it made me like you a little bit more."

"Wait, did you not like me very much before?"

"Aren't we losing track of what this oddly aggressive conversation was all about?"

Hana glanced down at the paper in her hand and then at her watch. Tamsin assumed the display showed what her own would. A point lost for lateness.

"Listen," Tamsin said, "we've already been docked for not showing up on time. We're already screwed, and I want to know what this weirdness is that you're accusing me of, so why don't we just skip?"

Old habits were hard to break. Tamsin would be sure to tell Wood that the next time he called her into his office.

"Skip?"

"Yes, skip."

"Skip where?"

Students found roving the halls of Maplethorpe when they were supposed to be in class were routinely rounded up and sent wherever they were supposed to be. But not Tamsin.

"I know a place." She liked the way it sounded mysterious when she said it like that.

Hana paused, sagging under the weight of her bags. The whirlwind of energy she'd brought to Tamsin's locker dispersed into the ether.

"What about turning over a new leaf?" Hana asked.

"Tomorrow's a new day." Tamsin took Hana by the arm, steering the other girl to the stairwell nearest her locker. There was a fire exit a flight down, with a disabled smoke alarm that no one had bothered to fix since the *last* time Tamsin had disabled it. She was beginning to think the facilities staff was slowly but surely being ground down under the heel of her stubbornness.

It was strange, bringing someone to the place she'd begun to think of as her secret lair, as childish a notion as it was. She saw people there, but they weren't friends. They were clients. And none of them seemed to want to be there. They went to Tamsin for a reason, and once she'd served her purpose, they departed as quickly as their feet could carry them out of the darkened building and into the sunlit lawns, far away from the Witch of Maplethorpe.

But Hana wasn't here for an exchange of funds and services. She was here on invitation. And that was something Tamsin had never extended to anyone. Ever.

As they slipped past the shoddy locks that provided only superficial discouragement from potential intruders, Tamsin glanced at Hana. The other girl had never been to this building. She wasn't one of Tamsin's regulars, had never gone to her for a reading. They'd never even exchanged words before that day in the shop. Yet here they were, sharing something truly bizarre, as if they'd been friends for years. It was a strange feeling, but Tamsin found she didn't quite hate it.

Hana looked around at the dilapidated furnishings and the cobwebs dangling in the corners. Motes of dust danced in the slanting sunlight. "This is nice," she said.

"It's not, but thanks for saying so." Tamsin made her way to the stairs, motioning for Hana to follow. "Come on. There's a room upstairs where I do tarot readings that's almost cozy."

She clomped up the steps, her heavy boots pounding out little clouds of dust. When she got to the landing, she turned just in time to see Hana sway, her weight carrying her back. Hana's hand groped for a banister, but there wasn't one. It had fallen off years before, left to rot with the rest of the building.

Tamsin grabbed Hana's jacket and yanked her forward onto the landing.

Hana collided with Tamsin, her body sagging forward. She righted herself quickly, but Tamsin kept a steadying hand on the other girl's arms.

"Sorry," Hana said, looking down, to the side, anywhere but at Tamsin. "Just got a little dizzy."

"Yeah, I noticed." Tamsin guided her to the room at the far end of the hall. There were at least cushions there, to break any more unexpected falls.

When they arrived, Hana sank onto one of them, folding on herself with enough grace to make it look more intentional than it probably was.

Tamsin watched her move. Her breath seemed labored, more than it ought to be, considering the girl was some kind of world-class athlete. Walking up a flight of stairs shouldn't take the wind out of her like that. Tamsin wasn't even breathing heavily and she didn't believe in exercise.

"Are you okay?" Tamsin asked, though it was obvious the other girl wasn't. But it felt polite to phrase it as a question instead of an accusation.

"Yeah," Hana lied smoothly, like she'd grown accustomed to doing it. "I'm fine."

Tamsin lowered herself onto a cushion next to Hana, the tarot card and the strange note pushed to the far corners of her mind. She looked at Hana, really looked at her.

Hana was small and thin, which wasn't entirely surprising given the sport in which she participated, but it wasn't a lithe sort of thin. The wrists that poked out of Hana's puffer jacket were bony, with skin so thin and pale stretched over them that Tamsin could see the fine tracery of veins under it in alarming detail. The collarbone Tamsin spied between the open throat of Hana's jacket was equally worrisome. She was all harsh lines and flat planes. Her muscles seemed to tremble with the exertion of holding her skeleton together.

Hana was not fine.

"So, the other day in the shop," Tamsin said, not sure if it was the right thing to say, but knowing she had to say something, "that wasn't the first dizzy spell you've had, was it?"

Hana's skeletal hands retreated into the safety of her sleeves, her fingers poking out just enough to pick at the cuffs. "No." She shook her head to get the bangs off her face and abruptly stilled, like the motion was too much for her brain to handle. "But it's not a big deal. It's just a thing that happens sometimes."

"You know it shouldn't, right?" Tamsin felt their conversation hovering on a precipice. Of what, she wasn't sure. But she was beginning to suspect.

Hana didn't answer. Instead, she thrust her hands into her pockets, pulling out the note she'd waved in front of Tamsin's face so menacingly just a few minutes prior.

"How about this super-weird note, huh?"

"Hana."

Only then did Hana look up, into Tamsin's eyes. The rest of her was still, but her eyes had the wild look of a caged animal. Something trapped that didn't know how to escape.

"What?"

"Have you eaten anything today?"

The question sat, heavy in the air between them. They both knew the answer, but it wasn't about the right answer. It was how they handled the lie they both knew was coming.

"Yeah. After practice."

Tamsin nodded. Pushing wouldn't do any good. The harder she pushed, the further Hana would retreat into the cocoon of her own suffering. Tamsin was surprised by the realization that she didn't want Hana to retreat from her.

"Okay," Tamsin said, even though it wasn't. Another lie, but a necessary one, in that moment. "Okay, just checking."

Hana pushed the note toward Tamsin. "If you didn't put this in my notebook, I don't know who did. Nobody touches that book but me."

Tamsin folded up the half-formed conversation about Hana's eating habits and set it aside. They could deal with it when they were both better equipped. When their friendship felt less like a possibility and more of a certainty.

Friendship.

Not a thing Tamsin had actively courted at Maplethorpe, but something she was starting to think she might like to develop.

Odd.

"What does it say?" Tamsin asked.

Hana opened the letter, laying it flat on the floor between them.

"'On the day of the prophet false,'" Hana recited, "'one mustn't dance a forbidden waltz. A copper found and a fortune told, all beside a box of gold.'"

"This is where it gets interesting." Tamsin rummaged in her backpack to retrieve the tarot card she'd found taped to her locker. She placed the card beside Hana's letter. The text of Hana's had been culled from various magazines, judging from the variance of fonts and paper textures.

"Holy . . . you got one, too?" Hana leaned closer to inspect the card, squinting at the tiny font. "When? Where?"

Tamsin shrugged. "A few days ago. Someone taped it to my locker."

Hana sat back. "On your locker? Anyone could have grabbed it there."

"I was the only person in the hallway," Tamsin said. "Wood had just called me into his office, so everyone else was in class."

Hana shook her head. "This doesn't make sense. Your locker is at least public. My notebook is private. Super private. And I always have it on me. I don't know how someone could have snuck a letter in there."

"Who has access to your stuff?" Tamsin asked.

"My mom and dad, I guess. Maybe some people at the rink, but I usually lock my stuff up when I'm there. I don't think I've ever left it in my locker at school . . ."

"That's it?"

"My world is really small." Hana shrugged. "It's basically just the rink, home, and school, and I spend most of my time at the rink."

"That's kind of sad," Tamsin said, before the part of her brain responsible for filtering insensitive remarks caught up with her mouth. It rarely got much exercise, so Tamsin couldn't blame it for being a little too slow. "Sorry, I didn't mean . . ."

"No," Hana said, "you're right. It's not ideal, I guess, but sometimes you have to make sacrifices if you want to succeed."

"And you've chosen to sacrifice having an actual life?"

Hana shrugged again. "I'd rather have an Olympic gold medal."

Tamsin felt herself at the edge of that great precipice. To step forward would risk destroying the fragile friendship she felt forming between them. But caution had never been her strong suit.

"Is a gold medal worth killing yourself for?"

Hana froze, her fingers hovering over the tarot card. Her eyes darted up to meet Tamsin's. They were wide, and she was blinking too fast.

"What are you talking about?" The tone of Hana's question contained the truth she didn't speak. She knew exactly what they were talking about, but denial was probably a reflex for her at this point.

"Have you eaten anything today? Like, for real?"

"I don't want to have this conversation with you," Hana said, each word sharpened to a fine point. "And I already told you I did."

"Okay, fine," Tamsin said. But the damage was done.

Hana stood, collecting her things. She shoved the note into her backpack, her movements stilted. "I've gotta go."

She didn't wait for Tamsin to say goodbye before she strode to the door and stomped down the stairs. Tamsin watched her go. Her smartwatch buzzed again. And again. She didn't bother looking at it.

CHAPTER 17

NOAH RAINIER

Noah tried to time his visits to Magnolia Children's Hospital when he knew his mother wasn't there. He was still avoiding his parents after the unexpected revelation of the blood test, but he'd never relished being at the hospital with her. She had a tendency to hover over Cece in a way both he and his sister found grating. Neither one of them complained—Noah couldn't imagine what it must feel like to have a terminally ill child, so he had no business telling his mother how to behave—but it was always something of a relief when she left.

Cece's main issue wasn't actually the hovering. It was their mother's draconian view of snack foods. The woman monitored every morsel of food that went into Cece's diet, but a twelve-year-old girl had needs, no matter how sick she was.

Which was why her smile nearly blinded Noah with its intensity when he held up the bag of goodies he'd smuggled in.

"I brought all your faves," he said as he dumped an unhealthy amount of candy on the bed. Every kind of chocolate imaginable, flavored with sea salt, caramel, raspberry, and mint. Sour gummy worms. Rainbow gummies shaped like little sharks. Raisins coated in yogurt. Lollipops with mystery centers. And a bag of chips in case she needed a little salt to counteract the sweet.

"You're a true hero," Cece said. She hugged him with one arm while the other swept the candy closer to her.

One of the first gifts he'd brought her during her first stay at Magnolia was a large stuffed bear that unzipped in the back, exposing a pouch large enough to hide all her illicit treats. The first few times Cece had glutted herself to the point of nausea, but with time she learned the beauty of rationing her supply. It lasted longer, and she wouldn't puke all the colors of the rainbow.

Noah perched on the edge of her bed as he watched her divvy up what to eat now and what to save for later.

He thought about not telling her. But a secret like that would fester if left on its own. He hadn't talked to his parents about it yet. There were too many emotions all jumbled up together to make it an easy conversation. But he wanted Cece to know. She had a right to know.

"Hey, spark plug," he said, "there's something I want to talk to you about."

She rolled her eyes at him. "I'm never gonna live down that fork in the electrical socket incident, am I?"

"Nope. Never."

"I was five," she said, with as much indignation as a twelve-year-old could muster, which was rather a lot.

"Doesn't matter. It's on your permanent record, *spark plug*." He ruffled her hair, smiling when she pulled away. With her hair all fluffed up, Noah finally noticed it was thinner than it had been.

"What is it?" Cece asked, sorting the gummy sharks into an orderly rainbow.

"I got tested," Noah said. "For my bone marrow."

Her hands paused, one still holding a green shark, as she raised her eyes to meet his. There was such expectation in them. Noah's chest constricted, like his rib cage was trying to crush his vital organs.

"I'm not a match."

A moment of silence passed between them, heavy with all the possibilities that simple statement had just washed away. But then Cece sighed and popped the green shark into her mouth. When she spoke, her words came out muffled.

"It was a long shot to begin with," she said. She paused to swallow. "But thanks for trying."

That was . . . not the reaction Noah had expected. He'd braced himself for crying. Maybe even a little anger. But she barely looked flustered by the news. Already, her attention had drifted away from him and back to her candy hoard. She wiggled her fingers over the pile before she settled on a bar of chocolate.

Might as well go all out, Noah thought to himself. He'd always told Cece everything. It would feel disingenuous to start hiding things from her now.

"That's not all," he said.

Cece didn't even look up at him as she tore open the candy wrapper. "Oh?"

"I'm adopted."

Cece looked at him, a handful of chocolate halfway to her mouth. "So?"

So?

So?

"So?" Noah repeated, because it was one of those things that bore repeating. "Wait, did you know?"

The idea that his twelve-year-old sister could have kept a secret of that magnitude was unthinkable. Once, years ago, she'd caught Noah pilfering five dollars from their mother's purse during a particularly sweltering summer. He'd wanted to buy a vanilla cone with rainbow sprinkles from the ice cream truck that drove through their neighborhood every day at two o'clock. She'd promised not to tell—provided he bought her one, too—and had lasted all of seven minutes before cracking. Their mother had simply asked if Cece had seen her car keys.

Cece shook her head, biting into the chocolate bar with crispy rice. Those were her favorites. "No. I just don't think it's that big a deal."

"But it is!" Noah's voice ticked up to an octave he hadn't realized he could hit.

A mere shrug was all Cece offered him. "I have a high threshold for big news."

"Oh my god, what twelve-year-old talks like that?"

"All I do is read all day. My vocabulary is epic."

"So wait," Noah said. He wasn't quite done torturing himself. "This doesn't bother you at all?"

"No." Cece looked at him like he was being exceptionally dense. "Why would it?

"Because . . . that's why I can't be your donor."

Cece put down the chocolate bar and leveled him with an eerily intense stare. "Noah, it's okay. It doesn't change anything. You're still my dumb brother and I'm still your exceptional sister. Everything is just like it was before, even if you are now burdened with a great and terrible knowledge that's, honestly, not that great or terrible."

"It felt pretty terrible," Noah muttered, pressing his thumb into the side of a pack of bubble gum.

"If it bothers you so much, you should talk to Mom and Dad about it."

Noah shrugged. "Yeah. Maybe."

Cece plucked the bubble gum away from him. "Plenty of people are adopted. Maybe you should just get over it. I know it sounds harsh, but I say that with love. Now stop messing with my candy."

That he could just get over it hadn't really occurred to Noah until that moment. And it was possible she had a point. Being a blood relation wouldn't have been a guarantee he'd have been a bone marrow match anyway. The odds would have been better, but by no means had it been a certainty. And it's not like his parents weren't his parents anymore. Javi had said as much at Lucky's, but it hadn't sunk in then. It still wasn't quite sinking fully in, but it was starting to penetrate the thick layer of indignation in which he'd wrapped himself.

"You're smiling," Cece said. "It's a dumb smile. Like you're thinking about a girl or something."

Noah blinked. Before he could stop himself, he said, "Not a girl."

Cece's grin widened. "A boy, then?"

So this was a conversation they were going to have now, too.

Great.

"Yeah," Noah said, and left it at that.

"Are you gay?" Cece asked. She had no filter. When she wanted to know something, she never wasted time fretting about it. She simply asked.

Noah picked at the edge of her bedspread. It was one from home that their grandmother had crocheted long before either of them were born. "I don't think so. I've liked girls before." And he had; his attraction to Javi didn't negate that. "I think I might be bi."

"Dude. You're just hitting me with all the revelations today," Cece said. "Maybe you should've spread them out a bit, saved some for slow news days."

Noah let out a small laugh. "Yeah, maybe I should have. I'll just have to come up with something even more outlandish next time."

"You better." Cece leaned in, her grin going slightly maniacal. "So, tell me everything about this boy. His name, his favorite color, his thoughts on how you pronounce 'GIF.'"

She said it with a hard *g*, like *gift*. Noah preferred a soft *g*, like *giraffe*. On this, they would never agree.

"Have you always been this nosy?" he asked as he watched her tear into another candy bar. "Or is this a new development?"

"There's not a lot of juicy gossip on the ward," she said, mouth full of half-chewed chocolate. It was gross, but also cute, because Cece was his little sister and she could do no wrong. "Do you like him? What are his intentions?"

"I don't know," Noah said.

"Which one?"

"Either."

Cece shoved another piece into her mouth as she mulled over his obviously inadequate answer. "How do you not know if you like a person? Isn't that the kind of thing where you either do or you don't?"

Noah shrugged and slowly moved his hand toward the diminishing bar of chocolate. Cece smacked him away. It was fine. He didn't really want it anyway.

He kind of did, but he wouldn't admit that.

"I barely know him," Noah said.

"So? I barely know the cute nurse who reads my vitals every morning, but I'm madly in love with him."

Cece was madly in love with a new person every week. Last week it had been the guitar player who came in every Friday to perform for the kids on her ward. The week before that it had been a med school student who was so nervous reading her chart that he'd dropped it twice.

"Oh, yeah?" Noah asked. "And what are *his* intentions?"

"To read my vitals. You're changing the subject."

Now Noah did steal a piece of her chocolate, purely out of spite. "Am not."

"Are, too." Cece's sigh sounded far older than it had any right to. "Listen. Life is short, bro."

Noah frowned. "I don't like it when you say things like that."

"Too bad. I'm not saying it because I'm sick. I'm saying it because it's true. And also, I'm smarter than you. If you find a cute boy, you should kiss him."

It wasn't terrible advice, Noah had to admit. He managed to ruffle her hair again before she could slap his hand away. "How did you get so wise?"

She blew a raspberry at him. "All the wisdom Mom and Dad tried to teach their children skipped you and landed on me. I am concentrated wisdom. I'm too powerful. Look upon me and despair."

"I'm your big brother. You're supposed to be nice to me."

"That is factually incorrect."

"Well, you should be nice to me," Noah said, "or I won't bring you forbidden snacks anymore."

They both knew it was a lie.

Noah's steps slowed as he neared his house. There was a person sitting on his porch. A person wearing large, noise-canceling headphones, typing fervently on his phone, designer sneakers tapping out a beat on the steps.

Javi. Javi was sitting on his front porch. Javi knew where he lived.

Noah walked closer, stopping at the base of the stairs. Javi's head jerked up when Noah's shadow fell across his phone.

That smile—the one that had haunted Noah's dreams since the first time he saw it—flashed across Javi's face. He whipped the headphones off, resting them against his neck in a way that made him look effortlessly cool. Noah could never look like that if he tried. Trying, he supposed, defeated the point of effortlessness in the first place.

"Hey," said Javi. "I was wondering when you'd get home. I was about to give up hope."

"Are you stalking me?" It was perhaps not the smoothest greeting.

Javi shrugged. "Maybe. Is that a problem?"

Noah shook his head. "No. But . . . how do you know where I live?"

Javi's grin turned sheepish, which only made it more powerful.

"I have my ways," he said.

Noah cocked his head to the side.

"Okay, fine," Javi sighed. "I sweet talked Mrs. Sullivan. Told her I needed to get to your place for a group assignment and couldn't get hold of you."

Mrs. Sullivan was Headmaster Wood's assistant. She was as much of a fixture at the school as the marble bust of the school's founder, or the stone foundation on which the entire edifice sat. Sullivan predated Wood's tenure as principal. She might have even predated Maplethorpe itself.

Noah shifted his keys from hand to hand. "So what *are* you doing here?"

Javi's smile dimmed. "I . . . wanted to see you. Sorry, did I misread things? I thought it would be okay . . ."

"It is," Noah said in a rush. "And you didn't." Well, he was making a mess of this. And Javi was still sitting on the porch. "Do you wanna come in?"

The wattage of Javi's smile increased. "Yeah. It's a nice porch, but my butt went numb like ten minutes ago."

Don't think about his butt, Noah told himself.

Noah led Javi into the Rainier home, trying to imagine what it looked like through a stranger's eyes. It was comfortable but a bit sparse, like a showroom at a furniture store. A few years ago, the living room had been a riot of toys, both his and Cece's. His parents had settled for a sort of ordered chaos. But with Cece sick and spending more and more time away, the house had become as sterile as the hospital. Noah's mother couldn't seem to bear the sight of her daughter's things without Cece there to play with them. And Noah had retreated into his own spaces. His bedroom. The darkroom.

"Can I get you something to drink?" Noah asked. It seemed like what one ought to ask a guest.

"Sure," Javi said. "Coke, if you have it."

They did. Noah led Javi to the kitchen and poured them two glasses. The carbonation fizzed, so fresh it almost burned. The sensation was bracing enough to ground him, to get him to think of things besides Javier Lucero sitting on a stool in his kitchen.

"I brought you something." Javi reached into his backpack. Leaning down like that gave Noah a nice view of his neck. It was long and elegant, and until that moment, Noah hadn't realized necks could be elegant.

Javi righted himself. In one hand, he held a video game controller, and in the other a large, black headset that would completely cover one's eyes. A logo of a leaping cat was stamped on the side of the headset.

"It's a virtual reality system," Javi said. He placed it on the counter with great care. "Panthera, one of my sponsors, sent it to me. I thought maybe your sister might like it."

Javi worried his lower lip between his teeth as he waited for Noah to respond.

"I . . . yeah. Yeah, Cece would love this," Noah said. But it seemed like too much. "Are you sure? It looks really expensive."

Javi shrugged. "Like I said, Panthera sent it to me. Didn't cost me a dime. They like it when I post about their stuff on social media. It boosts my rating and theirs. But honestly, VR isn't my thing. It makes me kind of nauseous."

Noah trailed his hands along the sleek surface of the headset. He'd told Javi about his little sister cooped up in a hospital room, and so Javi sought Noah out with the most thoughtful gift he could've imagined. It was almost too much for Noah to handle.

"Do you have flaws?" Noah asked, because Cece wasn't the only one in the family without a filter.

Javi smiled as he sipped at his Coke. "Oodles. But I like lulling people into a false sense of security before revealing them."

"That's . . . oddly comforting," Noah said. "But it doesn't feel right accepting this without giving you something in return."

Javi's laughter had a nice, warm sound about it. "That's literally how gifts work."

"I know, but . . ."

Javi canted his head to the side, studying Noah. "You're a photographer, right?"

Noah nodded. "Yeah. I mean, I like to think I am. I'm not a professional or anything, but yeah, I've been known to take a picture or two."

"Good," said Javi. "You can repay me in art. Got anything good?"

The thought that this seemingly flawless but allegedly flawed boy would want one of Noah's photographs did strange and wonderful things to Noah's stomach. "I have some stuff downstairs I just developed. In the darkroom."

Javi turned to him and smiled. "You have a darkroom? That's awesome. I'd kinda like to see it, if that's cool. Seems retro."

"Sure," Noah said, even as the thought of inviting a near stranger into his most private of spaces made his heart beat so frantically he thought it might bruise his ribs. His photography had always been a private thing, something he did just for himself. It was an interest he shared with his father, but parts of it belonged solely to Noah.

Unwelcome thoughts buzzed in his head like vengeful wasps as he led Javi to the basement. What if he wasn't as good as he thought he was? What if Javi noticed himself in one or two or three of the pictures and thought Noah was a complete freak? What if Javi hated every single one and only pretended to like them?

"Be careful with the lights," Noah said when they reached the door. "And watch out for the chemicals. I haven't put everything away."

"I'll look with my eyes," Javi promised, "not with my hands."

They entered the room. The red glow of the lights made the space feel a thousand times more intimate than the kitchen. Noah was suddenly aware that they were in a confined space. Unsupervised. With no school bells to save them.

Javi didn't seem to mind. He went straight to a series of photographs hanging from a cord strung from one wall to the other. His teeth gleamed in the dim light as he looked over his shoulder and smiled.

"Noah, these are amazing."

Noah liked the way his name sounded in Javi's mouth. He liked it a lot.

He hooked his thumbs in his pockets. He didn't know what to do with his hands. The darkroom felt so much smaller with Javi in it.

Noah didn't quite know what to make of Javi yet. Were they friends? At the start of the semester, he would have sworn that Javier Lucero hadn't even known he existed. And he hadn't even entertained the possibility that Javi would want to be friends with a notorious loner like Noah. The other boy radiated extroversion. Noah was as introverted as a human being could possibly be, while still doing things like leaving the house and interacting with other people. Even if he tried to keep the latter to a bare minimum.

"Thanks," Noah replied after he allowed the pause to stretch for too long. Javi didn't appear to notice the awkward silence. If he did, he didn't seem to mind.

"I'm serious." Javi turned to him, half of his face illuminated in red, the other half cloaked in sharp planes of shadow. "You're a true artist."

Noah's tongue felt oddly thick in his mouth. Had it always been that thick? And dry? He was pretty sure it was a new sensation.

Javi cocked his head to the side. "You okay?"

Nope.

Noah had to clear his throat before his voice obeyed his brain's command to answer. "Yeah. Yeah, I'm good. Super good."

When Javi smiled at that, Noah suspected that the other boy was laughing at him. But so long as it was a polite, internal laughter, Noah didn't much mind. His behavior *was* laughable, and he was powerless to stop it.

Javi's grin softened. "Thanks," he said.

"For what?" Noah croaked.

"For bringing me down here." Javi looked around the too-small space like Noah had shown him something precious. "I'm getting the feeling you don't allow a lot of people into your den."

His den. Not an inaccurate term, Noah supposed.

He shrugged, his hands kept firmly attached to his pockets. That way, he wouldn't do anything stupid with them, like reach out and touch the one part of Javi's face that wasn't sharpened by the red lights of the darkroom. Or his lips, which were curved and soft. Noah needed to destroy that train of thought before it went any further.

"Not really," he admitted. "Photography's always been my thing, you know? Something private."

"Well, in that case," Javi said, closing the distance between them with a slow step, "I'm honored to have been granted the privilege."

Noah took a step back, colliding with a tray of instruments on the counter. They clattered to the ground, the noise deafening in the silence.

Biting back a swear, he dropped to his knees to pick them up, glad that the semi-darkness was enough to mask his furious blush. Not enough to mask his utter stupidity, but it was something. A pair of hands reached out to help him gather the fallen tools. Noah kept his gaze down so he didn't have to look at the owner of those hands and promptly die of embarrassment.

"I'm sorry," Javi said.

Noah's head jerked up. "For what?"

"For misreading the situation." Now it was Javi who looked embarrassed. "I thought that you . . . that I . . . Never mind."

Noah dumped the instruments onto the tray, but made no move to place it back on the counter. "Wait. You thought . . . ?"

Javi shook his head and ran a hand through his hair, mussing up its artful arrangement. "Nothing. It's stupid. I'm an idiot."

"What? No."

Javi paused, his hand still half-raised. "No what?"

"You're not an idiot. I'm the idiot. I mean, look at me go."

That got a laugh out of Javi. "A little clumsy, maybe, but not an idiot."

Noah sat back on his heels. "What did you think?"

He had to know. He simply had to.

Javi sucked in a deep breath before answering. "That you were into this. Into me."

Was he? Of course he was. It seemed absurd now, that he'd hemmed and hawed when Cece had asked exactly that question. That was why he'd gazed at Javi through the lens of his camera on the first day of school. Why he'd tried to capture that dazzling smile on film. Why he'd stared at the photo for what felt like hours when he finally did. And why he would never ever admit to doing that to Javi. He'd take that shameful little secret to the grave if he had to.

Javi moved, as if to stand. "Look, I'm sorry. I should go. I've taken up enough of your—"

Noah shut him up with a kiss.

Well, he tried to. It wasn't a kiss so much as an artless collision of lips. His teeth bumped into Javi's teeth, which was probably not how a kiss was supposed to go, but since Noah had never actually kissed anyone before, he lacked the proper frame of reference with which to compare it.

A little oomph escaped Javi, muffled in the nearly nonexistent space between their mouths.

Noah was about to pull back, to apologize profusely, to perhaps die of mortification, his corpse beautifully illuminated in the crimson light of his darkroom, when Javi moved his lips against Noah's and all rational thought ceased to exist.

It wasn't a perfect kiss. Noah knew his lips were chapped. He had a tendency to bite them when he was anxious, which he was most of the time. He didn't know what to do with his hands, and he was a little congested and he couldn't really breathe through his nose, so he felt like he was suffocating in the best way possible.

It wasn't perfect. Except for all the ways in which it was.

Javi's lips. Those were perfect. They were soft and just the right amount of plump to have a little give to them, which Noah found he liked. A lot. Javi's soft laugh puffed against Noah's mouth as he pulled away for an interminable second for air. That was perfect, too.

"Was that okay?" Javi asked.

"'Okay,'" Noah said, "doesn't begin to cover it."

And to prove it, Noah leaned in and kissed him again. And again. And again.

CHAPTER 18
HANA SAKAMOTO

RATING: 75

The North Atlantic Regional Championships were the first step on the road to nationals. If Hana performed well enough at regionals, she would qualify for sectionals. And if she skated well enough at sectionals, she would qualify for nationals. Success at nationals would mean a possible berth on the team for worlds. It would mean assignments at competitions on the Grand Prix circuit. This was technically Hana's second year competing as a senior, but the first hardly counted. The injury had sidelined her for the majority of the season; she hadn't even had the chance to compete at nationals. This year was her true debut. And she was determined to make it spectacular.

Hana waited by the boards as the skater before her took her bows. First to the judges, as was right and proper, and then to the handful of spectators scattered about the arena. At a competition like this one, the only people who showed up were relatives of the skaters and occasionally very good friends. Hana's own parents were somewhere in the stands. She didn't know where they were sitting, but kept her eyes on the ice in front of her to discourage herself from searching for them. She hated when they watched her skate. It made her even more nervous than usual. She'd asked them to skip the competition, but they just stared at her as if she'd asked them to perform some absurdist circus act.

"But we're your parents," her mother had said in Japanese. She spoke Japanese when she thought Hana was being recalcitrant. Hana didn't think her request had qualified as such, but she wasn't a parent. She wouldn't know.

The girl who'd just skated stepped off the ice. Hana stepped aside to let her pass, trying to ignore the streaked mascara running down her cheeks. She didn't watch other skaters perform, but the look on the poor girl's face told Hana everything she needed to know. It hadn't gone well. And she'd forgotten to apply waterproof eye makeup. A rookie mistake.

"Next to skate," the announcer said, her voice booming across the mostly empty arena, "representing the Skating Club of Jackson Hills, Hana Sakamoto."

Polite applause shepherded Hana onto the ice. She raised her arms in presentation, as was also right and proper. Everything in skating was a show, not just the seven minutes spent on programs over the course of a competition. The judges watched the practices. They analyzed every move made on the ice, right down to the skaters' reactions to their own performances as they took their bows. Dmitriev always told her to never let her disappointment show if she made mistakes. The judges were human. If you acted like you had just given the worst performance of your life, they would think that you had. Hana straightened her back, bent deep into her edges, and skated to the center of the ice, her composure as solid as she could make it.

Her nerves were powerful enough to overwhelm the hunger gnawing at her stomach. She hadn't eaten anything that morning. She could never eat right before a competition.

The lights overhead caught the rhinestones sewn onto her sleeves. They sparkled beautifully against the dark blue fabric of her dress. As she took her starting pose, one hand draped delicately over her shoulder, a thought rose, unbidden and unwanted.

Tamsin's voice, asking questions Hana wished she wouldn't.

Is a gold medal worth killing yourself for?

The sounds of Rachmaninoff's Piano Concerto No. 2 drifted from the speakers, filling the cavernous space with almost enough noise to drown out the intrusive thoughts pushing at the edges of Hana's concentration.

Almost.

She pushed off the ice, tracing a semicircle with a strong and steady edge. Figure skating had ceased to be about tracing actual figures on the ice decades ago, but her coach was old-school enough to make her practice what used to be compulsory figures every day. Incorporating them into the beginning of her program was an excellent way to show off her skating skills, a valuable part of the program component score. But it was her technical element scores she was hoping would impress the judges.

It was only regionals. Not even sectionals. She didn't need the triple Axel to qualify for the next competition, but god she wanted it.

Her blades cut across the ice as she performed the footwork leading into her first jump. It was tricky skating into a triple Axel. Simple crossovers would have built up more speed, but the added footwork boosted the value of the element. She took a breath and flew into her jump preparation. Her blade skidded against the ice for a fraction of a second before she launched herself into the air from a forward edge.

Is a gold medal worth killing yourself for?

She rotated. Once, twice, three times—but not three and a half. Her feet were still crossed when her toepicks caught the ice. Her hip slammed into the ice as she collapsed, her legs tangled with each other. Hana pushed herself up as quickly as she could. Bits of snow clung to the fabric of her skirt, but she didn't brush it off. The element was behind her. She had to forget about it and move on, even if the bones in her hip were screaming in agony.

Her next jumps were in combination. A triple flip, double toe loop. Not the most difficult combination at the senior level but a serviceable one. After the understated crash on her opening jump, she needed a clean combo with a positive grade of execution. She could salvage the rest of the program. She had to.

Is a gold medal worth killing yourself for?

The triple flip was off the moment she kicked at the ice. Hana managed to crank out a landing, but it skidded so badly that she barely had enough speed to attempt the double toe. The second jump took off almost from a standstill. That would be a negative grade of execution on both jumps.

She was slow, too slow. Her body was still turning when her blade touched down. A skater was allowed only a quarter of a full rotation on the ice. Any more than that and the jump wouldn't count as fully rotated. If the technical caller was feeling kind, they would count it as an under-rotation, which wasn't nearly as costly as a downgrade. If they were feeling vicious, they'd call it a single.

Hana felt tears sting at her eyes, but she blinked them away. She had three and a half minutes left in her program.

Three and a half minutes to get it together and keep it together. In that moment, three and a half minutes felt like an eternity.

With every bobble and every balance check and every cheated landing, she felt herself die a fresh and horrible death. Nationals had felt so close just minutes ago. She'd been able to imagine the lights, the packed stadium, the weight of a medal as it was hung around her neck. The awed commentary about her triple Axel, a jump so difficult only a handful of American women had ever landed it.

But now those dreams were scattering further and further away, specks of dust on an uncaring wind.

The rest of the program went by in a blur. Tamsin's voice was louder than the Rachmaninoff piping through the speakers.

Is a gold medal worth killing yourself for?

She wanted to scream that it was. That it wasn't. She wanted to rip the skates off her feet and tear the bedazzled dress from her body. She wanted to quell the pain in her stomach that had become her most constant companion. She wanted to curl into a ball and fade into nothingness.

All that remained was her last combination spin. A flying camel into a doughnut spin into a backbreaking Biellmann. She spun, the velocity of it drying the tears on her cheeks. When had she started crying? Her back twinged as she reached behind her to grab the blade of her free leg and hoist it up behind herself, contorting herself into the Biellmann spin.

She let go of her leg and the twinge worsened. Something was wrong. But it didn't matter. Whatever injury was forming in her spine wasn't an excuse. Skating through pain was expected of her. By her coach. Her parents. By herself. Competition was supposed to be mind over matter, and in this, Hana knew she had failed. That sense of failure was so powerful, so visceral, that she wobbled as she exited the spin. Her body hadn't betrayed her. Her mind had.

The music came to an end, and Hana thrust her arms behind her in her final pose. It was designed to look triumphant. But triumph was the furthest thing from what she felt.

Her body went through the motions of saluting the judges. Bowing. Waving to the handful of people politely clapping for her disaster of a performance.

She skated to the boards, where Dmitriev wordlessly handed over her skate guards. Tense silence accompanied them to the kiss and cry—a glib name for the section of the rink where Hana sat down to receive a score she didn't want to see. Beside her, Dmitriev sat as still as stone. There were no words of condolence, no admonishments. The admonishments, at least, would come later. The condolences, probably never.

The top four would advance to sectionals. Everyone else would have to come back and try again next year.

At the sound of the announcer's voice, Hana closed her eyes.

"And now, the scores for Hana Sakamoto . . ."

She didn't listen. She didn't want to know. If she hummed loudly, she could distort the sound of the announcer's voice enough to muddle the numbers. Dmitriev would hold them over her head at their next practice anyway. They would haunt her, long after this.

But what she couldn't block out were the vibrations against her wrist.

Her rating, docked to reflect her poor performance. The official judges were not the only souls sitting in judgment of Hana and every other skater who took the ice. Anyone in the crowd could weigh in. They could cast pity votes for skaters who fell and tried to rally. They could condemn the ones who failed to live up to whatever overused, bombastic music their coaches had saddled them with. Performing to *Carmen* or *The Phantom of the Opera* or *Swan Lake* was practically begging for a bad rating.

She didn't look at her watch either. The numbers would not lie. They would reflect the brutal truth of her performance, but she didn't need numbers to testify to that. She had skated it. She had lived it. And even with the pain still throbbing in her hips, there was only one thought floating through her mind on an endless loop.

Tamsin's voice, soft with concern.

Is a gold medal worth killing yourself for?

"Man is born free; and everywhere he is in chains."

A very smart man wrote those words, at a very volatile time in history.

It is true of all civilizations. We come to love our chains, especially if they are all we have ever known. We find a certain comfort in their weight. We are soothed by the limitations they place upon us. There is little chance for failure if we can only extend ourselves so far. Predestination is in many ways preferable to the unknown future before us.

But it is a false security peddled by false prophets.

None more false than the man who built our chains.

The red spray paint is more than a little dramatic. The blue and black are downright vulgar. But it looks so nice, so loud, against the white marble. It is a statement, made boldly, as the best statements ought to be made.

It is a key sliding into a lock. A door being opened. A chain breaking under the tide of change.

The rest is simply theater.

CHAPTER 19

HANA SAKAMOTO

RATING: 70

Five days before the Founder's Day Dance, a second act of vandalism put the first to shame.

And Hana was lucky enough to see it with her own two eyes.

She had skipped practice that morning. Her parents normally forced her to go unless she had a good reason—bones sticking out of the skin was their minimum threshold for good reasons—but her parents weren't in Jackson Hills. They were somewhere on the other side of the world, competing for more gold medals to add to their collection. Something as trivial as having a child—birthing or raising one—was hardly reason enough to slow Mariko Sakamoto down. Equestrian sports were the opposite of figure skating in so many ways. Skaters had the lifespans of mayflies. Their careers were often over before they could legally buy a beer. Equestrians like Hana's mother could compete well into middle age and beyond. There was a guy in his seventies at the London Olympics. Hana could easily envision her mother trying to break that record. She lived on her horse, and she'd probably be happy to die on one.

Hana had called Dmitriev at five o'clock in the morning and informed him that she had a vicious stomach virus.

Blasting out of both ends were the words she used. No one asked for specifics after that.

He'd merely grunted out, "с Богом," and hung up.

Go with God in Russian. It was the same thing he said to her before competitions.

After the disaster at regionals, she really should have been working herself to the bone to prepare for sectionals. She'd only just squeaked by to qualify. But the thought of spending another cold morning at the rink trying to be faster, higher, and stronger than she was the day before, while her stomach ate itself and her bones creaked with their increasing brittleness, seemed so unappealing.

Recovery was an important part of training. It wasn't important to Dmitriev—who was Russian enough to expect his athletes to skate to their fullest potential every day—but Hana had heard that it was important to other coaches. So she was recovering.

It was odd, how much recovery felt like slacking off.

But Hana was markedly less conflicted when she arrived at Maplethorpe Academy that morning and walked right into what was likely the most scandalous thing to happen in the school's illustrious history.

The marble bust of John Maplethorpe—founder of the academy that bore his name, father of the Rating System, and architect of their society—had been vandalized.

The word *vandalized* didn't do it justice. This was an act of desecration. A demolition of the sacred.

Paint smeared the stern countenance of John Maplethorpe. Downward slashes of blue over his eyes. Red splashed across his gently disapproving frown. Strategic dashes of black to complete the look.

His face resembled a harlequin mask. A jester. It looked just like the stickers that had been slapped onto the security cameras outside the school's front doors.

But the desecration did not end there.

On the plinth, the vandal had spray-painted another phrase, this one more esoteric than the last.

Man is born free, and everywhere he is in chains.

A few members of the faculty had formed a loose human shield around the statue, trying to prevent students from getting too close. Someone behind Hana jostled her to get a better look. She recognized the girl from some of her classes. Monica. Melanie. Melody? Perhaps. She was an art student, about as far removed from Hana's lived experience as one could possibly be while also occasionally breathing the same air.

"Sorry," the girl who was probably named Melody said. "Just wanted to see what it said."

Hana stepped a few inches to the side so the other girl could peer over her shoulder.

"'Man is born free,'" Melody or maybe Melanie read, "'and everywhere he is in chains.'" A frown marred the girl's delicate features. "What the heck does that mean?"

It was a good question. Not one for which Hana had an answer, but a good one nonetheless.

Someone else jostled Maybe-Melody from behind, and was less polite about it.

"Move," came a familiar voice. Melody frowned at the interloper, but she moved to the side, allowing her in.

"Hey," Tamsin said, nudging her shoulder into Hana's in what was either a greeting or an accident. Hana wasn't quite sure.

"Hey," Hana replied.

Tamsin studied her for a brief but significant moment. They hadn't spoken since that day in the abandoned music building, when Tamsin had prodded at wounds Hana was desperately trying to pretend weren't there. She'd forced Hana to confront how infected those wounds had become, how the poison had seeped from them into every part of her existence.

"Are we cool?" Tamsin asked. She was evidently the kind of person who could just ask straightforward questions like that. Hana envied her the ability.

Were they?

Hana was still upset, but she knew she wasn't truly mad at Tamsin. She was upset with herself. Tamsin just made an easy target, and that wasn't fair. To either one of them.

"Yeah," she said. "We're cool."

Tamsin nodded, and only then did Hana realize how their previous conversation must have weighed on the other girl. If Hana had been haunted by it, maybe Tamsin had been as well. Hana got the feeling that Tamsin didn't have a lot of friends. Now that Hana had started paying attention to the other girl, she noticed how much Tamsin kept to herself. Hana could relate. Navigating friendships was turning out to be much harder than she'd thought it would be. After all, she had so little practice doing it.

She took a deep breath. "Listen, I wanted to say I'm s—"

"Out of the way, Sabrina the Teenage Witch."

Summer Rawlins and her flock cut through the crowd like sharks through a school of terrified fish. Hana had never interacted with the girl much—she didn't interact with many Maplethorpe students, but Summer had felt particularly distant—and the few encounters they'd shared had left Hana unimpressed. Summer was the queen of the academy, but the academy was such a small, isolated place. Her power was a puny thing and she didn't even realize it.

In her hands, Summer held a stack of bright pink flyers. Hana angled her head just enough to read them upside down.

FOUNDER'S DAY DANCE
FRIDAY 7 P.M. TO 9 P.M.
AFTER-PARTY AT THE RAWLINS MANOR
10 P.M. TO WHENEVER

A manor. Who even lived in those?

"One for you." Summer handed a flyer to Melody, who accepted it with a cheery thanks. Summer's gaze slid from Hana, to Tamsin, and then back again. "And one for you." Summer held a flyer out to Hana. "I don't see you around school often but you seem cool. You should come."

Hana blinked down at the flyer. She took it but only because it felt awkward not to.

"Oh, what? I don't get one?" Tamsin's pout dripped with insincerity.

"I'm sure you have much better things to do on Friday night," Summer said with a toxic sugar smile. "Like dancing naked under a full moon or communing with the Prince of Darkness." Summer wiggled her fingers at Hana and Melody in a way that was likely meant to be funny. "Bye. Hope to see you girls there."

Hana's smartwatch buzzed. She glanced down. Her rating had climbed a point. She looked up just in time to catch Summer's eye. The other girl smiled at her. That was odd. Summer had never given her a positive or a negative before.

Tamsin glared at Summer's back as the other girl weaved her way through the crowd, dispensing flyers to those deemed worthy and cold derision to those who weren't. "I'd rather dance naked over hot coals than spend a minute inside that girl's Barbie Dreamhouse, full moon or not."

"Wait," Hana said, still holding the wilting flyer in her hands, "you don't really dance naked under the full moon, do you?"

"Would it make me sound more intimidating if I said yes?" Tamsin asked.

"Kind of."

"Okay, then yes."

Hana felt a smile tickling at her lips. It was nice, this banter. She could get used to it. But not here.

The faculty had finally managed to rope off the scene of the crime, and teachers were hustling students away from the sight of the defaced John Maplethorpe. They had a few minutes before the bell rang, signaling that they needed to be in their seats for morning assembly, and Hana was in no particular rush to get there. She couldn't remember the last time she'd attended a morning assembly. She wasn't sure she'd even know where to sit.

Tamsin tugged Hana away from the crowd and toward a recessed alcove that housed a large silver trophy. There were names inscribed on it, but for what Hana wasn't sure. She'd heard it referred to as the school spirit trophy, but since Summer Rawlins had won it the year before, Hana wasn't certain what they were calling spirit these days.

The alcove was barely large enough for the trophy and its plinth, much less two teenage girls. Hana had never had a growth spurt, but she was still waiting—dreading—one. If she got any taller, she'd have to relearn all her triple jumps from scratch.

Tamsin leaned in close enough to whisper to Hana without passersby overhearing.

"This isn't a coincidence," Tamsin said. "The graffiti. The notes. The statue. They're all connected somehow. They've gotta be."

"Okay, yeah," Hana agreed. "But why? What's the point of any of it?"

Tamsin wrapped her hands around the straps of her backpack. The black polish on her nails was chipped unevenly, like she'd been picking at it. "I don't know. But there's gotta be a reason."

"Sure, but again, why? Why do any of this? Why go around saying the ratings aren't real? Why put clown makeup on the statue of a dead old man?"

Tamsin nodded along but then stopped abruptly. Her face lit up. She looked a lot less Goth like that. "False prophets," Tamsin said.

"False . . ."

The note. The poem. That awful little rhyme that haunted Hana's sleep like the worst kind of lullaby.

"He's the false prophet," Tamsin said.

"John Maplethorpe?" It made a certain amount of sense, if one considered the facts.

Fact: The graffiti artist wanted to convey to their audience that the ratings were an arbitrary invention.

Fact: John Maplethorpe invented the ratings.

Conclusion: The graffiti artist was not a fan of John Maplethorpe.

"Okay," Hana said, "but what about the rest of it? The copper and the gold and all that."

And just like that, Tamsin deflated. She scraped at the polish on her index finger with her thumbnail, without letting go of her backpack straps. "I don't know."

The shrill sound of the bell ringing made Hana jump. Her hip bumped into the plinth supporting the trophy. It jostled on its base, and both Hana and Tamsin reached out to steady it.

"Teamwork makes the dream work," Tamsin said.

Hana righted the trophy, frowning when she saw how their fingerprints had smudged it. She pulled the sleeve of her sweater down over her hand and used it to wipe away the offending marks. She might not have held the school spirit trophy in high esteem, but she'd polished enough trophies in her life that it was almost a reflex to clean this one.

"We better go," Hana said. She wasn't quite as keen to flout school rules as Tamsin. Maybe one day she would be. She had, after all, lied her way out of skating practice. Who knew where that slippery slope led?

"Yeah," Tamsin said. "Listen, do you wanna meet up at lunch and go over that poem again? See if we can figure it out now that we have a clue?"

Lunch. With another person. The thought was almost unbearable. But it wasn't lunch to eat. It was lunch to brainstorm. Hana could do that.

"Sure," Hana said. Somehow, she didn't dread the thought of spending her lunch break with another human being as much as she thought she would. Baby steps, for sure.

CHAPTER 20
BEX JOHNSON

RATING: 90

The second act of vandalism caused an even greater stir than the first. The first had been an appetizer. An amuse-bouche for the palate of the mind. The second . . . the second had drama.

Bex stood on the fringes of the group crowded around the defaced bust of John Maplethorpe. She had to elbow a few people aside to get a good look at the writing on the plinth, but once she did, her breath caught in her throat.

She backed out of the crowd with as much grace as she'd made her way through it in the first place. None. Popping up onto her toes, she scanned the sea of students milling about the foyer and congregating on the steps. The dirty-blond head of hair she was searching for was nowhere to be found. With a grumbled curse at the universe, she continued to elbow her way through the front doors and onto the wide steps out front. She scaled the short dividing wall at the top—and purposefully did not look down at the ten-foot drop below. It was tall enough to let her see over the heads of the students surrounding her.

In the distance, standing next to a weeping birch that Bex was rather fond of, was Chase. A few of his teammates lingered around the tree as well, but none seemed particularly captivated by the commotion. They simply looked happy to be outside and not in assembly.

Bex clambered down from the wall and tried to shove her way down the steps as delicately as possible. Hurting someone in her zeal to get to Chase would be a bad look for a number of reasons, the most significant of which was that she didn't want anyone to stop her.

Her steps slowed as she approached the group. Athletes were almost an entirely different species. Bex had tried her hand at sports—anything to pad a résumé—but the only one in which she'd excelled was bowling. It lacked the jock factor of more traditional team sports like baseball, and so she found it difficult to deal with those athletes in large groups. Individually, they were fine. En masse, they became something other.

But the gods of social interactions smiled on Bex, and Chase noticed her before she had to do something awkward to get his attention, like clearing her throat really loud or risking her voice squeaking when she said hello.

"Hey," Chase said, an easy smile gracing his lips as she approached. It was almost like he didn't mind their two worlds melding.

Bex liked to keep people separate. Chase belonged to one bubble. Melody to another. Her parents to their own bubble, far, far away from all the friend bubbles.

"What's going on?" Chase said. "I didn't want to brave the crowd to find out."

Before Bex could answer, one of Chase's friends looped an arm around his shoulders to peer at her. Perhaps peer wasn't quite the word. Leer was more like it. A mild leer, but a leer nonetheless.

"Who's your friend?"

Perhaps Bex was as unusual an entity to this guy as he was to her. She thought she was fairly well-known around school. She did hold offices in five or six clubs at any given time, but maybe the goings-on of organizations like the *Lantern* and the Mathletes weren't particularly thrilling to baseball players.

"This is Bex. Bex, Steve." Chase slid Steve's arm off his shoulder with a shrug that managed not to look dismissive. Bex wouldn't have been able to pull that move off as gracefully.

"Hello, Bex," Steve said. He stretched the *o* of the *hello* out a second longer than was seemly. "What brings you to our huddle?"

"School stuff," Bex said. It wasn't a lie. Not technically.

"What kind of stuff?"

"She's tutoring me," Chase said. "Gotta keep those grades up to stay on the team."

The slight twinge of Chase's jaw muscle told Bex that he didn't like saying that. But it's not like the ratings were a secret. Everyone knew everyone else's number. You might not know someone's GPA, but the ratings never lied.

"Then, Bex, you're doing a public service." Steve punched Chase in the upper arm hard enough to hurt at least a little. "We need this guy if we're gonna win the championships this year."

"Yes," Bex said. "The height of all accomplishments. Chase, can I talk to you for a second?"

Chase frowned at her. Her comment must have irked him. She hadn't meant it. Not really. But sometimes she found her parents' words coming out of her mouth without even meaning to speak them.

But still, he nodded. "Sure. See you later, Steve."

"Aw, come on," Steve whined. "Stay a while. Hang out with us."

"Maybe next time," Bex said. "Chase?"

She took Chase by the elbow, her fingers digging into the thick material of his letter jacket. She'd always hated those letter jackets. It wasn't fair, in her opinion, that athletes received visible markers of their accomplishments while students who excelled in arenas outside sports were given a pat on the back and, if they were lucky, a trophy for academic excellence at the end of the year. But she didn't hate the jacket on Chase. He wore it well.

She refused to examine that thought any further.

Chase was still frowning as he allowed her to tug him along, farther down the lawn, away from his friends who were jostling one another and laughing about something. Probably her.

"I'm sorry for saying that about the championship," Bex said. "I didn't mean it."

"It's okay." Chase gave her a little nudge with his elbow. "It's not really that big a deal. But that's as far as most of the guys are gonna get, so they take it really seriously. I just want the scouts to see me play."

Oh. That made her feel like slightly less of a snob.

Chase jerked his chin toward the front doors of the school, where the faculty was still having very little luck relocating the horde of curious students crowding around the entryway. "What's going on over there? Did the Jester strike again?"

"Yup. And not just that."

She grabbed his jacket again, ignoring his grumbling, and led him closer to the crowd. It was thinner now as the novelty of the sight wore off. Chase was tall enough to see over most of the heads between them and John Maplethorpe.

He squinted. "What does that say?"

"'Man is born free,'" Bex recited, "'and everywhere he is in chains.'"

"Um. Okay. What?"

"I know that quote," she murmured, keeping her voice quiet enough so that no one else could hear.

He leaned down a bit, to lessen their dramatic height difference. "What's it from?"

Bex darted a glance around them. There were too many students and faculty clustered around the graffiti. It wasn't safe to discuss it there. Anyone could overhear.

You're being paranoid, she told herself. But then, was it really paranoia if it was entirely justifiable?

Someone was evading the notice of campus security, even after it had doubled in the wake of the original incident. Someone was also leaving cryptic messages for Chase and who knew who else to find. The two could not be mere coincidence. If this was a prank, the culprit was going about it in a very risky, very bizarre way.

Without uttering another word, Bex tugged on Chase's elbow, dragging him away from the crowd. He mumbled something under his breath that she didn't catch, but he followed her with little resistance. She liked that he was obedient like that.

Once she was confident they were out of earshot, she said, "Rousseau."

"Who-sseau?"

Bex rolled her eyes at him. "Jean-Jacques Rousseau."

Chase lifted his broad shoulders in a shrug. "Yeah, that doesn't really clear anything up."

"Swiss philosopher," Bex said. "He wrote *Emile*."

"What's *Emile*?"

"God, you're lucky you're pretty." The words were out before Bex could smother them to death in her throat.

"Wait, what?" Chase asked. Now she had his attention. "You think I'm pretty?"

"Whatever. No. Shut up." Bex thought about whipping out her tablet to search for *Emile* online, but she didn't want anything related to the graffiti in her search history.

Paranoia, thy name is Bex.

"I did a project on banned books in the third grade," Bex said.

"Of course you did."

"My mom wouldn't let me submit it, so I had to do another book report in its place, but I remember Rousseau. He also wrote something called *The Social Contract* that's almost impossible to find online."

Chase blinked at her. "What third grader reads Swiss philosophers?"

"Me," Bex said. "Now seriously, shut up."

Before Chase could say something—he was quickly becoming less obedient—a deep voice cut him off. A long shadow cut across the grass as Headmaster Wood approached them, the lines of his sand-colored suit emphasizing the tension corded through his muscles.

"I take it the tutoring is going well," Headmaster Wood remarked. "But if you could follow your classmates into the building, I would appreciate it."

"Sure," Bex said. She didn't realize that she'd still been holding Chase's jacket, but it served her well now. She tugged on his sleeve, leading him away from Wood and toward the school. "No problem. See you later, Dr. Wood."

"Bye," Chase said with a wave. Once they ascended the steps, he added, "You know, it's not often I get dragged around by a girl half my size."

"Would you prefer being dragged around by a girl twice your size?" Bex asked.

"Don't know," Chase said. "Could be fun. Where are we going?"

"Assembly. But slowly."

Bex slowed her steps. Chase did the same until they were lingering well behind the wave of students heading toward the auditorium.

"Do you think the same person who sent me that message did it?" Chase asked.

"Possibly. It could be a copycat or someone just messing around, but I don't think it is. It's too bizarre, too weirdly literary." Bex shook her head. "No, there has to be some meaning behind it. Some way they're connected."

Chase nudged her gently with his elbow. "Well, you're the brains. Any ideas?"

Bex chewed at her lower lip. It was getting even more chapped. She rummaged in her pockets, looking for her lip balm. They were empty.

"What are you looking for?" Chase asked.

"ChapStick."

Chase reached into his own pocket and retrieved a tube of strawberry-flavored ChapStick. He offered it to her, and she accepted it.

"Strawberry? Really?"

"My other choices were original and cherry. Strawberry is clearly the superior flavor."

"Can't argue with that."

Bex rubbed the ChapStick over her lips, trying not to think about how the same ChapStick had, at one point or even several points, touched Chase's lips.

"I hate saying this, but I don't know what to do. I recognize the quote, but I don't know what good that does us."

"So we go to the library and check out the book," Chase said. "See what's what."

Bex shook her head. "I doubt they'll have a copy. Like I said, it's banned in most school districts. It's really hard to find. As far as I know, it's been out of print for years."

"Yeah, but Maplethorpe's not most schools. It's worth looking, isn't it?"

There was a gleam in Chase's eyes she'd never seen before. She thought maybe that same gleam was reflected in her own eyes.

It wasn't just a message left in someone's locker. It wasn't just a bit of spray-painted rebellion. It was starting to feel like *something*.

She didn't know what that something was, but she was going to find out.

"Meet me after school," she said. "I have an idea."

Rebecca Lee Johnson had never skipped class. Not once. She'd never even considered doing it. Not even in sophomore year when she'd contracted some kind of terrible virus that had her regurgitating everything she'd ever eaten in her life. (Her teacher had dismissed her when it looked like Bex might actually spew all over the whiteboard as she rose to solve for x.) Not even when she'd screwed up her timetable freshman year, gotten the date of a test wrong, and shown up entirely unprepared. (She got an eighty-nine and had yet to live it down with her parents.) Not even when she and Melody had gotten into a vicious fight about something so stupid neither one of them could remember it, and Melody had convinced the rest of the class to literally turn their backs on Bex when she walked in the door. (That was in sixth grade.)

But today . . . today she skipped first period.

It took a little extra time for her smartwatch to buzz against her wrist.

Her comparative literature professor, Mr. Hutchins (or Hutch, as he insisted they call him, though no one ever did), had probably given her the benefit of the doubt. Reputation mattered when it came to ratings. But the minutes ticked by and Bex was still in the library, combing the shelves for a book she didn't have much hope of finding.

She didn't look at her watch. She didn't feel that same sense of immediate, breath-stealing panic she did whenever she thought her number was sliding. She didn't feel that same powerlessness that had plagued her every day of her life until she'd cracked 90.

Something had changed in her. It could be that she'd finally reached her limit, that her mind had decided to reject her constant pursuit of perfection in order to save her from herself. Or maybe it was more than that. Seeing that graffiti on the first day of school had triggered a change so subtle she hadn't noticed it at first. It had surfaced when she'd stood up to her parents during family dinner. It was surfacing again now, as she flagrantly broke the same school rules she'd followed so slavishly her entire life.

And it felt good. Really, really good.

Her fingers skimmed the spines of books tucked into a dismal, dusty corner of the library. The shelves were tidy, but there was a fine layer of dust on top of books no one had checked out in years. Maplethorpe prided itself in its library as much as every other state-of-the-art amenity it provided for its students, but no one had seen fit to update the oldest collection they had. It felt forgotten, this faraway shelf. It wasn't visible from the librarian's desk or from any of the tables or chairs in the main reading room.

The odds of Maplethorpe's library carrying the book were so small, they were infinitesimal. Nonexistent.

Except . . .

Bex's hand stopped as her fingers landed on a slim leather-bound tome.

"*Du contrat social*," Bex whispered to the books, "*ou Principes du droit politique*."

The title in its original French. *The Social Contract, or Principles of Political Rights*.

Of course Maplethorpe didn't carry the book in English. It was on too many banned lists. But no one ever looked closely at the foreign texts. Who had the time?

Bex slid the book off the shelf. It was thin; the reddish-brown cover was pockmarked with water stains. Not even a hundred pages in total.

Easy to slip something so small into a pocket.

Easier to walk right out the door, past the librarian who offered Bex a smile and a good morning.

Easiest thing Bex had ever done.

Bex had never cut a class before, had never stolen anything before, had never realized just how simple it could be doing all the things one really shouldn't do. It should have worried her how quickly, how readily, she took to a life of crime. It didn't. And that was perhaps the most worrisome thing of all.

CHAPTER 21

TAMSIN MOORE

Tamsin hated the cafeteria of Maplethorpe Academy. She hated the way it always smelled like stale french fry grease, no matter how thoroughly it was cleaned. She hated the round tables the Maplethorpe board had insisted upon to make it look more welcoming and less cafeteria-esque. They each seated only about six students, so space was tight. And sitting at a round table made it harder to eat by yourself while ignoring everyone around you. Round tables forced eye contact upon the unwilling, something Tamsin could not forgive.

Normally, she would take her lunch in her music building hideout, but she'd promised Hana she would meet her in the cafeteria. Tamsin would just have to swallow her distaste and be there. She'd been surprised when Hana had texted her earlier that day, in the scant minutes between second and third period.

Thoughts on lunch today? I'm free during fifth.

Tamsin also happened to have a free period then. That Hana had offered to meet someplace where food was sold seemed like a big step for the girl. Tamsin wasn't going to let her down. It was obvious that Hana was struggling with some kind of disordered eating. The way she'd rebuffed Tamsin so staunchly the other day made it seem like she wasn't interested in the "admitting you have a problem" part of recovery. Maybe now she was ready.

The possibility was worth braving the uncomfortably intimate Maplethorpe cafeteria. Tamsin didn't know Hana that well, but she was already the closest thing Tamsin had to a friend at their godforsaken school. She would try to be a good one.

Tamsin got to the cafeteria early to find a table. Most students had lunch during fourth or fifth period. Some unlucky souls had to wait until sixth, when they had to engage in gladiator-style combat for the last order of onion rings on the rare days they were served. Maplethorpe never ran out of healthy food—the school's brochure boasted of their wholesome, nutritious offerings—but they did run out of anything fried.

So when someone slammed a pile of heavy textbooks on the table, Tamsin wasn't entirely surprised. She was, after all, expecting company. But when she looked up, it wasn't Hana standing by the table. It was a much less welcome visitor.

"Hello, Summer," Tamsin said, injecting as much frost into her voice as possible. "To what do I owe the displeasure?"

Summer sneered. "How did you know?"

Tamsin glanced toward the doors leading into the cafeteria, willing Hana to walk through them. "How did I know what?"

"About my boyfriend, stupid."

Tamsin narrowed her eyes at the girl. To Summer's credit, she didn't flinch from what Tamsin knew to be a highly effective glare. "Is there really a need for name-calling?"

"How did you know?" Summer asked again.

At first glance, the girl looked as put together as she always did, but the more Tamsin studied her, the more obvious her frayed seams became. Her ponytail wasn't as perky as it usually was. Her cardigan was slightly askew. Her lips were chapped, as if she'd been chewing on them. And the liner around her eyes was just a hair too thick, like she'd applied it, removed it, and applied it again.

"I have no idea what you're talking about, Summer," said Tamsin. "And I don't appreciate being ambushed. Just say whatever it is you came to say and put us both out of our misery."

Summer's nostrils flared, making her look briefly like an angry bull. "Steve. He was cheating on me with Sasha."

Summer. Steve. Sasha. It was like a bad alliterative soap opera.

"I don't even know who that is."

"Sasha!" Summer exclaimed, as if it explained anything.

Tamsin merely shrugged in response.

"Who told you?" Summer asked. "I know you're not some kind of witch. Magic isn't real. But somebody had to have told you and I want to know who."

And that was when it clicked.

The reading. The Ten of Swords and the Lovers.

Oops.

Tamsin had only been trying to be mean. She hadn't been trying to be prescient.

Maybe magic was real. Maybe Tamsin really could read the future in the cards.

Or maybe Steve was just a terrible human being.

"Look, I'm sorry your boyfriend's a jerk," Tamsin said, "but I didn't need anyone to tell me that. Anyone with eyes and two working brain cells could have told you." She wiggled her fingers at Summer, whose frown deepened. "He's always had wandering eyes and grabby hands. Not my fault you picked him."

It was perhaps not the most sympathetic thing Tamsin could have said, but her sympathy was a finite resource. The well ran dry with Summer's rotten attitude.

Summer leaned over the table, looking like she was ready to spit in Tamsin's face. "Listen, you rotten b—"

"Hey, guys." Hana's voice was a touch too loud, but it was a welcome interruption.

"Hey, Hana. Have a seat. Join the fun." Tamsin patted the chair beside her. Hana dumped her bag onto it but did not sit.

Hana looked between Summer and Tamsin, eyes wary at the pairing. Already she must have known it meant nothing good. "What's going on here?"

"Oh, nothing," Summer said.

"Really? Because it looks like something," Hana said, crossing her arms over her stomach. It made her look even smaller, and Tamsin had thought that was impossible.

"What do you care? Are you friends with her?" Summer asked. Her tone implied that being friends with Tamsin was some kind of mortal sin, just below murder and adultery.

Hana shrugged. "So what if I am?"

Summer made a disgusted little noise in the back of her throat. "Ugh. I thought you had better taste than that."

"We've never had a real conversation, Summer," Hana

said. "You don't know me at all. And I'm kind of okay with that, if this is how you talk to people."

No one had ever come to Tamsin's defense quite like that. She'd been a loner since the first day of school, so she hadn't exactly spent her time collecting a defense squad of friends and allies. It felt nice to have someone take her side. She felt oddly warm. Not in a bad way. Just in a way she'd never really felt before.

But Hana's words seemed to have little impact on Summer. That hard glare returned to Tamsin.

"You know, it's a good thing Maplethorpe has standards," Summer sneered. "Trash like you won't linger around long enough to stink up the place." She turned her gaze to Hana. "You might want to watch yourself, Hana. You don't wanna get caught in Tamsin's blast radius."

"Okay, now that's a bit much." A dawning realization tickled at the corners of Tamsin's mind, but she didn't want to entertain it just yet. Not with Summer looking at her like that. "How about we pump the brakes and go back to existing in our own spheres of influence? Yours as far away from mine as possible."

"Gladly," Summer said. "Not that it'll make much of a difference for you."

"Okay, honestly, I have no idea what you're talking about," Tamsin said. Though she thought maybe she did.

"Hope you've been enjoying your ratings." A poisonous smile spread across Summer's face. It was too unpleasant to be anything but a baring of fangs. "The best is yet to come."

With that, she sauntered away, a spring in her step that hadn't been there when she'd first confronted Tamsin. It was like ruining someone else's day made Summer's.

"Well, that was pleasant." Hana moved her backpack off the seat beside Tamsin and plopped down. She propped her elbows on the table and dropped her chin into her hand.

"Yeah, about as pleasant as a warm jar of mayonnaise on a hot summer's day." A buzz against her wrist made Tamsin look down at her smartwatch.

19.

Her rating. It had ticked down another point. And then, immediately, another.

"What the fudge?" Tamsin asked, though she had her answer.

"It's Summer, isn't it?" Hana leaned over to peer at Tamsin's number. "She's doing this. Or at least orchestrating it."

A loud burst of laughter sounded from the other side of the cafeteria. Tamsin raised her eyes from that abysmal number and caught Summer's gaze from across the room. Vicious mirth danced in them, visible even from a distance. The girl bowed her head as she whispered something to the others at her table. Another round of laughter pealed like bells at a funeral. Steve approached their table, unperturbed by the withering glare Summer shot him. He leaned down to whisper something in Summer's ear. Whatever it was wiped the frown off Summer's face. She beamed up at him as he pulled up a chair to sit next to her, his arm draped around the back of her chair.

Tamsin couldn't see who contributed to her ratings, positively or negatively, but she knew who'd just dinged hers. Steve, to win points with his jilted girlfriend.

"Yeah," Tamsin said. "Summer's behind it."

"Why, though?" Hana asked. "I mean, I get that you don't like each other, but it seems extreme."

Another vibration. Another negative. Another round of venomous laughter. Tamsin's gut churned. This must be what foreboding felt like.

"She's trying to get me kicked out of Maplethorpe."

CHAPTER 22

CHASE DONOVAN

RATING: 55

Chase didn't share a single class with Bex. Their lunch periods didn't even line up, and he doubted she took hers, anyway. She probably spent it trying to find the cure for cancer or solving Fermat's last theorem or doing something else equally intellectually dazzling. He'd gotten two tests back that day. Both failing grades. His rating had dipped, putting him right on the cusp. Again. He tried not to think about it. He didn't want Bex to know how much of a lost cause he was.

He waited for her by her locker, ignoring the incessant buzzing from his phone. He'd already told Coach Jenkins that he wasn't going to make practice that afternoon. Tutoring made for a wonderful excuse, one not even Coach could argue with. The rest of the team still tried, though. The group chat was a litany of complaints, all directed at him.

A smack to his back made Chase jump. He turned to see Steve grinning at him, with a few of the other guys from the team in tow. "Hey, buddy. Waiting for your girlfriend? Coach said you had tutoring."

"She's not my girlfriend," Chase said. He spotted Bex rounding the corner and coming toward them. "And yeah, I do. Shouldn't you guys be at practice?"

"I figured you weren't checking your messages," Steve said, "but I thought maybe I was more convincing in person. Ditch her and come to practice. Your tutor's cute and all, but the team needs you, buddy."

"Shut up, Steve," Chase hissed just as Bex got close enough to hear. Her eyes darted from Chase to Steve as a frown pulled at her lips.

"Hi," Chase said, hoping Steve would go away.

Steve did not go away.

He tossed his arm around Chase's shoulders, his gaze raking up from Bex's shoes to the top of her head. "Anything we can do to convince you not to steal our best pitcher for the day?"

"Nope." Chase knocked Steve's arm off his shoulder. "Bye."

Steve and the others took the hint—not that it was subtle—that their presence was undesired and left, their voices low enough to make their words indistinguishable. The tone of their laughter was anything but. He could imagine the sorts of things they were saying about Bex, because he'd heard them say things about girls before. None of it was fit for polite company.

Bex watched them go, a little wrinkle forming between her brows. "Are you ashamed to be seen with me?"

Oh god.

"No, no way, absolutely not," Chase said in a rush. "I'm ashamed to be seen with them. They're Neanderthals. Honestly." He liked the way she smiled at that. "What's up?"

An uncharacteristically mischievous grin spread across Bex's face. "I found it."

"Found what?" Chase asked.

Bex rolled her eyes. He got the feeling she did that a lot when engaging with lesser beings such as himself.

"The book," Bex said. She slipped her backpack off one shoulder so she could sling it in front of her. She opened the zipper just enough to grant him a glance of a slender book sandwiched between her tablet and a frighteningly thick binder.

"Oh," Chase said. The book. With the quote. "The library had it? You checked it out."

She zipped her backpack shut quickly, her eyes darting around to see if anyone had noticed their illicit exchange. No one had.

"Yes, the library had it," Bex said. "But no, I didn't check it out."

"What do you . . . ?"

Oh. Oh. She didn't check it out. She *stole* it.

Chase clucked his tongue at her, thoroughly delighted. "Bex Johnson, you naughty girl."

Her face contorted in disgust. "Okay, first of all, never say that again."

"Sorry," Chase said with a laugh, "but I'm just so proud. Look at you, a baby delinquent. Didn't think you had it in you."

It could have been his imagination, but he was pretty sure Bex was actually flattered.

"Neither did I," she said. There was a light in her eyes he'd never really seen before. "I can't believe I stole a book!"

Chase couldn't believe it either, but then, he still couldn't quite believe he'd formed a friendship with Rebecca "Inevitable

Valedictorian" Johnson at all, so he supposed stranger things had happened.

"I didn't have time to go through it," Bex said, "but I thought maybe . . ."

She hefted her backpack onto her shoulder again. It looked at least twice as heavy as Chase's. Maybe three times as heavy. He thought about offering to carry it for her, but Bex didn't seem like the type of girl who'd be into that.

"Maybe what?" Chase prompted, when she let the silence hang too long.

"We could try going over it at my place? You know, if you want. I mean, if you don't, that's cool."

Chase smiled at Bex as he watched her fingers nervously dance over the strap of her backpack. Not smiling at her would have involved a Herculean effort and he wasn't interested in resisting the urge. It was a nice urge, so he gave in to it.

He leaned against his locker. "Don't you have a million things to do after school? Like clarinet practice or Model UN or, I don't know, performing open-heart surgery?"

"Okay, first of all," Bex said, "I play the flute."

"Dorky woodwind instrument. Tomayto, tomahto."

"Hilarious." Bex glanced at her watch, her brow pinching as she looked at her rating. Her face always did that when she checked her number. Chase wasn't sure why. Hers was miles beyond most Maplethorpe students, but she never seemed pleased about it. Chase would have donated all his unnecessary organs and at least half of the necessary ones to crack 90. "I skipped out on the Mathletes today, and they're not happy about it."

"Can't please 'em all," Chase said. "And yeah, we can go to your place."

Better hers than his.

"And on the way," he added, "how about we stop by Lucky's and get some burgers and shakes?"

He'd pinched enough money from his father's wallet to pay this time.

The frown fled Bex's expression at the mention of empty calories and copious sugar. "Yeah," she said. "That'd be nice. Let's go."

And that was how Chase found himself sitting on a rooftop in the more affluent section of Jackson Hills, quite literally on the other side of the tracks from where he lived. It was too dark to see the railroad tracks, but he could imagine the undulating line that cut across the landscape, dividing the haves from the have-nots. The highly rated and the poor. He'd dreamed of crossing that line as a child and now he had. Just not in the way he thought he would.

"Oh my god." Bex's voice pulled him from his thoughts, which was honestly for the best. "Look at this thing. It's the size of my head."

The thing was a cheeseburger, and Bex's assessment was only a mild exaggeration. The Lucky Penny didn't make small cheeseburgers. Small cheeseburgers were for the weak. They made monsters.

"I don't remember the last time I ate a cheeseburger." Bex unwrapped hers so delicately that Chase wanted to die a little bit. She seemed like the kind of person who hated being called adorable, so he kept his thoughts to himself.

Fast food comprised a percentage of Chase's diet that was unhealthy at best and potentially catastrophic at worst. He compensated by working out, but he had a feeling that one day the trans fats or cholesterol or whatever it was in fast food that made it so delicious would catch up to him. Then he'd develop the Donovan paunch his father boasted. But burgers and fries were an efficient way of getting enough calories into his system on the nights when his father couldn't be bothered to cook. Which was most nights. It wasn't the worst thing in the world, though. Chase loved a generous serving of meat, cheese, and bread.

"A life lived without cheeseburgers," Chase said, "isn't a life lived to its fullest."

He nodded to the book Bex had brought up along with their feast. There was a very real possibility someone was going to smear grease all over it, but surprisingly Bex didn't seem to mind.

"So, any idea why the Jester stole that quote from that book?"

Bex nodded as she chewed a dainty bite of her burger. She swallowed, then said, "Yeah. It's all about the rights of the people and trying to build a fair and free society. I think it's safe to say our good friend the Jester doesn't think ours fits that description."

"Can't argue with that," Chase said. He held up his wrist and pointed to the smartwatch. The display was dimmed so he didn't have to see his rating. "Not when these things call the shots."

"What I want to know is why that quote specifically." Bex wiped her hands on a napkin, picked up the book, and flipped through the pages. "Gimme a light?"

Chase picked up his phone and switched on the flashlight,

illuminating the pages for her. "Do you actually remember what page it's from?"

"It's how the book starts," Bex said as she skimmed the text. "Just gotta get past the front matter . . . people love adding a lengthy foreword to things like this. And it's all in French so . . ." She stopped, her fingers tracing the lines of a page as she silently mouthed words as she read. "Got it."

"Man, you're good."

"I try."

Bex pointed to the quote on the page. "This is it, but . . . wait." She put her hands on his and directed the flashlight to the top of the page.

Someone had scribbled a series of numbers in the margins.

Chase leaned closer to get a better look. "Are those GPS coordinates?"

"I think so." Bex pulled her phone from her pocket and punched the numbers into her maps app. She frowned when she saw the location.

"So? Where is it?"

"Maplethorpe," Bex said. "Literally, our school."

She held out her phone as if he needed extra convincing. He didn't.

"That's . . . odd?" And unsatisfying. "What good is a scavenger hunt that sends you right back to the same place you found the clue?"

"I don't know." Bex angrily shoved an onion ring into her mouth. Even her chewing seemed displeased.

"Can I take a look at it?" Chase asked, holding his hand out for the book.

Bex shrugged. "Be my guest."

Chase held his own flashlight as he flipped through the pages, while Bex grumpily ate her burger beside him. Nothing else was written in the margins on any other page. No words were underlined, no page numbers circled. Nothing. He flipped to the last page of the book. There was a paper pocket affixed to the back cover, with a library checkout card inside.

"Huh. Haven't seen one of these in ages." Chase slipped the card out of the sleeve and turned it over. "Bex."

She grunted something that sounded like "Yes?" around a mouthful of burger.

He held up the card, one finger pointing to the date stamped at the top.

Bex leaned in, squinting to read it in the harsh glare of the phone light. When she realized why he'd pointed it out, her eyes went wide.

"This book hasn't been checked out in ages, if the dust is anything to go by," Chase said. "But this date is in the future. A week after Founder's Day. And I'm pretty sure the four zeroes after it mean midnight. Military time."

Bex swallowed what had to be a painful lump of cheeseburger. "It has to be a sign! Coordinates! And a date! We go there on this date! At this time!"

"Yes. Yes, we absolutely will. We're doing this." It felt right. Chase couldn't fight the goofy grin on his face. He didn't really want to. But there was something else, something that didn't quite fit. "Wait . . . how does this relate to the other message? The one I got?"

Bex fumbled for her tablet. "I wrote it down," she said. "And I think I figured it out."

"When?"

"During calculus." She tapped the screen a few times, and when she'd found her notes, she held them out proudly.

"'On the day of the prophet false,'" she recited. "That's gotta be Founder's Day. I wasn't sure, but after the stunt with the statue of John Maplethorpe and the thing about the ratings not being real—being false—it adds up."

"'One mustn't dance a forbidden waltz,'" Chase read. "The dance. The Founder's Day Dance. Is it telling us not to go?"

Bex nodded. Her excitement was contagious. "Yeah. It wants us to go somewhere else while everyone else is at the dance."

"Okay, but where?"

"A copper found," Bex said. *"A copper found."*

Chase puzzled over the words for a moment before it dawned on him. "The Lucky Penny."

"Oh my god, yes," Bex said. "I don't know what a fortune told means, but I can guess the last line."

"'All beside a box of gold,'" Chase said. "The jukebox."

"The only one with the gold trim," Bex confirmed.

"So, on the day of the Founder's Day Dance we're supposed to go to Lucky's, and hang out at the booth with the gold jukebox?"

"Sounds like it," Bex said.

"Okay . . ." Chase stole one of Bex's onion rings. She didn't seem to mind. "I'm down with that, but what do we do until then?"

Bex looked at him, blinking against the light of his phone. He turned it off. It took a moment for his eyes to readjust to the darkness. Bex's soft laugh came out of the gloaming.

"I have no idea," she said. "Guess we could actually get some studying in."

"Oh," Chase said. "Studying. I was sort of hoping you'd forgotten about that."

Bex barked out a short laugh. "I never forget about studying."

Chase flicked a renegade crumb off his shirt. "Though to be honest, I don't even know why I bother. I'm never gonna do well enough to keep my scholarship."

Bex angled herself to look straight at him. "Don't say that. You're going to pull through."

"But how can you be so sure?"

"Because failure's not an option." The conviction in her voice was almost enough to convince Chase. Almost, but not quite. "That's like my mantra. And it's a lot less soul-crushing when I apply it to helping someone else achieve something."

"Instead of you trying to be perfect all the time?" Chase asked.

Bex plucked a fry out of the greasy paper bag between them. "Bingo. So long as you're cool with a little hard work, everything's going to be okay. I can feel it in my bones."

"Ah, yes. The bones," said Chase. "They're never wrong."

Bex offered him one of her fries. She'd gotten the curly kind while he'd opted for the standard straight-cut. "Will you laugh at me if I attempt a sports analogy?"

"Probably . . . but go on."

That earned a wisp of a smile from Bex. Pleased, Chase stole another of her curly fries. She didn't protest.

"Okay, so," Bex began. "Baseball's always struck me as a sport rooted in strategy. It's not just about who runs the fastest or throws the hardest or hits the ball the farthest, though those things are important, right?"

Chase nodded. "Yeah. All that stuff is great, but it's not worth much if you don't have a good strategy to back it up."

"Right, exactly." Bex, Chase observed, started talking with her hands when she was excited about something. He found it endearing. "So our study time is a lot like baseball. You and I are going to come up with strategies to help you score that game-winning touchdown."

Chase nearly choked to death on a curly fry. "Oh man. You were doing so well, but you just couldn't stick the landing, could you?"

"Mocking my failed sports analogy with one of your own." Now it was Bex stealing Chase's french fries. "Devious."

As he chewed, he mulled over Bex's scattered metaphor.

"You know . . . that does actually make a lot of sense. Even if you did veer into my least favorite sport at the end."

"What, football?" Bex asked. "Wasn't your dad on the Maplethorpe team like a million years ago?"

"He was," Chase replied, "but how did you know that?"

"There's a gigantic silver football with 'Chase Donovan' stamped on it in the trophy case I walk by every day to get to my locker. And since it's clearly older than you are, I figured it must be a relative. It's always bugged me that the athletics department gets those huge awards while the academic achievements get teeny tiny ribbons at the end of the year."

"Now that you mention it, that does kind of stink," Chase said. "But yeah, football was my dad's thing. Baseball's mine."

"You didn't want to follow in his footsteps?" Bex asked. It

was an innocent question, but it made that sick feeling in his stomach swell.

"When I was little, I did . . . but not so much anymore."

Bex was quiet for a long moment. When she spoke again, her voice was softer, as though she knew she was treading on fragile ground. "What happened?"

The direction the conversation was taking made something twist deep in Chase's gut. It was the same sense of foreboding he always felt when the subject of his home life came up with friends or their parents. Usually he lied, to cover up his father's bad behavior. Chase wasn't sure who those lies were meant to protect. His father or himself.

But Bex's rooftop had the feeling of a sacred place. There was no one to eavesdrop on their conversation. Anything Chase said was between him, Bex, and the stars.

"My mom left about six years ago. My dad changed after that. He started drinking. Sometimes, he got violent."

"Chase . . ." The tenderness in Bex's voice made his skin itchy all over.

He shrugged, attempting to dislodge that feeling. "But yeah . . . football reminds me of him. It's bad enough we share a first name. I picked baseball because I wanted something that was just mine."

He tried to lighten his voice at the end, but the frown forming on Bex's face told him he'd failed miserably.

She reached for him. Chase went still. When her fingers brushed the cut on his cheek, he flinched. She pulled her hand back, as if worried she'd caused him actual pain.

"Did he do that to you?"

237

Chase looked away from her. He had to. Her voice and her touch and everything about her in that moment was so gentle. Too gentle. He didn't know what to do with it.

A part of him felt good to get that off his chest. He'd never told anyone about his father, not even his closest friends on the team. But another part was screaming at him to clam back up. It was too much, too soon, in what he wasn't even sure was a real friendship. He felt scrubbed raw. Vulnerable. It wasn't a nice feeling at all. His heart was thudding wildly in his chest. He felt like some kind of prey animal, scampering to safety in the woods. He'd never opened himself up like that before. He didn't hate the way it felt, but it was a new and terrifying experience all the same.

"Look, it's fine," he told Bex, even though it clearly wasn't. "I just have to stick it out until graduation, then I'm out of that house for good."

"Chase, that's not okay. You shouldn't have to live like that."

How easy it must be for her to say that. Her pressure cooker of a life may not have been emotionally ideal, but at least she was *safe*.

"I shouldn't have to, but I do. It is what it is, okay? Can we drop it?" And then, because she didn't deserve to be snapped at like that, Chase added, "Please?"

Bex worried her bottom lip between her teeth for an interminable moment. Then she nodded.

Silence stretched between them as they finished their meal.

Chase tilted his head up toward the stars. They were far enough from the lights of downtown Jackson Hills that he could actually pick out half-remembered constellations. His first-grade teacher, Ms. Redding, had pinned a large star map to the wall of their classroom, and she'd told them stories to go with the connect-the-dot constellations drawn on it. He'd liked her. She was patient when he stumbled over passages in even the simplest of chapter books. And she never mentioned the Rating System in class once. She'd only taught at Jackson Hills Elementary for a year. He never saw Ms. Redding after that, and a part of him always wondered what had become of her.

"Sometimes," Bex said, her voice soft and buttery smooth in the darkness, "when things get to be too much, I come up here."

Chase pulled his gaze from the stars to settle it on her.

"It's quiet," she continued. "And if you just look up, you can't really see anything else. It's easy to forget that there's a whole world out there."

"What are you trying to forget?" Chase asked.

"How stressed I am, mostly."

He nodded. He understood that. But it seemed like so much of Bex's stress was self-inflicted. "Why do you work so hard?"

Bex shrugged. "To have a better life, I guess."

Chase spread his arms wide. The suburban neighborhood below glittered with the soft lights of people living their lives inside their stately homes. "Better than this? Man, you really won't be satisfied until you take over the world, will you?"

Bex smiled, but it was the barest whisper of one.

"I don't know." Her voice held the air of a confession. "I guess I never really thought about why. I just did things because they were the things you were supposed to do."

"But what about the things you *want* to do?" Chase asked. It seemed to him such an obvious question, but he was beginning to suspect that it wasn't as obvious to Bex. Her life was so different from his own. Greatness was expected of them both but in very different ways. Chase had to be good at one thing. Bex had to be good at everything. Just the thought of trying to master all the skills she did made his stomach twist in anxiety.

Again, she shrugged. "I never really thought about that either. I've always just known that I was going to be a doctor, like my mom. Or a scientist, like my dad. Getting to choose which one almost felt like freedom. But now . . . I don't know. I want to do lots of things. I want to see all the things outside Jackson Hills."

"I don't know, Bex, that's an awful lot of things," Chase said. "Wanna narrow it down a bit?"

Her smile was more genuine this time. "I want to go to Egypt and see the pyramids. I want to run a marathon just to see if I can finish. I want to eat strawberry crepes and drink gross, bitter, fancy coffee as I sit at a wrought-iron table overlooking the Seine."

"That is extremely specific."

"I could settle for a chocolate crepe, I'm not picky," Bex said. "What about you? What do *you* want to do with your life? Do you want to play baseball professionally?"

"Not really," Chase said. It was oddly liberating, admitting that out loud. "I want to play in college because I'm pretty sure that's the only way I'll get into a decent one. But to be honest, baseball's just the means to an end for me."

"What sort of end?" Bex asked.

"I have this idea," Chase began. "But . . . it's stupid—never mind."

"No! I want to know. Tell me," Bex pleaded. "My roof, my rules. You have to."

"Well, if you're gonna twist my arm . . ." Chase steeled himself. He'd never shared this with anyone either. "I have this idea that if I can just get into a good school—find my way and maybe become successful enough to have people listen to me—then I can use that platform to make a difference. I want to help kids like me who are stuck in bad situations and don't have anyone else."

"You have me now." Chase met Bex's gaze. Her eyes were wide, as if she'd surprised herself with that statement. But she nodded resolutely. "And that's not stupid. That's brilliant. I'm in total support of this plan."

Chase was glad it was dark enough to hide his blush. He'd told Bex more about his inner thoughts than he'd ever shared with anyone. And she'd welcomed them. But then reality pressed in, as it always did.

"Yeah, well, none of it's going to matter if I lose my scholarship before the championship at the end of the year," said Chase. "Coach told me some scouts already made it clear they were interested in me, but it'll all be for nothing if they don't see me play."

"That's not going to happen," Bex said. "I'm going to make sure you're at that game, scoring goals and nailing free throws, if it's the last thing I do."

Chase laughed. The knot that had been forming in his gut loosened. "Okay, now you're just messing with me."

"Yup." Bex offered him the last curly fry. He accepted it, then offered her the last regular fry. She accepted that. "You know, I think this is the start of something good. You've got a bright future ahead of you."

"Let me guess," Chase said, "you feel it in your bones?"

"You know the bones. They're never wrong." Bex wiped her palms on her jeans and fixed Chase with a determined smile. "Now grab your chemistry textbook. We have work to do."

CHAPTER 23

NOAH RAINIER

RATING: 63

Noah's lips were still tingling long after Javi had left that day in the darkroom. They'd texted almost constantly after his departure, about everything from the little old ladies gossiping on the bus behind Javi, to Noah's worry for Cece, to their mutual love of truly terrible B movies. (The campier, the better.)

Over the course of the next week, Javi became a constant presence in Noah's life, even outside school. He was always there, one short text away. Noah had been so distracted that morning that he forgot to pay the bus fee as he got on, prompting the driver to huff and send him a negative. But his rating didn't matter. Not when he felt like he was walking on air.

His thoughts drifted to Javi as he set the table for dinner. Noah's mother had made his favorite food (macaroni and cheese, elevated by the addition of expensive Gruyère). He wondered if Javi was also just sitting down for dinner. What he'd be eating. What it would sound like to have so many siblings clustered around a dinner table. Would the noise be louder than the overwhelming silence of the Rainier household? Noah adjusted the napkin at his seat and fiddled with the fork and knife. His mother placed the dish of fancy mac and cheese on a trivet in the center of the table. She sank a serving spoon into it with an obscene squelch. His father lowered himself onto his chair at the head of the table, and then said the worst four words in the English language.

"We have to talk."

Noah paused, a heaping spoonful of cheesy pasta frozen between the Pyrex dish and his plate. A small clump toppled off the mound and landed on the tablecloth.

"Noah, honestly," his mother said, snapping him out of his state of frightened suspension.

He mumbled an apology and tried to wipe away the stain with his napkin. All he succeeded in doing was smearing it around even more. It was her fault really, for buying a white tablecloth. It begged for stains. Noah plopped the remaining mac and cheese on his plate. It looked vastly less appetizing than it had a mere forty-five seconds ago.

Nothing good ever came after someone said *we have to talk*. Not once in the history of their species.

Noah looked to his mother when his father remained silent. She looked somber, but not surprised. Whatever it was his dad had to say, his mom already knew. The news, then, was meant specifically for Noah. Cold dread coiled in his gut. There weren't many things that could put that strained look on his mother's face.

"Is it Cece?" Noah asked. "Is she okay? Did something happen?"

"Your sister's fine," his dad said. "It's just . . . there are going to be some changes in the near future."

Noah's eyes darted between his parents. He didn't like how cagey this sounded. He especially didn't like that they were tip-toeing around the announcement. He much preferred the truth dealt in a single blow. An immediate impact hurt less than prolonged torment.

"Dad, what happened?"

"I lost my job."

With a wordless sound of disgust, Noah's mother threw her napkin down on the table and stood. The news didn't appear to shock as much as infuriate her. So it wasn't *news* to her. She grabbed a bottle of wine from the rack on the sideboard and left. Noah's father didn't watch her leave. His eyes remained on the congealing macaroni at the center of the table.

"What?" Noah asked. He'd heard, but he couldn't quite wrap his head around it. For as long as Noah could remember, his father had been a photographer for the largest newspaper in Jackson Hills. He'd given Noah his first camera, a dinky little point-and-shoot, and taught him everything about lighting and exposure and f-stops. "Why? Was it something you did?"

That earned a startled chuckle from his dad. "No. At least I don't think so, unless I have the power to topple large corporations all on my own. No, it wasn't me. At least it wasn't just me. The whole staff was let go. The paper is being shuttered."

That seemed even more unthinkable. A copy of the *Jackson Hills Tribune* was delivered to nearly every home in the city each morning. Their subscription rate, at least according to the last time his dad had boasted about it, was higher than ever.

"Why?" Noah asked. "I thought it was doing well."

His dad shrugged. "It was, but that's just the way of the times. Print is dying."

Noah wasn't convinced. It sounded like his father was repeating a line. Something he'd been told to repeat. Noah thought about the school paper closing. They *couldn't* be connected—a high school paper and the *Tribune* were such different beasts they were barely the same species—but the thought was there, tying them together like a flimsy string.

But was it so flimsy?

Bex, the *Lantern*'s intimidating editor in chief, had believed that the paper was shuttered because the administration didn't want them talking about the vandalism. Noah had assumed the school simply wanted to silence the rumor mill. But perhaps there was something more to it. Perhaps everything was connected.

Noah poked at his rapidly cooling macaroni. It had fused into a small mountain, held together by Gruyère they probably wouldn't be able to afford in the future.

"We'll all have to tighten our belts for now, at least until I can find something else. Your mother might go back to work, but . . ."

He didn't have to finish his sentence for Noah to know what he meant. His mother had quit her job as an adjunct instructor at Jackson Hills Community College when Cece fell ill. She was at the hospital more often than she was home. She still covered the occasional class as a substitute, but she'd devoted her life to her daughter, at the expense of all else. Reentering the work force after an extended absence was no simple thing. It wouldn't be easy.

"But that's not what I wanted to talk to you about."

"It gets worse?" Noah asked.

His dad sighed. "Everything's going to be fine," he said without an ounce of conviction. "But Cece is going to have to move to a different hospital."

Noah gripped his fork so hard, he thought he might actually bend the metal. "Why?"

He knew why. But he needed to hear. He needed his father's voice to shape the words, to give them sound. To air the wild injustice that was about to be done to a sick child, who had deserved none of the rotten luck fate dealt her.

"Without a steady job, my rating isn't what it was." His dad held up his wrist and tapped on the screen of his smartwatch. The display lit up.

Noah's throat constricted, like he might throw up.

52.

His father's rating had fallen thirty points since that morning.

Thirty points lost, through no fault of his own.

"The hospital," his father went on, though his voice sounded distant and muffled, like he was speaking through a heavy curtain, miles away, "is the best in the state. It has a minimum rating for its patients. Cece's just a kid, so it's ours that matters."

As a stay-at-home mom, Noah's mother's rating was also tied to his father's. One bad day, and their fortunes had shifted. They'd never been rich, not really, but they had never suffered for want of a thing. The inheritance his mother's family had left her paid for their house and his tuition. It provided enough of a cushion to make their lives comfortable. Cece's hospital bills had been covered by their father's insurance. By the *Tribune*.

"Where's she gonna go?" Noah had to force the words out.

"She'll be moved to Jackson Hills General by the end of the month, unless I can get this"—he tapped on the smartwatch, where the damning number was still glowing—"back up to seventy-five. There's a grace period . . ."

Noah stopped listening. The public hospital was open to all, regardless of rating, but nobody wanted to go there. Nobody wanted to work there either. The best pediatric oncologists went to Magnolia Children's Hospital. The ones who'd graduated at the bottom of their classes, with the lowest ratings, wound up at Jackson Hills General.

"I don't want her to go there." Noah hated the way his voice sounded. Like a child. Like a dumb kid, crying about how unfair the world was. The sight of his father went blurry at the edges. Noah blinked rapidly, clearing away tears he would not allow to fall. They weren't sad tears. They were angry ones, and those burned even worse.

"I don't either, kid. But it's going to be okay." His father reached for his hand, the one still gripping the fork hard enough to bend stainless steel. Noah slowly loosened his hold on the utensil. It clattered onto porcelain, the tines poking into the mass of cheese and pasta. "I'll find another job soon."

Noah did not believe him. He didn't think his father believed himself. But maybe that was just what parents had to say. When the world was too ugly to bear, they peddled flimsy little lies to their children.

Noah bit his bottom lip so hard he felt the skin break under his teeth. He sucked his lip into his mouth, tasting the metallic tinge of his own blood. He didn't want to sit there a moment longer, but his father was finally being honest with him. Perhaps now was the time to ask the question that had been plaguing him since his meeting with Dr. Lowe.

"Why didn't you tell me?" Noah asked.

His father frowned. "Tell you what? About my job? It just happened. It caught me by surprise, too."

Noah shook his head. "No, not about that."

"Then about what?"

"That I was adopted."

Silence fell between them, stretching unbearably long. Noah stared at his plate. He didn't want to look at his father. He couldn't. If he did, he'd fall apart.

Finally, his father spoke. "How did you find out?"

"I had my bone marrow tested." Noah's tongue had gone dry. It felt oddly thick in his mouth. "I wanted to find out if I was a match for Cece. I wanted to know if I could save her."

"Oh, Noah . . ."

Only then did Noah look up. His father had buried his face in his hands. The silver of his wedding band stood out starkly against his skin. He scrubbed at his face before finding Noah's gaze.

"It's not your job to save her." His dad extended his hand, as if contemplating taking Noah's again. But he let it fall to the table. "That's not on you."

"I know," Noah said. "Even if we were related, it was still a long shot, but—"

"You are related," his father interrupted, "in all the ways that really matter."

"But why didn't you tell me?" Noah's voice broke halfway through the question.

"Because I didn't know how. I know that sounds like a cop-out, but it's the truth. You were our first kid. We were flying blind on everything, not just that. You mother and I talked about telling you. We'd planned to do it. And then Cece got sick and everything else sort of fell by the wayside."

Noah wished the reason didn't sound so . . . reasonable.

But his father wasn't done.

"Yes, we adopted you. We chose you when you were just a little baby. A newborn. You were a sickly little thing back then. You'd been born a few weeks premature. Your skin was a little bit yellow, too. Jaundice. The doctors had to keep you under special lights to get you back to normal. But after that, you were fit as a fiddle."

Unlike Cece.

"The older you got, the harder it became to tell you," his father continued. "I put it off. Your mother's been over-whelmed with Cece's illness." His father rested both hands flat on the table. "We screwed up. We should have told you, but we didn't. And for that, I'm sorry."

Noah swallowed past the lump forming in his throat. The mac and cheese blurred as he gazed upon it.

When he didn't speak, his father asked, "Do you think you can forgive me?"

His father's question sounded so plaintive.

Noah wanted to say no. His anger and his disappointment and his hurt all wanted him to say no.

But he didn't.

"Yeah," Noah said. "I just . . . I need some time with this. Is that okay?"

His father nodded. He reached across the distance between them to clasp Noah's shoulder. "Of course, buddy. Take as much time as you need."

Noah nodded. The motion was jerky enough to dislodge some of the tears clinging to his eyelashes. He wasn't even sure why he was crying. For himself. For his sister. For his parents, maybe. "May I be excused?"

His dad sighed. It was such an alien sound coming from his father. It made him sound old and tired in a way Noah had never encountered before.

"Yeah. Sure."

Noah pushed away from the table, not knowing where he was going, but knowing he couldn't stay there.

CHAPTER 24
JAVI LUCERO

RATING: 89

Javi was just logging into *Polaris* when his phone buzzed. He glanced down at it to find a text message alert.

From Noah.

He bit his bottom lip to prevent himself from smiling like a lunatic. Not that there was anyone around to see.

Can I come over? Please say yes.

Yes, Javi typed back quickly. He added his address a second later.

It wouldn't take Noah long to get here from his house. They were only a few stops away on the bus. Javi could probably squeeze in a quick round of PvP if he was brutally efficient.

He loaded *Polaris* with that stupid smile still on his face. Noah was coming over. *Noah was coming over.*

"Feels good, man," Javi said to himself, because he was apparently a lunatic.

Once the game loaded, he looked at the team roster. Rouge's name was grayed out, which meant she wasn't online. He clicked through to her profile to see how many days it had been since she'd last logged in.

Seven. That was odd.

The team had enough members that there was always someone available to step in if they needed the numbers for PvP or a raid, but Rouge was one of their constants. The only times she ever disappeared like that were during her exams, and as far as Javi knew, her university wouldn't have those for months.

His eyes fell on his phone, sitting on the desk beside his large bottle of intensely caffeinated soda. In her last message, Rouge had said that she was going to look into the graffiti on her campus, but then she'd never followed up. He'd told her to be careful, not really believing she would need to be, but maybe . . .

He didn't want to think any further than that. Speculation was a fool's game, and Javi was no fool. He pulled up the team chat and switched his mic on.

"Hey, guys, has anyone heard from Rouge lately?"

"Nope," Domino said. "I was just wondering the same thing. You know something we don't?"

He did, but he didn't. Not really. There were any number of reasons for her absence. Maybe she was just busy. She was probably just busy. Probably.

"Nope," Javi said, perhaps a little too quickly. He hoped he sounded convincing. "Who's up for some PvP?"

It was as good a distraction as any. From Rouge, and from Noah.

Javi did have enough time to get in a quick round, but he wasn't his usual self. They still won but not by the large margin they were used to. Even so, his rating ticked up a point, likely from the people watching his team stream their game. Livestreams were always good for that sort of thing.

"Sorry, guys," Javi said. "My head's not in the game. Literally."

"No worries," Domino said. "We all have off days."

Before Javi could say anything else, the doorbell rang.

"Sorry, gotta run, bye!" He logged out at lightning speed and tossed his headset off. He needed to get to Noah before his family did. He loved them all, but they were A Lot.

Javi bounded down the stairs, but when he arrived at the foot of the staircase, he saw that he was too late.

Eva had already opened the door. She stood on the threshold, staring up at Noah. The boy had his hands in his pockets as he gazed down at Javi's frowning sister.

"Who are you?" Eva asked, in lieu of a proper greeting. She looked like a little lioness ready to defend her den. She was a savage child, and while Javi normally enjoyed her savagery, he didn't want it directed at Noah.

"I'm Noah. I'm a friend of Javi's."

There was nothing wrong with what Noah said. It's just that Javi never had friends over. He was always too busy gaming to have *anyone* over. He knew exactly what conclusion the younger Luceros would draw from so innocuous a statement.

Noah caught Javi's eye just as a chorus of frenzied *ooh*s erupted from his siblings.

"Ooh, Javi's got a boyfriend."

"How come you haven't said anything, Javi?"

"Are you dating?" Eva asked as she ushered Noah inside. And then, assuming that the answer to her inquiry was yes, she asked, "How long have you been dating?"

Javi buried his face in his hands. "Oh my god. Please shut up, all of you."

"Look at him," his grandmother chimed in. "All skin and bones."

Noah patted his stomach self-consciously.

"Don't overthink it," Javi said. "She says that to everybody."

His abuela shot him a look that softened when it then landed on Noah. "I cooked."

Javi's grandmother always cooked. Her baseline state of existence was cooking. With a small child army at her command, there was always someone to eat her offerings. But that did nothing to abate her insatiable need for even more mouths to feed.

"I made mofongo."

Noah leaned closer to Javi to whisper in his ear, "What's mofongo?"

"A dish made out of plantains. It's not my favorite."

"I also made tostones," his grandmother said. "You like those."

"What're tostones?" Noah asked.

"Another plantain dish," Javi said. "They're mashed and fried into salty discs of deliciousness."

"That actually sounds really good," Noah said. He smiled at Javi's grandmother. She beamed back at him.

"Abuela, if I take a plate of tostones, will you leave us alone?" Javi asked.

"Sí," she said, though they both knew she was lying. Within ten minutes, she'd probably be banging Javi's door open, telling them to make sure they left room for the Holy Ghost.

She beckoned them into the kitchen, which, he had to admit, smelled divine. Javi accepted a large plate piled high with tostones. Noah took the two glasses of iced tea Javi's abuela thrust at him without complaint.

"Thanks, Mrs. Lucero," Noah said. Javi had mentioned that his grandmother was his dad's mom, so it wasn't really a surprise that Noah got her name right. But it still warmed something inside Javi that Noah remembered such a minor detail.

His grandmother patted Noah's cheek and smiled. Nothing made her happier than someone shutting up and eating her food.

"Be good, you two. Don't do anything I wouldn't do."

"Abuela!"

Her cackle followed them up the stairs and into Javi's room. He kicked the door shut behind him.

"I am so sorry." Javi placed the plate on the center of his bed and sat to one side of it. Noah sat on the other. "They're a lot to handle."

"It's okay," Noah said. "They seem nice." He picked up one of the tostones and sniffed it.

Javi smiled at him. "You're supposed to put a little bit of the mojo on them and eat them like that."

"What's mojo?"

"A garlicky type of sauce. I don't know what else is in it, to be honest, but it's good. I wouldn't recommend it right now, though."

"Why's that?"

"Because I don't want to taste like garlic when I do this."

Javi leaned forward, driven by impulse, and kissed Noah.

It was even nicer than he remembered. He hadn't thought

it was possible, but every time their lips touched was better than the last.

There was a poster of Javi rolled up under his bed, of him holding an ergonomic Panthera controller and smiling at the camera, the words *Practice makes perfect* scrawled across the bottom in some kind of futuristic font. He'd thought it was just a stupid aphorism, but now Javi had a greater appreciation for the sentiment. The more he kissed Noah, the more he learned how. He was learning just how much pressure to apply, when to press on and when to pull back. When to—

"Oooooh, I'm telling Abuela!"

Javi jerked back fast enough to hit his head on the wall behind him. The pain was bad but not bad enough to interfere with his aim when he grabbed a sneaker off the floor and hurled it toward the doorway, where Daniela and Dario stood ogling at him.

"Get out!" Javi hollered loud enough for the entire house to hear him. Two pairs of feet scampered down the hallway, leaving a trill of giggles in their wake.

Eva peered into the room after the twins departed, her expression somber. "Don't worry. I'll make sure they won't tell."

"And you're not?" Javi asked, incredulous.

Eva shrugged. "I ain't a narc."

With that, she left, thoughtfully closing the door behind her.

"How does she even know what a narc is?" Noah asked, laughter lightening his voice.

"Oh my god." Javi buried his face in his hands. He could

feel the warmth in his cheeks against his palms. "Kill me now."

"No, thanks," Noah said. "I kind of like you alive. And this is good. I needed a distraction."

Javi wanted to kiss Noah again. He wanted it very, very badly. But there was something about the way Noah held himself, something stiff and pained, that gave him pause.

"What happened?" Javi asked.

"It's my sister," Noah started. He stopped, letting that awful sentence hang in the air.

"Is she okay?" Javi couldn't imagine what he would say or do if Noah said she wasn't. If it was one of Javi's siblings, there'd be nothing anyone could say or do to comfort *him*. His hand itched to take Noah's. He resisted the urge for less than a second before deciding that maybe Noah needed him to. Noah didn't seem to mind.

"Cece's fine . . . It's just . . ." He sighed heavily, picking apart his food and leaving a small mountain of fried plantain crumbs on the plate. "She has to leave the hospital she's in. Magnolia Children's Hospital."

"The good one." A few years ago, Eva had fallen out of a tree Javi told her not to climb and broken her leg. Javi's rating had been just good enough to get her in the front door. The level of care she'd received had been miles better than Javi's own experience at the public hospital.

It was just a few months after the accident, when the grass hadn't quite grown over his parents' graves. Javi got into a fight with some kids in the neighborhood. He'd started it, but they had finished it. His grandmother had taken him to the Jackson Hills General emergency room, where they waited eleven hours before a doctor deigned to tend to Javi's broken wrist. No one went to Jackson Hills General if they had better options. His abuela's rating hadn't been high enough for anything else. That was the night Javi had sworn that he would do anything he could to make sure his brothers and sisters had more than he did.

"Yeah. My dad got laid off and his rating tanked." Noah swallowed thickly. Javi watched the movement of his Adam's apple. He wanted to do more than hold Noah's hand, but he didn't. Not yet. "They won't let her stay if he doesn't get it back up. They'll move her to Jackson Hills General."

The not so good one. Javi kept that observation to himself.

Javi swore, once in English, then again in Spanish for good measure. "That's not fair."

"No, it's not." Noah's voice was thick with bitterness. He looked down at his hands. The nails had been bitten to the quick. "And there isn't a thing anyone can do about it."

"Actually," Javi ventured, "there might be."

Noah's eyes shot up. He somehow managed to look both guarded and hopeful, all at once. "What? What is it?"

Javi looked over his shoulder to make sure the door was still shut. It wouldn't do to have any curious ears overhear what he was about to propose. "Tell me . . . do you have any moral reservations when it comes to hacking?"

And so it begins.

CHAPTER 25
CHASE DONOVAN

RATING: 55

Founder's Day approached with a flurry of activity. The school took John Maplethorpe's birthday seriously. Too seriously, if you asked Chase. Nobody did.

The gymnasium was decorated in rich maroon and shimmering gold, transforming it from a utilitarian space to something that could almost resemble a ballroom. Someone had placed a little wreath of flowers on Maplethorpe's bust in the foyer of the main building. The remnants of paint on his face had been washed away as much as possible, but you could still see minuscule flecks of color if you looked hard enough.

It was a lot of worship for a false prophet, as Chase had come to think of him.

Any other year, Chase would have looked forward to the dance. Tickets were sold at the door, but if you were wearing a Maplethorpe letter jacket, you could just walk right in without paying. It wasn't fair, but then neither was life, so Chase didn't feel particularly bothered by that small act of inequality. It was a free way to have a fun time, to do something besides stress about his future and his grades and his dad and his house.

But not this year.

This year, he left at the same time he would have if he were going to the dance. His father was out, probably at the bar a few blocks away where he liked to watch football games. There was no one to ask Chase questions as he left. But instead of heading to the school, he took a different route. Twenty minutes later, he was waiting outside Bex's house, in the part of town that might as well have been another universe for Chase.

She'd asked him to text when he got there instead of ringing the doorbell.

"My parents wouldn't approve," she'd said.

"Of me?" Chase had asked.

"Of your gender. And, well, of the general fact of your existence," she'd replied. "It's not personal. They think boys are a distraction I don't have time for. So just text me when you hit my block and I'll meet you outside."

Chase quite liked the notion that he might be distracting. As promised, he texted her when he turned the corner onto her block. By the time he reached her house, she was bounding down the walkway toward him.

There was a sparkle in her eyes that wasn't normally there. Her voice was high and breathy with excitement when she asked, "You ready?"

"As I'll ever be." He offered her his arm. They weren't going to the dance, but that was no excuse not to at least pretend to be a gentleman. "Let's go to Lucky's and find out what this weirdness is all about."

The Lucky Penny was emptier than Chase had ever seen it.

On a normal Friday night, it would be packed with Maplethorpe students, but tonight it was practically devoid of patrons.

Except for two.

"They're sitting at the booth," Bex whispered to Chase. "The one with the gold jukebox."

They were. Two boys, both in Chase's year. He recognized one of them. Javi Lucero. An athlete of sorts, if one considered e-sports to be actual sports, which Chase didn't. But still, he was a pleasant enough dude. Chase had shared a few classes with him over the years.

"That's Javi, but who's the pale kid?" Chase asked Bex as they slowly approached the booth.

"Noah Rainier," she said. "He does photography. I was going to recruit him for the *Lantern*, but . . . well, you know."

When they reached the booth, both boys looked up at them.

"Can we help you with something?" Javi asked. His gaze wandered from Bex to Chase and back again, as if he was trying to solve the puzzle of their odd pairing.

"So, this might sound weird, but . . . we need this booth," Bex said. It did sound weird, but Chase supposed there was no better way to put it.

The pale kid—Noah—frowned. "So do we."

The bell above the door jingled, and four heads swiveled in its direction. Two more Maplethorpe students entered. The shorter one was the figure skater, Hana. Chase had always been a little in awe of her. He was good at baseball, but as an elite athlete, she was on another level entirely. She competed internationally, in places Chase had only ever dreamed of visiting.

The girl beside her frowned when she saw the four of them at the booth. Chase knew her, too, but only by reputation. Tamsin was the weird witchy girl who charged forty bucks for fortunes Chase was pretty sure she just made up. The heavy makeup around her eyes made her frown look especially severe. After saying something to Hana in a soft voice, she marched up to the table with the gold jukebox, the many bangles around her wrists jingling as she moved.

"You guys are gonna have to move," Tamsin said by way of greeting.

"Hello to you, too," Javi said.

"We need to sit here," said Tamsin.

"Why?" Bex asked.

Hana drew up beside them, her lips pressed together in a tight line. She looked worried and a little confused.

"Why do *you* need to be here?" Tamsin asked. Chase wondered if she talked to everyone this way, or if she was being aggressive just for their benefit.

This was getting them nowhere.

Chase reached into his pocket and retrieved the letter he'd carried with him every day since he and Bex had first discovered it.

He held it up, displaying the jester affixed to the front. "I got an engraved invitation. How about you?"

A few impossibly long seconds passed before heads nodded all around. Tamsin took out a tarot card. Hana, a page covered in letters cut out of magazines, like a ransom note in a bad movie. Noah, a photograph with words written on the back. Javi pulled up a picture on his phone of an image on a computer screen. Each one displayed the same poem that had led Bex and Chase to the Lucky Penny on the night of the Founder's Day Dance.

"I didn't think things could possibly get weirder," Tamsin said. "And yet, here we are."

"How about we all sit down and try to look normal?" Bex suggested.

They tried. And failed. The assortment of wildly disparate personalities crowding into a booth at the back of the Lucky Penny looked like the setup for a bad joke.

A jock, a Goth, and a handful of nerds walk into a diner . . .

Chase shook the thought away. He didn't want to guess what the punch line would be. Perhaps they *were* the punch line. A group of teenagers, each from a very different walk of life, comparing notes on a conspiracy theory about a deranged clown.

It was all very funny, but none of the studiously serious faces around the table were laughing.

The lone waitress working that night came by to take their order. It was the same blonde who'd been there the night he and Bex found their note. Chase hadn't planned on getting anything, but Bex insisted. It would have looked odd, she said to him in a hushed whisper, if none of them ordered. It was a diner, after all.

Bex ordered a strawberry milkshake and asked for an extra straw when it became apparent to her that Chase had no intention—and no money—to order anything. Javi asked for a cheeseburger deluxe, Noah a grilled cheese, and Tamsin a black-and-white shake. Hana asked, in a voice so quiet the waitress had to bend down to hear her, for just a Diet Coke.

They waited in tense, awkward silence for the waitress to leave. When she was finally back behind the counter, Javi spoke.

"So," he started, "which one of you sent the messages?"

No one answered. They looked at one another with varying degrees of suspicion.

"Oh, great," Tamsin said. "I was worried tonight was gonna be too straightforward."

Bex spread her hands on the table, leaning forward. "If none of us sent the messages, then someone else did. Someone who wants us to come together."

"Yes," Hana said. "But *why?*"

"Million-dollar question," Tamsin said, popping her bubble gum.

"Another thing I don't get," said Noah, "is what these messages have to do with the vandalism of the Maplethorpe statue." He shared a look with Javi. "We know they've gotta be connected somehow."

Chase traded glances with Bex. They were both thinking about the book, safely tucked away in Bex's backpack.

"I don't know . . ." she said.

"We've gotten this far by working together," said Chase. "We should show them, Bex."

"Show us what?" Tamsin asked, her eyes narrowing.

"The quote on the base of the statue," Bex said. "I found the book it's from."

Chase shuffled a few inches to the side to allow Bex to pull her backpack up from where it rested at her feet. She took the book out and placed it on the table. It sat there under the neon lights reflecting off the windows, looking like an object of great significance, out of place among a bunch of glossy diner menus.

A battered copy of Jean-Jacques Rousseau's *The Social Contract*—in the original French—calmly absorbed their stares.

"Ah, yes," Javi said. "A book. I am familiar with such things."

Tamsin, the Goth/witch/whatever-she-was, snorted. Chase had never gone to her for a tarot reading—he didn't believe in such nonsense—but a few of his buddies had. All their readings had taken on distinctly dire tones that Chase suspected had more to do with Tamsin's general view of athletes than it did with *mystical divination*.

A part of him did wonder if Tamsin had seen this fascinating grouping in the cards. It seemed too outlandish for even the spirits to predict.

"It's not just a book," Bex said. She opened the cover with reverent slowness, stretching the moment as if she were luxuriating in the reveal. "It's the next step."

"The what?" Hana asked.

Bex opened the book to the page she'd marked with a small Post-it flag. "The numbers in the margins. They're coordinates."

"This is so freaking awesome," Javi said, his voice soft with childlike awe.

"Where do they lead?" Noah asked.

"Maplethorpe," Bex replied. She pulled up a map and entered the coordinates. They passed her phone around so everyone could see. "Not sure where, though."

Tamsin touched her fingers to the screen to zoom in. "I know where this is."

"Do tell," Javi said.

"The music building. The old one no one ever bothered knocking down."

"Isn't that where you read fortunes?" Chase asked. He

remembered Steve going there once and coming back a little paler than when he'd entered.

"Read, invent," Tamsin said with a flippant gesture. "Same difference."

"That's cool and all," Noah said, "but what good is a location without any context?"

"That's what I said, until Chase noticed something else." Bex flipped through the book's yellowed pages until she got to the back cover. With gentle fingers, as if she were handling some priceless artifact, she slipped the library checkout card from its sleeve. "Look at the due date."

They all leaned over the table, bringing their heads together over the card. A little tingle of satisfaction danced through Chase at Bex's acknowledgment of his part in that discovery.

"That's next week," Javi said.

"Yup," Chase said. "And I don't know about you guys, but I want to find out what this is all about."

One by one, they nodded, voicing their agreement. There was no hesitation. No doubt. They were in this together, all of them, for better or worse. Some outside force may have driven them to that table, at that diner, on that day, but the decision to accept the challenge, now that it had been laid out in front of them, was their own.

They wanted to know what came next. Chase needed to know. He hadn't realized how much he'd needed something else, something outside baseball and his dad and his team and his own desperation.

Bex fingered the corner of the book's pages, flicking a few up and down. "But . . . I don't know . . ."

Chase gently nudged her with his elbow. "Don't know what?"

"You guys all got letters. Messages specifically meant for you." Bex absently chewed at her lower lip. "What if I'm not meant to go? What if they just want you guys and not me?"

"You know," Chase said, "for someone so smart, you're being kind of dense."

Bex frowned at him. He was willing to bet it was the first time someone had ever called her that. "What do you mean?"

"The graffiti," Chase said. "On John Maplethorpe's statue. That was your message. You're the one who recognized the book it came from. You stole it from the library. You knew where to look. None of us did, right?"

"Nope."

"Definitely not."

"I have literally never heard of Rousseau until just now."

"You think so?" Bex asked.

"I know so," Chase said. "This was meant for you to find. And *you* are gonna lead us to the next step in this super-weird scavenger hunt."

A shadow fell across their table and silence fell along with it. The waitress stood next to him, her arms laden with heavy plates and a tray full of milkshakes. She paused at their table long enough to peer at the open book in Bex's hands.

"What are you kids reading that's got you so excited?"

"Oh, nothing," Bex said, the lie spilling forth with ease. She closed the book in such a way that her hand obscured the title. "Just something for a group project."

The waitress wrinkled her nose. "Ugh. I used to hate those. Nobody else ever did the work."

Bex shared a conspiratorial look with the others at the table. Chase wondered if she was beginning to think of them as her minions. She looked like she was having fun. Probably the most fun she'd ever had in her strictly regimented life. "Oh, I think we'll do all right."

The waitress seemed satisfied with that answer and left, carrying her tray to the kitchen.

"So I take it this means we're all gonna show up at the old music building at midnight a week from tonight?"

"I am," Noah said firmly.

"We've come this far," Hana said. "There's no sense stopping now."

Tamsin stabbed a fry into a little tub of ketchup. "And it'll be extra illicit, because I doubt I'll even be a Maplethorpe student by then."

"What do you mean?" Chase asked.

Tamsin held up her forearm and pulled down her sleeve. On her wrist, she wore the same utilitarian display Chase had. Her number glowed a stark, unforgiving white against the black background of her screen.

17.

Chase winced. "Yikes."

"Holy cannoli," Javi said. "They're gonna kick you out."

"Yup." Tamsin rolled her sleeve down and crossed her arms. The gesture was likely intended to look defiant, but it just made her appear defensive. "Summer and her goons have sent me way below Maplethorpe's bare minimum."

"It's not fair," Hana said. She was the only one at the table who didn't seem surprised by Tamsin's abysmal number. "Maybe if you told someone . . ."

"No one will care, Hana." Tamsin tugged her sleeves even farther down, stretching the black fabric over her balled-up hands. "I was already living on the edge of the ratings. All it took was one good push to send me over. It was my own fault I made it so easy for them."

"But that doesn't make it right," Hana insisted. "The system isn't supposed to work like that."

"Don't you get it?" Tamsin asked, loud enough to draw the disapproving stare of the waitress behind the counter. She pitched her voice lower as she continued. "The system doesn't work, period. Full stop. We've been served a big old plate of nonsense, and we've been eating it all up our entire lives."

"Hana's right," said Javi. "It's not fair . . . but there might be something we could do about it."

Noah put a hand on Javi's arm, his mouth pulling into a concerned frown. "Are you talking about what I think you're talking about?"

Javi nodded. "Yeah. If I can do it for you, I can do it for Tamsin."

"Do what?" Bex asked.

"Yeah," Tamsin chimed in, "who's doing what to me?"

A bell rang, making them all jump a little. It was the kitchen, signaling that an order was up. The waitress walked by their table on her way to the open window that divided the diner from the kitchen. Javi waited until she was out of earshot before he went on.

"Manipulating the ratings," he said. "I think I figured out how to do it."

That made Chase perk up. So much of the stress in his life was rooted in the ratings and his ongoing battle with his own. If there was a way to game the system, he needed to know.

"How?" Chase asked. "And why?"

"It was for me," Noah said. "Well, for my sister. She's sick. My dad got laid off and our rating isn't high enough to keep her at her hospital."

"The only problem," Javi said, "is that it would be a lot easier for Noah's sister if I had access to Magnolia's database."

"Magnolia?" Bex said. "My mom works there. She's the chief neurosurgeon. If you need access, I can get you in."

A languid smile curled the corners of Javi's mouth. "That would work." He turned to Tamsin, who arched a dark eyebrow at him. "And as for you, all we need is to get our hands on Summer's smartwatch."

"And what are you gonna do with it?" Chase asked, though he knew. He just wanted to hear it out loud.

Javi looked at them in turn, perhaps gauging how serious they were. Chase had no complaints. Summer had always been kind of a monster. "We're going to depose a queen."

CHAPTER 26
NOAH RAINIER

RATING: 63

They didn't dare linger around Lucky's longer than necessary. The place was fairly empty save for the staff and a few college-age guys picking up takeout, but Noah still thought that maybe someone was watching them. It could have been the person who'd sent them the messages, or it could have been someone else. Whatever the case, the clandestine nature of it all was getting to him.

The six of them exchanged numbers and went their separate ways, promising to work out the finer details of their dastardly plan via text. Noah's bus arrived first. Before he got on, Javi darted close and pressed a quick kiss to his cheek. A furious blush accompanied him onto the bus. As it drove away, he caught sight of Tamsin giving him a thumbs-up.

What they were proposing was illegal. It had always been illegal. Meddling with Summer's rating was probably slightly less illegal than hacking a hospital database to reflect a higher rating for the Rainier family, but it was still definitely, without question, super illegal.

And they were going to do it anyway.

The bus rolled to a stuttering stop a few blocks down from Lucky's. Noah rested his forehead against the window. His breath fogged up the glass. He dragged his finger through the condensation, drawing a question mark.

They knew what they had to do. But not how they were going to do it.

Unless . . .

He fumbled in his pocket for his phone as an idea occurred to him, his fingers flying over the screen frustratingly slow compared to the thoughts racing in his head.

He started a group chat and added everyone to the contacts.

Noah: I just had an idea.

He added a few lightbulb emojis because why not?

Chase: Hit me.
Hana: hit ~*us*~
Javi: Oh look at all these delightful weirdos texting me
Noah: I have a Plan.
Javi: A Plan? Not a plan?
Noah: A Plan. Capital P and everything.
Javi: My breath is bated.
Chase: A plan to do what?
Bex: Oh, god, why are we in a group chat?
Tamsin: Yeah who let this happen
Chase: I like group chats
Tamsin: You would.
Chase: whats that supposed to mean?
Bex: Play nice, everybody.
Tamsin: Don't know how. Skipped that day in kindergarten.

Tamsin: Wait, I don't think I even went to kindergarten. My mom wanted to homeschool me until she realized she'd have to teach me math.

Noah: I always thought homeschooling would be kind of nice.

Javi: Noah. The Plan?

Noah: RIGHT. The Plan.

Noah: so summer is having that party tonight after the founder's day dance . . . why don't we just steal her device then?

Bex: I don't think I know where her house is.

Chase: me neither. I've never actually been there

Javi: hey noah remember when I said I asked mrs sullivan for your address? I lied. I just hacked the school database to find it myself

Noah: dude that's weird

Hana: That's actually kind of sweet

Tamsin: Yeah, in a stalkery sort of way

Javi: nvm I shouldn't have said anything

Chase: yeah u really shouldn't have

Bex: You*

Chase: omfg dont

Bex: Don't*

Noah: GUYS

Javi: so anywaaaaaay anything you fine folks need off the school servers . . . I got u

Bex: Don't you start, too.

Javi: u u u u u u u u

Chase: my dude

Chase: so how r we gonna do this

Bex: Are*

Chase: bex i s2g

Bex: swear to god*

Chase: friendship canceled

Bex: I'm sorry.

Chase: lol no ur not

Bex: You're not wrong.

Chase: So anyway when ARE we going to do this? Happy, Rebecca?

Bex: Type however you want so long as you never call me Rebecca again.

Tamsin: I think my crashing this lil shindig might be detrimental to ~*The Plan*~

Hana: oooh I like that ~*the plan*~

Bex: I don't think I've ever gone to a party before. I'd stick out like a sore thumb.

Hana: Summer gave me a flyer the other day . . .

Chase: the whole team was invited. i can go with u. meet u there at 10ish?

Tamsin: Oh good, our two best jocks are on the case

Hana: I'm not a jock

Tamsin: You're a jock in sequins

Chase: i think id look good in sequins. maybe we should make it a thing

Chase: bex u should come too

Hana: Wear something with sequins, it's our look now

Bex: idk . . .

Chase: I don't know*

Bex: I've taught you well. Okay, just for that, I'll go.

Noah: omg this is like working with children

Tamsin: For realsies, the clock is ticking

Javi: no one says for realsies

Tamsin: I'm bringing it back. I'm making it cool again.

Javi: OK SO hana, chase, and bex will infiltrate the rawlins manor

Chase: but what if someone tries to stop us while we're infiltrating

Hana: I will fight them (ง'-')ง

Tamsin: Can I bring popcorn? I wanna see Hana throw down

Noah: GUYS focus

Noah: you two go in, get summer's necklace thingie, get out, bring it to me and javi

Javi: You and me?

Noah: yeah I was gonna go over to your place if that was ok

Javi: def ok

Tamsin: ooooooooohhhh

Hana: ooooohhhhhhh~

Chase: oooooooooo

Bex: Oooooooooh.

Javi: oOoOoOoOoOoO

Noah: once this is done, you're all dead to me

CHAPTER 27

HANA SAKAMOTO

RATING: 71

Hana did actually wear sequins to Summer's Founder's Day after-party. Silver ones, on a tank top. It was too cold to wear it alone, so she added a simple black jacket on top (pilfered from her mother's closet). She thought she looked like a teenager ready to party.

She wasn't surprised that Bex had not worn sequins. But traveling for competitions her entire life had taught Hana never to go anywhere unprepared.

As they stood a few feet from the front door of the ostentatiously named Rawlins Manor, Bex stared at the sparkly rose-gold cardigan Hana held out to her like it was a smallpox-ridden blanket.

"Just put it on," Hana said. "It'll look nice on you."

Bex looked down at her outfit. Dark blue jeans (boot-cut), purple-and-gray sneakers (utilitarian), and a simple white shirt (unadorned). "What's wrong with what I'm wearing?"

"Nothing," Hana said. "It just doesn't scream, 'I'm here to party.'"

"But I'm not here to party."

Chase took the sweater from Hana and draped it across Bex's shoulders. She frowned at him, but only slightly. "True, but we don't want anyone else to know that."

"Yeah," Hana said, "we need to blend in. So blend."

With a mumbled token protest, Bex slid her arms through the sleeves of the cardigan. It did look nice on her, nicer than it looked on Hana. The rose gold complemented her darker skin much better.

"You know," Hana said, "you should just keep that."

"Yeah, you look nice," said Chase. "Not that you didn't look nice before or anything but, um . . ." He looked at Hana like she was the last lifeboat on his sinking ship. He cleared his throat and flailed for a subject change. "Did you bring any sequins for me?"

"Sorry," Hana said, "I didn't have anything in your size."

The door swung open before Hana could touch the knob. A tallish guy in a maroon Maplethorpe jacket stood on the threshold, both hands bearing red plastic cups.

"Chase! My man, what is up?"

"Hey, Steve." Chase offered the other boy a little wave. He didn't look overly pleased to see him. Hana couldn't blame him. Ten seconds spent in Steve's company and she already didn't like him, or the way he looked at her and Bex.

"And you brought two girls. Nice." Steve held out a red Solo cup to Hana, who took it with absolutely no intention of ingesting whatever vile liquid it held. "Bottoms up, babe."

He drained the contents of his own cup and backed into the house, beckoning for them to follow.

Hana daintily dumped out her cup into one of the very expensive-looking planters bracketing the door and followed Steve inside. Dmitriev would have her hide if he found out she'd taken so much as a sip, but she didn't want to draw attention to herself by turning the drink down. They were there to blend. Hopefully, the plant would survive.

Summer's house looked exactly the way Hana thought it would.

Everything was white and gold, from the gold-flecked marble floor of the foyer to the gilded banisters running along the staircase. Small porcelain figurines sat on side tables of dubious necessity. Some were fairies, suspended with their tiny wings flared, but most were unicorns. There were unicorns in repose, resting their slender heads on bent legs. Unicorns mid-canter, their hooves frozen at the height of their stride. And even unicorns in flight, which Hana supposed were actually Pegasuses. Pegasi?

"Hey, Bex?" Hana looped her arm around the other girl's elbow, speaking close to her ear to be heard over the music. "What's the plural of 'Pegasus'?"

"There isn't a plural form," Bex replied. "There was only one Pegasus, the equine child of Poseidon and Medusa. He was born after Perseus chopped off her head."

"Oh." Hana thought she liked the way Pegasi sounded better, even if it was grammatically incorrect, so she was going to go with that.

Chase split from their group and went off with Steve, while Bex and Hana surveyed the party. They all had their roles to play and they knew them, but it still took Hana a moment to adjust to the atmosphere.

"Why did we think this was a good idea?" Hana asked Bex.

"I was just wondering the same thing myself," Bex said.

Neither one of them had ever been to a high school party. The last party Hana remembered attending was the eighth birthday of another skater at the rink. There had been cake and balloons and little bags with party favors. Her coach had confiscated the slice of cake Hana had been handed by the skater's mother before she could manage even a single bite.

"No," he'd said. His accent had been thicker then, before he'd lived in the States long enough to dull its sharp Russian edges. "Cake makes you fat."

She hadn't attempted to eat cake since.

"What are we supposed to do?" Hana whispered.

Bex shrugged. "Like you said, blend in. Or, you know, try to."

Drinks were ladled out of a cut crystal bowl surrounded by matching crystal bowls full of chips, all on a table at the side of the main sitting room. The punch was the unnaturally vivid red of a brand-new crayon. Hana served herself a cup and handed one to Bex. Neither of them drank, but holding the red plastic cup gave her something to do with her hands.

"Bex! You made it!"

Hana had just enough time to step aside before a human-shaped cannonball launched itself at Bex. She plucked the drink out of Bex's hand before it could spill. A dark-haired girl threw her arms around Bex's neck and squeezed her tight.

Hana knew the girl's name only because she'd been called it more than once by teachers at Maplethorpe. Melody's family was Korean and Hana's was Japanese, but that didn't seem to matter to people who thought they looked alike, despite the fact that Melody was a good six inches taller than Hana.

"Oh my god." Judging by the flush in Melody's cheeks, she was enjoying the party. "I'm so glad you came." She grabbed Bex's hand and started to drag her off. "Come on, let's go check out the kitchen."

Bex shot Hana an apologetic look over Melody's shoulder, but she seemed powerless to stop the tide. It occurred to Hana only then that Melody hadn't even said hi to her.

"Oh well," Hana said to no one. She absently took a sip of her drink and immediately regretted it. It managed to taste even worse than it smelled. Truly, an impressive feat.

From her position near the table, Hana was in the perfect spot to watch Chase put their plan into motion. He let Steve lead him over to their group of friends, all athletes and cheer-leaders. They congregated around the plush white couch where Summer held court.

Chase said something and they all laughed. Hana wondered what it would be like to blend in as seamlessly as he did. He seemed different from the rest of the jocks, but then, before that day at Lucky's, she'd thought they were all the same.

She observed the scene from a distance. Steve said something, but he was the only one who laughed. Summer shot him a deadly look, then said something to him that looked like an order. With a grumble, Steve got up and made his way to the snack table. Hana inched away from it, keeping her back to the wall. In Steve's absence, Summer scooted closer to Chase and wrapped a manicured hand around his bicep.

"Could she be more obvious?" Hana muttered into her cup.

"What?" asked a girl to Hana's left she hadn't noticed. The girl was piling a handful of potato chips onto a plate. The kind with ridges. Hana's favorite. She hadn't had one in years. Her stomach cramped, empty and dissatisfied.

"Nothing," Hana said.

With a shrug, the girl walked off.

Hana turned back to the group on the couch. Things had progressed in the seconds her attention had been elsewhere. The group had thinned, with most pairing off into separate conversations. Steve was now chatting to another girl by the snack table, oblivious to what was going on mere feet away.

Summer leaned in close to Chase. Hana winced on his behalf. Summer walked her hands up his chest, tracing the contours of the *M* on his jacket before spreading her hand to cover it. Hana inched even closer to hear what she was saying.

"Steve didn't know what he had," Summer muttered. "You wouldn't be so horrible to me, though, would you, Chase?"

Her body was slotted against his, connecting them in an unbroken line from hip to shoulder. His hands hovered awkwardly behind her and a little off to the side. He looked like he didn't know where to put them. "Um, yeah. No. Definitely not."

As Summer laid her head on Chase's shoulder, mumbling something about ungrateful boyfriends and all the things she did for hers, Chase wiggled his fingers at Hana. It was very jazz-hands–y. And then it hit her. The plan wouldn't work if he didn't have a drink in his hand.

Hana hopped away from the wall, pushing through the crowd of partying teens, away from the table heaped high with snacks, punch, and the red plastic cups. Before tonight, Hana had believed those cups existed solely in movies about stupid high school parties, and not at *actual* stupid high school parties.

With as much subtlety as she could manage, Hana handed the cup to Chase and kept walking. She stopped when she reached the opposite wall. She leaned back against it and waited. No one paid her any mind.

Chase wasted no time. He gesticulated wildly with his hands while he spoke to Summer. Half the punch sloshed out of the cup and onto Summer's very tight and very white dress.

Summer leaped to her feet with an indignant shout. With a look over his shoulder, Chase nodded slightly at Hana.

Now it was her turn.

She sprung into action, grabbing a handful of napkins from the snack table and rushing to Summer's side.

"Oh my god, your dress!" Hana offered Summer the napkins. "Come here, let me help you get cleaned up."

She took Summer's hands and led her away from the sitting room and into the hall. Only then did she realize she had no idea where to go.

Summer patted uselessly at her dress with the wad of napkins. "Thanks," she said forlornly. "But I think this dress is ruined."

It absolutely was. A bright red stain spread across the snowy fabric, right over Summer's stomach.

"Where's your room?" Hana ventured. "I can help you pick out something else."

Summer looked at Hana, really looked at her, for maybe the first time that night. "I . . . yeah. Thanks. That's really sweet."

A faint tendril of guilt tickled at Hana's brain, but it was easy enough to brush it away. Summer was actively trying to ruin the life of someone Hana now considered a friend. That wasn't something that could be forgiven just because Summer showed an inkling of humanity. Righting a wrong had to take precedence.

Summer's bedroom was as absurdly luxurious as the rest of the house. A large four-poster bed dominated the room, with gauzy white curtains hanging around the mattress. She even had her own en suite bathroom, tiled in the same white marble as the foyer.

Hana watched as Summer slipped off her necklace and dumped it onto her vanity. As Summer slid out of her soiled dress, Hana's fingers itched. So close.

She waited while Summer turned to her closet (a walk-in) and began rummaging through racks of dresses (designer). While the girl's back was turned, Hana slipped the necklace off the vanity and into her pocket. She just hoped Summer was too preoccupied to notice.

"What about this one?" Summer asked as she turned around, holding up a canary-yellow bandage dress.

It actually suited her red hair rather nicely. Hana didn't even have to lie when she said, "It's perfect."

Summer beamed. She was a pretty girl when she wasn't sneering. It was a shame her personality was so ugly. Hana took her phone out of her other pocket and pulled up the group chat.

Phase one complete.

CHAPTER 28

BEX JOHNSON

RATING: 91

The kitchen of Rawlins Manor—Bex was still not over that name—was a crush of bodies, but Melody didn't appear to mind as she dragged Bex through the crowd. A few people recognized Bex from school. Most seemed surprised to see her there but not displeased. A handful even shot her positive ratings. The music wasn't as loud in the kitchen, but it was no less noisy. A tray of tiny cups filled with multicolored liquid sat on the counter. Melody picked up two, one for herself and one for Bex.

Whatever it was, Bex didn't want it. And Melody knew Bex didn't drink. She had too much on her plate.

But even so, Melody held out the small plastic cup. Apparently, tiny disposable glasses were a thing. It was filled with a bright green substance that jiggled like gelatin.

"No, thanks," Bex said, offering it back to Melody.

Melody refused. She pushed it back toward Bex with that same insistence that Bex both loved and hated about her.

"Oh, come on. It'll be fun."

Bex looked around for a place to dispose of the drink, but there wasn't anywhere obvious to put trash. It simply accumulated on every available surface. Bex placed it on the counter. Let it be someone else's problem. "Melody, why are you here? You don't even like Summer."

Melody quirked her shoulders up in a little shrug. "Summer's kinda cool actually. She said if I helped her with this thing, then maybe I could go to her family's ski chalet over winter break. It's super exclusive. Can you imagine the ratings spike I'd get?"

Bex was only aware that her expression had pulled into a frown when Melody reached out and smoothed the wrinkle that formed between Bex's eyebrows whenever she did. "What thing, Melody?"

"Oh, nothing major." Melody shrugged, but she refused to meet Bex's eyes. Her gaze bounced around the kitchen, from the crumb-covered tray that held a lone cupcake to the oblivious couple making out against the fridge. "There was just some girl who needed to be put in her place is all."

"Tamsin?" Blood rushed to Bex's face. She wasn't mad. Mad was too soft a word. She was . . . *incensed*. How could she reconcile Melody—the girl who slept over at her house and hated board games because they were *too competitive*—with this strange partygoer engaged in a crowdsourced bullying campaign? "Melody, why would you do that?"

"It's not a big deal," Melody said with another shrug. "Besides, she was rude to me. She kind of had it coming."

"Melody . . ." Bex started. She didn't know how to finish. Melody knew it was wrong. That was why she wouldn't look Bex straight in the eye. But Bex's disapproval had only ever gone so far with her friend. Melody always did exactly what she wanted, whatever the consequences.

This was what the system bred. It swallowed up good people and made them do things they otherwise wouldn't for the quick high of a ratings bump and the validation of people who shouldn't have mattered.

"You know, Bex, one of these days you're gonna have to unclench." Melody snagged a drink off the tray before leaving Bex alone in that cramped kitchen. "See you Monday. Maybe you'll be more fun by then."

It took Bex longer to find a door to the back garden than felt reasonable. The house—no, the manor—was just that big. It was probably the biggest residence in town. The Rawlinses were the wealthiest family in Jackson Hills, and they wanted everyone to know it.

Once outside, Bex sucked in a deep lungful of air. It was getting chilly, but she vastly preferred the brisk evening to the claustrophobic warmth of the party. The garden wasn't completely devoid of people, but they were sparsely scattered around. A couple on a nearby bench was making out with as much vigor as the pair in the kitchen. Bex couldn't imagine shoving her tongue down someone's throat like that, much less doing it in public. She walked to the other side of the garden, where a gazebo sat, bathed in the soft glow of fairy lights wrapped around its pillars.

Out here, she was almost alone. Alone enough to breathe. Her ears rang in the relative silence. She hadn't realized how loud it was inside until the noise fell away, relegated to a distant thrumming of the bass drifting from open windows.

"Thought I'd find you out here."

Bex started. Chase stood behind her, at the base of the short steps leading to the gazebo. His hands were shoved in his pockets, and he gave her an apologetic smile. "Sorry, didn't mean to scare you."

"It's okay," Bex said, though her heart was still pounding hard enough that she could feel it in her throat. "I just needed some air. Parties aren't really my thing."

"It's cool." Chase climbed the steps in a single bound—his legs were long enough for it—and came to stand beside her. "It's not really my scene either."

"I find that hard to believe," Bex said.

"Oh, yeah? Why's that?"

Bex shrugged and waved a hand at the manor, packed full of people who didn't just accept Chase's presence among them. They welcomed it. They courted it. They tolerated Bex, but they *wanted* him. "Aren't they your people?"

Chase turned and leaned against the railing, half sitting on it. "Not really. They like having me around because I'm a really good pitcher. That's sort of where our interests align, but if it wasn't for baseball, I wouldn't be here." He placed one hand on the nearest column, fingers tracing the intricate carving of leaves winding around it. "This is about as far from where I come from as you can get."

He went silent then. Bex felt like there was a layer to his words beneath the ones he actually spoke out loud. The possibility of excavating that hidden meaning was so tantalizing, so close, she could almost taste it on her tongue.

The soft lighting was kind to him. It emphasized the sharpness of his cheekbones, the angle of his jaw. Her heart was still pounding but for an entirely different reason. One she didn't quite understand.

So she changed the subject.

"Where's Hana?" Bex asked.

"She's hanging back so it doesn't look like we're leaving together," Chase replied. "I think she's actually helping Summer look for this."

He slipped the necklace out of his pocket and dangled it in front of Bex's face.

"She slipped it to me right after she left Summer's room. Summer didn't notice a thing. Hana's, like, a scary good actress. Maybe it's all that emoting skaters do."

Bex wrapped her hands around Chase's and pressed the necklace into his fists. "Oh my god, Chase, put that away before someone sees."

He laughed, but he tucked the necklace away. Then his eyes widened. "Oh, I can't believe I forgot to show you this before."

From his pocket, Chase pulled out a crumpled test booklet, misshapen from having been shoved in his jacket. "Behold, my latest chem test."

Bex snatched the booklet from him and opened it so quickly she nearly tore off the front page. When she saw the number scrawled in red ink, she nearly dropped the booklet.

76.

"Chase! You passed!"

Chase glanced down, suddenly bashful. "Barely, but yeah."

"Don't sell yourself short. This is amazing." Bex cradled the booklet in her hands. In that moment, it was more precious to her than any 100 she'd ever received. She only reluctantly offered it back to him, and Chase returned the pages to the pocket with the stolen necklace. "I'm really proud of you, Chase."

He looked at her then, canting his head to the side.

"You know," said Chase, "that cardigan does look really nice on you."

Bex shrugged. It was a little snug through the shoulders, which wasn't surprising considering how petite Hana was. "It's just a sweater."

"Take the compliment, Bex."

"Okay. Fine. Thank you."

There was a wry curl to his lips when he smiled. "You know I'm not actually talking about the sweater, right?"

Only then did Bex realize that she was still touching one of his hands. He'd only pulled one away to put the necklace back in his pocket. The other had remained under hers.

Oh.

Slowly, painfully slowly, Chase turned his hand in her grasp, unfurling his fingers like a flower opening its petals. He gave her ample time to pull away. When she didn't, he curled his fingers around hers, linking their hands.

"Would it be okay," Chase said, as slowly as he'd taken her hand, "if I kissed you right now?"

Bex answered without thought, without hesitation, without doubt. "Yes."

And he did.

His lips were shockingly soft. They moved against hers, slowly, as if he was still seeking permission. As if he was testing to see this was actually okay.

It was. It very much was.

A twig snapped and Bex jumped away from Chase, dropping his hand. The loss felt monumental.

"Oh, I—sorry." Hana was standing at the base of the gazebo steps, one foot raised a few inches above a thin broken branch. "I can, um, leave. I just—we're done, so we can . . . go." She started walking backward. "Or I can just go and you two can just . . . yeah. I'm gonna go."

"No, wait," Chase said, his words warm and soft with mirth. "It's fine. I'm glad no one caught you. Though your timing could use some work."

Hana shuffled her feet in place, looking as though she was unsure if she should approach or retreat. "Honestly, I don't mind. I can go back in if . . ."

"No," Bex said, maybe a little too quickly. Her mother was right. Boys were a distraction. But a really, really, *really* nice one. "We should get the necklace to Javi ASAP."

"To be continued?" Chase asked, voice light with hope.

"Awkward," Hana said as she started walking toward the front lawn and away from the scene of their crime. Chase held out his hand for Bex. After a slender moment's hesitation, she took it.

"Yeah," Bex said. "To be continued."

CHAPTER 29

JAVI LUCERO

RATING: 90

"I feel like a third wheel," Tamsin said from her perch on the corner of Javi's bed. She flipped through an e-sports magazine that featured his grinning likeness on the cover. She'd arrived shortly after Noah.

As nice as it would have been for Javi to have Noah all to himself, Tamsin was a necessary part of the plan. There would be other nights for a metaphorical romantic vehicle with only two wheels.

Javi glanced over his shoulder at her. She didn't appear to be overly concerned about her third-wheelness. Her posture was relaxed, or as relaxed as it could be considering they were about to commit several misdemeanors and at least one downright felony. Noah put a few inches between himself and Javi; he was standing by Javi's chair, looking over his shoulder as Javi explained how to access the ratings database. Each city had its own localized server, and the one in Jackson Hills was shockingly easy to get into if you knew what to do. Javi did.

"You know," he said, "I used to joke that when the e-sports money ran dry, I could have a lucrative career in cybercrime."

The e-sports money was good at the moment. The headsets were on their third production run. His rating had just cracked 90. But the cybercrimes were shaping up to be more fun.

"The two aren't mutually exclusive," Noah said. "Look at you, multitasking like a champ."

Javi smiled up at Noah, who smiled down at him.

"Yup," Tamsin said. "Definitely a third wheel. I can go outside and hang out with your siblings if you guys want a moment to canoodle. I'm pretty sure there's enough of them for me to start my own softball league."

"Ha, ha. But I respect your use of the word 'canoodle' in a sentence." Javi inched his chair closer to Noah so his shoulder was brushing against Noah's stomach. He liked the contact. It helped him focus. A few more firewalls to bypass and then, "We're in."

"Seriously?" Tamsin asked. She unfolded her legs and came to stand at Javi's other side. "That quickly?"

Javi offered her an insouciant shrug. "Their security is good, but I'm better."

"Awesome," Noah said. "Now all we need is Summer's necklace and—"

As if on cue, the doorbell rang. Javi sprang from his desk chair to intercept whoever it was before his siblings could pepper the poor soul(s) with inappropriate questions. He managed to make it downstairs before anyone else got to the door. He flung it open to find Bex, Chase, and Hana standing on his stoop.

"Hey, guys." He held open the door to let them in. "Welcome to mi casa."

His grandmother shuffled her slippered feet into the room to see who was visiting so late at night. She was wrapped in a quilted housecoat.

"Mijo, what are all these people doing here? It's so late."

"Study group, Abuela. Big test coming up." He began shepherding them up the stairs and toward his room.

His grandmother was not appeased by his answer. "Pero es viernes."

"Yeah, it's Friday, but the test is on Monday. No such thing as too much studying."

She hummed unhappily in the back of her throat but seemed to accept the answer. "You can't study on an empty stomach. Let me get you something to eat."

"No, Abuela, it's okay," Javi started, but she was already on her way to the kitchen.

"Your grandma is super cute," Hana said.

"And honestly," said Chase, "I could eat."

"Fine, fine," Javi said. "Go upstairs. I'll bring snacks. Noah and Tamsin are in my room. Last door on the left."

Javi followed his grandmother into the kitchen. The microwave was spinning as she warmed up a plate of tostones. She made them in batches too huge even for a family of their size.

"You've never had so many friends over at once," she commented as they waited for the microwave to ding.

Javi wasn't sure if they were all friends, or if they were all just a bunch of individuals thrown together by circumstance. Or if there was a difference between the two.

"Yeah," Javi said. "It's nice. They're actually pretty cool."

"I'm happy." The microwave beeped as the timer hit zero. She turned to take the plate out. "You spend too much time on that computer. You should talk to people more, face-to-face."

"Yeah, I know." It was an old topic of conversation. His grandmother had never been able to comprehend that most of

Javi's meaningful relationships were conducted over the internet. He was friendly with people from school, but being friendly wasn't quite the same as being friends. But tonight he was just glad that the novelty of living, breathing humans in their house, by Javi's invitation, was enough for her to overlook the oddity of their eleven o'clock study group. "Thanks, Abuela. Now go back to bed. You work too hard."

She patted his cheek. "You're a good boy, mijo."

He accepted the heaping plate of tostones and gently coaxed her out of the doorway but not before he caught sight of the delighted little smile gracing her face. Nothing made her happier than extra mouths to feed. Nothing.

The others fell on his grandmother's tostones like ravenous beasts once he presented them with the plate. All except Hana. Tamsin offered her one, but she politely demurred.

Tamsin frowned. "Please?"

Javi watched as Hana hesitated, then reluctantly took a tostón. She broke it in half and took a dainty bite before setting the other half back down. Tamsin looked inordinately pleased by this.

There was something going on there, but it was probably not Javi's business.

"Holy crap," Chase said, his mouth full. "These are amazing. Can your grandma adopt me?"

"I'm sure she'd love to. She's never had an athletic appetite to feed. She'd live for the challenge."

"Nice." Chase helped himself to another tostón. "I'll have my people draw up the paperwork."

"Here's Summer's device." Bex offered Javi the necklace by its long golden chain. The actual device looked like a locket with the Rawlins family crest emblazoned on the front. Javi was deeply amused that they had a crest at all. He pressed the clasp on the side to open it. Summer's rating blinked into existence on the display.

81.

"Not for long," Javi said with a dark chuckle.

"Your evil laugh is unsettling," Noah said as he perched on the arm of Javi's desk chair. "But I kind of like it."

"Good, because honestly, it feels really natural. I think a life of crime suits me." Javi set the pendant on his desk and adjusted his lamp to shine directly on it. It would take very fine, delicate tools and steady hands to remove the back paneling and access the tiny chip inside. No one's hands were steadier than Javi's. He ranked in the top 5 percent on headshots from a distance in *Polaris*, after all.

The others ate and paid only vague attention to what Javi was doing. He didn't mind. He had Noah there to help him if he needed it. And it was kind of nice to not be alone in his room, playing video games in the dark. Not that he'd ever admit that to his abuela. She'd be unbearably smug about it.

"Tamsin," Javi said. "I need your smartwatch."

She slipped it off and tossed it to Noah, who caught it before it could smack Javi on the side of the head. "Sorry," she said. "What do you need it for?"

"You'll see."

With both chips out of their casings and inserted into the not entirely legal microchip reader he'd purchased from a not entirely legal website that may or may not have existed on the dark web, he got to work.

"What are you doing?" Noah asked. His breath ghosted over the shell of Javi's ear. It tickled a bit, but in a good way.

"Tweaking the algorithm," Javi said as his hands flew over his keyboard. He was in the zone. Nothing could stop him when he was in the zone.

"Okay, cool," Noah said. After a beat he added, "What does that mean?"

Nothing could stop him save for the opportunity to explain his brilliance to a willing audience. "I'm altering the settings of Summer's rating interface. Whenever someone tries to dock Tamsin's rating, it'll bypass her and add a positive rating to Summer's numerical score."

"Wait what?" Tamsin fixed Javi with a glare that could have seared the skin off a weaker man. "Why are we boosting her rating?"

Javi smiled, slow and languid. "Tell 'em, Noah."

"Because," Noah said, "nothing gets you on the administration's radar faster than a sudden and inexplicable surge in your number. Accounts that show a wild uptick in positive activity are automatically flagged for review."

"And," Javi added, "since I'm such a genius—"

"And modest, too," Noah said.

"—I left a few breadcrumbs for the authorities to find when they investigate Summer Rawlins."

"What kind of breadcrumbs?" Bex asked.

"Enough to make it look like she hacked the system herself." Javi relished the way Noah grinned at him, proud and devious. "When they dive into her base code, they'll see that alterations were made using her own device. All roads lead back to Summer."

"Where does that leave me?" Tamsin asked.

"That leaves you the poor unfortunate victim of Summer's cruelty. She deliberately tried to sabotage your rating by orchestrating a pile-on, and these markers will make it look like she tried to boost her own at the same time. Sloppily. Your account will also get flagged for review. They'll reset your rating to what it was before this tragic, precipitous drop. I bet those kids who hopped on Summer's mean-girl bandwagon will also find their own ratings docked."

Tamsin let out a low, impressed whistle. "Dude. You're good. Like, crazy good."

Javi preened. "I know. Now eat up and pull out some books or something before my grandma realizes we're not actually studying."

CHAPTER 30
TAMSIN MOORE

RATING: 34

On Monday, Tamsin walked out of Headmaster Wood's office trying to fight the too-wide grin that desperately wanted to blossom on her face.

Summer Rawlins had been suspended. She was currently being investigated for ratings malfeasance, both her own and Tamsin's. Maplethorpe had a zero-tolerance policy for such behavior, Headmaster Wood had insisted. They would closely monitor Summer's activity as well as her circle of friends (minions, Tamsin's brain supplied) to make sure there were no further incidents. He had relayed the information to Tamsin in a tone dripping with apology. He probably wanted to make sure she didn't raise a stink about the school's inaction when it was clear she was being targeted by Summer's smear campaign. And she wouldn't. The less attention she drew to herself and her new friends the better.

It was odd, thinking of them as friends, but nothing brought people together like a crime jointly committed. That was the sort of thing that expedited the friendship process.

It felt different, walking out to the school's lawn during Rest Period and knowing there were people waiting for her at one of the wooden picnic tables she usually avoided. They were the homes of cliques and clubs, not loners like her. But she wasn't alone now. It was different. Not bad different, but good different.

The message Tamsin had sent to the group chat before her meeting said to meet at the table by the old oak tree, the one farthest from the main building. All the better to avoid being overheard by curious students and nosy faculty. She knew the others would be dying for an update.

When she reached the table, Hana scooted over to let Tamsin sit beside her. There was a salad of mixed greens and tomatoes in a bento box in front of Hana, and it looked like she was actually eating it. It wasn't much, but maybe it was a start.

"What did Wood say?" Bex asked.

It did not escape Tamsin's notice that a too-large maroon Maplethorpe jacket was draped over Bex's shoulders. Tamsin winked at Chase, who quirked an eyebrow at her, daring her to comment. She didn't. Already she was growing as a person!

Noah and Javi sat side by side, sharing an order of fries from the cafeteria. Javi had mentioned that the lunch lady always put some aside for him in case he missed the fourth-period rush.

Lucky.

"Summer got suspended," Tamsin said. "And they reset my rating." She held up her wrist so the others could see her new number, which was really her old number. "Still sucks, but it's not expulsion level of suck."

"So, what do we do now?" Chase asked. "Do we stop here or . . ."

"Or do we find other sad sacks like me to help?" Tamsin ventured.

"You're not a sad sack," Hana said. She popped a cherry tomato in her mouth and offered one to Tamsin. She accepted it. It exploded on her tongue in a burst of flavor.

"That's kind of you to say." Tamsin only half meant it. She was still trying to accept the fact that these people she hardly knew put themselves on the line for her. They didn't even know her. Maybe if they did, they wouldn't want to help her. She wasn't a nice person. She'd never tried to be one. But maybe, just maybe, she wasn't as bad as she thought she was.

"A friend of mine said there was similar graffiti at her university in London," Javi said. "About the ratings not being real. This could be way bigger than Maplethorpe."

"London?" Tamsin asked. "As in England?"

"Like an ocean away?" Bex's voice was tinged with the same budding excitement she'd shown on that fateful night at Lucky's, when an unseen force had thrown them all together.

"That would be the one, yeah," Javi said. "Could be something to follow up on."

"Guess we have our next mission," Noah said. "After my sister."

"So, are we like a team now?" Hana asked. "Is this what we do?"

"Crime-fighting cyber vigilantes," Chase said. "Wicked."

"Are we fighting crime, or are we fighting something else entirely?" Noah asked.

Hana frowned, puzzled. "What do you mean?"

"I mean," Noah said, "what we did was fight something that was technically legal, so it's not a crime. But we all knew it was wrong."

Bex nodded. "Like how tweaking the Magnolia hospital records to keep your sister there isn't legal, but it is right." She turned to Javi. "By the way, what do you need for that?"

"Access to a hospital computer terminal would be great. Can you get me in?" Javi asked.

"My mom did say there was an internship position available . . ."

"That could work," Javi said. "All we need is a reason to be there without arousing too much suspicion."

"Man, you guys are crafty," Tamsin said. "Though I'm not surprised. I'd expect nothing less from the girl who convinced her parents to let her boyfriend move in."

Chase barked out a laugh as he darted in to kiss Bex on the cheek. "That's my girl. A criminal mastermind."

Bex sank her teeth into her lower lip to quell her wicked grin. "It really wasn't that hard. All I had to do was mention that Chase needed a place to stay and that doing something charitable for a member of the Maplethorpe community was in their best interest."

"And it helped when Headmaster Wood told them the school's board of trustees would make sure their ratings got a nice bump."

"Did it bother your dad when you moved out?" Hana asked.

Chase shrugged. It didn't escape Tamsin's notice that he would close off at the mention of his father. From what she'd been able to glean, the elder Donovan was a real piece of work.

"Nope. He didn't even put up a fight. Doubt he even notices I'm gone."

Bex wrapped her hand around Chase's and gave it a gentle squeeze.

"Forget him," Tamsin said. "You have a new family now. A crime family."

Javi nudged Chase on the shoulder with his fist. It was too soft to be called a punch. "That's right. And to think, we already have our next job lined up, all thanks to Bex's cunning."

"Does it worry anyone else how quickly we've taken to this?" Hana asked.

"Not really."

"Nope."

"Nah."

"Do you want out?" Tamsin asked.

Hana shook her head. "No. I just . . . didn't really see myself joining a high school cybercrime syndicate is all."

Javi laughed as he dipped a fry into a small container of what looked like barbecue sauce. Gross. "That's not an unreasonable expectation to have," he said, "but isn't it kind of fun?"

On this, they agreed. There was a sense of liberation in what they had done. No longer were they victims of circumstance or dehumanized numbers in a system. They had control. They had agency. They saw something wrong, and they did something about it.

It felt a lot better than misanthropy ever had. Not that Tamsin would admit that out loud. She had a reputation to maintain.

"Hey," Hana said, "is that Summer?"

They all turned to see a girl storming out of the doors—the very same ones that had been spray-painted what felt like a lifetime ago—and stomp down the stairs. With a huff, she threw herself down on a stone bench near the front of the school and began furiously typing something on her phone. Texting her minions, most likely. Tamsin wondered how many of them would stick by her side now that she'd lost her crown. No one wanted to be associated with ratings malfeasance. If Summer wasn't already persona non grata with her old court, she would be soon.

"I'll be right back." Tamsin pushed up and away from the table. "There's something I gotta do first."

"Are you sure that's a good idea?" Bex asked.

"Yeah," Chase said. "Maybe don't poke the bear."

Tamsin snagged one of Noah and Javi's fries. "I'm gonna poke the bear."

"Tamsin, just leave it," Hana said, but Tamsin was already walking toward the bench.

She saw the moment Summer recognized her as she drew closer. The girl's posture changed from angry to defensive, like a wild animal bracing for attack. Her back straightened and her face hardened into a scowl. She scrubbed at her eyes with her sleeve. She'd been crying.

"What do *you* want?" Summer asked. "Come here to gloat?"

"I don't know what you're talking about," Tamsin said.

With a disbelieving snort, Summer reached into the pocket of her Maplethorpe blazer and produced a packet of bubble gum. She held Tamsin's gaze as she drew a strip out of the package and popped it in her mouth. She chewed, loudly, then blew an obnoxiously large bubble. Its pop was even more obnoxious. Gum was banned on Maplethorpe's campus, mainly to discourage students from sticking it under desks or spitting it on walkways. Students caught with such sugary contraband were subjected to an automatic one-point deduction.

"Gum?" Tamsin asked. "On school grounds? Scandalous."

Summer smacked her gum. The sound was obnoxiously loud. "What are they gonna do? Kick me out? Pretty sure Wood's already working on that."

"Might as well rebel while you're at it, huh?"

Summer heaved a drawn-out sigh. "What do you want, Tamsin? I don't know how you did it, but you won. You don't have to rub it in."

The defiance seemed to bleed out of Summer in slow spurts, like a wound expelling the last blood pumped by a dying heart. She looked small in a way she never had before.

"They won't talk to me, you know." Summer held up her phone and wiggled it at Tamsin. "No one's responding to my texts. It's like I don't even exist."

Tamsin really didn't want to ask what she was about to ask. She didn't. She really, really didn't. Except, she kind of did. Maybe it was morbid curiosity, but the sight of the girl who'd nearly tormented her to expulsion sitting on a stump and crying wasn't as satisfying as she thought it would be.

"Are you okay?" Tamsin asked.

Summer hastily wiped at her eyes again. All it did was smudge her eyeliner. "What do you care?"

"Because I'm not a complete jerk," Tamsin said.

Summer snorted. That was answer enough.

"Okay, fine. I'm kind of a jerk, but I'm trying this new thing where I'm not as much of one," Tamsin said. And because she *was* kind of a jerk, she added, "You should try it some time."

Summer let out a startled little laugh. "Yeah. Maybe."

Tamsin sat down on the bench beside Summer. The other girl shot her a confused glare but didn't object. Not out loud anyway.

"It's just . . . why?"

Why did you try to ruin my life? Why are you like this? Why are you so cruel? Why was I cruel in return? All those questions, filtered into a single, effective word.

"When Steve was with Sasha, he showed her the stuff I sent him. Like, all of it. Every text. Every email. Every photo I'd ever sent. Even the ones I'd only ever meant for him to see."

"Oh," Tamsin said. "That's messed up."

"And that wasn't even the worst part. They put them online. The texts . . . those weren't a big deal, but the pictures . . ." Summer scrubbed at her tearstained cheeks with her sleeve. "My parents saw them. And I just . . . I cannot explain to you how mortifying that was. My parents tried to get them taken down but . . ."

"But once something's on the internet, it's on there forever." A twinge of sympathy coiled in Tamsin's gut. No one deserved that. Not even Summer.

"Yeah, and they told me you did it. That someone sent you the pics and you put them up. I could just imagine you up in that music room laughing at me. It drove me crazy."

"That sucks and all," said Tamsin, "but you know that wasn't my fault."

"I know," Summer said. "I never really believed it was. None of us would ever be caught dead texting you, it's just that . . . god, you made such an easy target."

"Wow," Tamsin said with a startled laugh. "It's kind of impressive how you can just come out and say that."

Summer shrugged. "What have I got to lose? I'm about to get kicked out of Maplethorpe. Every generation of Rawlins has graduated from this school for the past hundred years. I'll be the first to leave in disgrace. Might as well clear my conscience as well as my locker."

"Oh, I'm sure you'll be back," Tamsin said. "There's nothing Rawlins money can't buy."

Summer snorted. "You're not wrong there."

Tamsin looked out over the rolling hills of the Maplethorpe campus. The verdant trees just beginning to change. In a few weeks, instead of a sea of green, the school would be surrounded by waves of autumn gold and crimson. "It's kind of messed up when you think about it."

Summer just shrugged. "It's how the world works."

"Yeah," Tamsin said. "For now."

Summer took her gum out of her mouth, holding it in a dainty grip between two fingers, and then flicked it toward the center of the walkway. Perfect for someone to step on later. "Never would have pegged you for the optimistic type." She stood, wiping her hands on her artfully ripped jeans. "Well, I'm out. Try not to burn the place down while I'm gone."

"I make no promises," Tamsin said. She really, really didn't.

"Course not."

"I never hated you, you know." Tamsin wasn't sure why she said it, only that it felt right to say it.

"I don't know why," Summer said. "I'm pretty easy to hate."

"Maybe that's why we don't get along," said Tamsin. "We've got too much in common."

For perhaps the first time since they'd both started at Maplethorpe as two opposing poles of the social spectrum, Summer Rawlins and Tamsin Moore smiled at each other. And they both almost meant it.

EPILOGUE

On the appointed day, at the appointed time, six teenagers approached the abandoned music building on Maplethorpe's campus. Flashlights illuminated their path. The security system had been disabled—another act of Tamsin's brilliance—but they tried to be quiet anyway. It wouldn't do to get caught this close to having answers. Real, substantial answers.

Tamsin led the way. She didn't need a flashlight to illuminate the ground before her. She knew the path by heart. The building had been her refuge from a place that never belonged to her and to which she had never belonged. Until the possibility that it would be taken away from her became alarmingly real, she hadn't thought she would ever miss it. But Maplethorpe, with all its flaws, all its blemishes and sins, had forged her into the person she felt herself becoming. She would always be a misanthropic cynic, but she was beginning to think that maybe she could be that and more.

Hana held on to the sleeve of Tamsin's wool sweater (a nice deep eggplant color to complement the rest of her outfit). She worried about tripping over something in the dark, like a rock or a fallen branch. She'd run out of excuses to skip practice with Dmitriev. In six hours, she had to be on the ice, ready to give the triple Axel another try. She knew she would likely fall, again and again and again, but nothing was ever gained by giving up. Her coach had also made an appointment for her after school in lieu of practice. He hadn't said what the appointment was for, but she'd googled the name of the doctor. A sports psychologist with experience dealing with elite athletes. Hana didn't protest. She hadn't thanked him either; she wasn't sure yet if she was grateful for the intervention, but she was aware that she needed it.

Bex wrapped her arms tight around her middle. It was cold, despite the fact that autumn had only just begun to set in. The Hudson Valley was like that. Warm one minute and then cold as an arctic wind the next. Chase's jacket hung from her shoulders, sealing in some of her body heat. She hadn't asked for it. She'd simply shivered and then felt its solid weight dropped onto her shoulders. She glanced at him. He was close enough that she could just make out his facial expression. A small smile and a hand self-consciously rubbing the back of his neck. She whispered a soft thanks and tried to make it not so obvious when she breathed in the scent of him from the collar of the jacket. It was nice. And it would probably distract her a great deal in the days to come, but maybe, just maybe, distractions weren't all bad. It certainly felt nicer than having her brain run circles around itself like a distressed Pomeranian.

Chase was cold. He tried not to show it, but it was cold out. But the sight of Bex being swallowed up by his jacket warmed something deep inside that he couldn't quite name. Earning that letter jacket had meant so much to him. It had symbolized all the things he craved so desperately. A chance to be something, to be someone. A road out of Jackson Hills and away from a life that fit him so poorly. He'd never let anyone else touch it. He'd cared for it, spot cleaning it in the privacy of his own room while his father relived the glory of his own letter jacket days downstairs. It had been a lifeline. An opportunity. But now, he thought that maybe Bex wore it better than he ever did. And now that he was living in her guest room, he'd get the chance to see her wearing it a lot more often.

Noah's hand was warm in Javi's. Neither of them had spoken when Javi reached out and took it. A part of him had worried that Noah wouldn't be receptive to the sort of casual contact Javi craved. An even bigger part of him thrilled when Noah gave his hand a quick squeeze in return, holding on as they walked toward the music building. Javi was a tactile person. Always had been. He'd stepped into the void left by his parents, cared for his little brothers and sisters when they were sick and his abuela was overextended. He'd tucked them into bed, and felt their foreheads for fevers, and rubbed their backs when they cried, and held them when they had nightmares and crawled into his bed, their faces sticky with tears. Love meant being there, physically. He knew it was too early to drop a bomb like that on Noah, but the feeling still exploded in his chest in the most pleasurable way. *One day*, Javi thought. One day, he'd tell him.

It was nice, Noah thought, *to be touched like that*. He hadn't realized how starved for touch he'd been until Javi had started doing it so casually. A shoulder leaning against Noah's own. Their thighs touching under a table at Lucky's. A hand holding his as they picked their way across the Maplethorpe lawn, toward what he hoped would be a conclusion to the odd series of events that had led them to this moment. Every time Javi's skin brushed his own, Noah was reminded that he was there. He was present. He was wonderfully alive. He'd thought he liked experiencing the world through the filter of a lens, had found comfort in the distance, but he was beginning to think that maybe immersion could be just as fascinating as observation.

When they reached the building, Tamsin paused, one hand on the door. "You guys sure about this?"

"Not really," Bex admitted.

Chase just shrugged. "What's the worst that could happen?"

"There could be an ax murderer lying in wait," Hana supplied.

"Yeah, but what are the odds of that happening?" Javi asked.

"That sounds like exactly the sort of thing someone would say right before they got ax-murdered in a horror movie," Noah said.

"Okay, great, so we're all gonna die." Tamsin rolled her eyes and pushed the door open, the creaking of its hinges loud in the quiet of the night. "Let's go."

They went.

It was dark inside, but a sliver of light shined from the upstairs landing. They shared glances ranging from curiosity to concern. But still, they went, following the siren song of that light up the groaning staircase. Tamsin knew which steps to avoid to keep her tread light, but the others didn't. This was her domain, not theirs.

The door at the end of the hall was open just enough to emit a triangle of amber light. It flickered as they approached. Candlelight then, perfect for dancing in the persistent breezes that made their way through the building's old bones.

The door swung open under Tamsin's gentle push, silent and slow. They crowded at the threshold, each of them just as silent.

Chase broke first. "What the—"

"Headmaster Wood?" Bex pushed her way to the forefront of their little group.

The headmaster was alone. He wasn't dressed the way he normally was at school. Gone were the immaculately tailored suits and the pressed slacks and the shining wingtips. He looked younger, clad in dark jeans and a thick burgundy sweater. He smiled when he saw them.

"Oh, good. You all decided to come. I was a bit worried one or two of you would get cold feet."

"Again," Chase said, "what the—"

"Is this a trick?" Tamsin asked. "Are we getting expelled? Are you messing with us?"

Wood held up his hands in a gesture of placation. "No one's getting expelled. Especially not now that you've cracked the code."

"The code in the messages?" Noah asked. "Or . . ."

"The ratings code," Javi said, his tone hushed with realization. "It was a test."

Tamsin's glare darted from Wood to Javi and back again. "Excuse me?"

"Yeah, wait, what?" Hana looked as puzzled as Tamsin, if not as outraged.

"You made it look easy, Javier," Wood said. "It's not. Trust me, we would know."

"Who's we?" Bex asked. She stood in front of the group, the shortest of them all but no less fierce for her stature.

"I think you know, Rebecca." Wood gestured for them to come farther into the room. They did but not without a great deal of reluctance. Of all the faces to find behind that door, his was not the one they were expecting to see.

"What do you mean it was a test?" Tamsin asked.

A strangled little laugh escaped Bex. "To see if we could manipulate the Rating System."

"And not just that," Wood said. "We wanted to see if you would do it for someone else. If you would work together for the benefit of a person you barely knew."

"Why?" Chase asked.

"Because it was the right thing to do. We had to make sure that you understood the distinction between legal and right. Between crime and sin. How one isn't always the other."

"That's super philosophical and all," Noah said. "But why us?"

"Wait, wait, wait." Tamsin waved her hands, shushing the others. "I was a test. *A test?* You almost ruined my life for a test?"

Wood had the decency to look at least somewhat apologetic. "It needed to be real. There had to be something at stake. Something important."

"Oh my god." Tamsin threw her head back, laughing a deep, full-bodied laugh that made the others jump. It was more of a cackle than anything else. "The Hanged Man. I was the freaking Hanged Man for your weird social experiment."

"Why would you do that to her?" Hana was less puzzled, but her outrage was building.

"Because," Bex said, "it brought us together. It brought us here."

"But why?" Noah added. "Why us?"

"Change has to start somewhere," Wood said. "It has to start with you. With people like you. People who look at something wrong and say, 'No more.' People who see the chains we've built for ourselves."

"'Man is born free,'" Bex recited. "'And everywhere he is in chains.'"

Wood smiled at that. "I'm glad that message reached you. I was worried it wouldn't. After all, how many kids remember the things they read ten years ago?"

"Bex would," Chase muttered.

"Indeed." Wood sat on the corner of a table and clasped his hands loosely across his lap. "I have to admit, defacing poor old John Maplethorpe wasn't my idea, but you can't deny the efficacy of good theater."

"You haven't answered my question." Noah walked farther into the room. He'd dropped Javi's hand, but the warmth of it clung to him still. It made him feel stronger. Not quite invincible but almost. "Why us *specifically*?"

"A number of reasons," Wood said. "Some of you have reasons to hate the system." He looked at Noah, like the tragic backstory of his life was written across his skin. At Chase, like he could see the ghosts of faded bruises. At Tamsin, who had never hid her disdain for something that always felt so unfair. "Some of you are already uniquely poised to take up positions of influence, to become people others look to for guidance." He looked at Bex as he said it. "For inspiration." Now at Hana. "Or for their unique skills." Javi. "All that matters. All that *will* matter."

"You want us to change the world," Bex said. She'd understood from the moment she'd stepped over that threshold.

Perhaps a part of her had always understood precisely what was being asked of them.

Wood nodded. "To go big, sometimes you have to start small. Tamsin was a test case."

"Still not sure I appreciate that by the way," Tamsin interjected.

"But," Wood continued, "things will get harder from here on out. Helping one person is only the start. We mean to help a lot more people than that. And eventually, we want the ratings to disappear. We want them to be nothing more than a dark chapter in our history. One we can look back on and learn from."

"What if we don't want any part of this?" Hana asked.

Wood gestured toward the door. "You're welcome to leave."

"Bull," Tamsin said. "We know too much."

"Maybe so." Wood fixed her with a knowing look. "But I don't think any of you want to leave. You came here for a reason. You helped one another for a reason. You didn't turn around the second you saw me—for a reason."

The words resonated in the silence.

"So," Hana started, her voice soft, "I can leave?"

Tamsin's lips pressed into a thin line, but she said nothing.

"You can," Wood replied. "But do you want to?"

Hana looked at each of her friends in turn, Tamsin last. "No. No, I don't."

"You realize," Javi said, "that you're encouraging us to commit illegal activity for the sake of destabilizing a governmental agency, right?"

"Is that a complaint?" Wood asked.

Javi smiled. Noah smiled with him. "No way."

Tamsin giggled. She hadn't thought herself capable of such a sound, but she supposed stranger things had happened. Stranger things were happening in that moment. "This is wild. I'm in."

"So am I," Chase said. He was almost taken aback by his own readiness, but he couldn't deny the rightness of it. It felt like an anchor, like a certainty, when all he'd ever felt was anything but. He reached for Bex's hand, brushing aside the thick fabric of his own letter jacket to take it.

Bex looked at him. Then she looked at the others. Her resolve solidified. It felt right. It felt good. "I'm in, too."

"I just have one question . . . how did you get the messages to us?" Hana asked. "Mine was hidden in my diary."

"And mine was on the back of a photo I took," Noah added.

"Mine was in my locker," said Chase.

"And mine was taped to my locker when I was in your office," Tamsin said. *"With you."*

Wood's smile was equal parts pleased and enigmatic. "This isn't a one-man operation. There are plenty of people who want to see this system burn. They helped."

"And let me guess: You're not gonna tell us who those people are," Javi said.

"Let's just say they're the ones you least expect. People you don't take much notice of. Even people who seem to enjoy the status quo."

"That's nice and vague," said Tamsin.

"Sometimes, the less you know, the better. At least for now. It helps maintain the security of the operation. If one channel goes down, there are others."

"I don't like the way that sounds," Bex said with a frown.

"Is it weird," Javi asked, "that I kind of do?"

"Yes," Noah said, but he was still smiling.

"I just have one more question." It was a question that had been plaguing Bex since the very first day of school that semester, when the first message had been left in a messy scrawl at the entrance to Maplethorpe Academy. "Why jesters?"

Mirth danced in Wood's eyes. "Jesters made fools of kings and their kingdoms. They spoke truth to the power. And they got away with it, in part because they were underestimated—after all, who would take them seriously? But also because deep down, even the most powerful among their targets knew that their jabs and japes rung true. And there's another reason, one more arcane than that."

He looked to Tamsin then, expectation written across his face.

"The fool," she said. "Another term for a jester. Also the first card in the Major Arcana of most tarot decks." She smiled, appreciating the circuitous nature of the sentiment. Where one cycle ended, another began. "It's the start of something new. A journey. An adventure."

Wood pushed himself away from the table to stand before them. "It's dangerous, what we're proposing. Change won't come easy and it won't come cheap. But I think you all know that it must come. The way we live now . . . it's not right. And I don't think I'm mistaken in believing that you all feel the same."

One by one, they nodded. Bex and Chase and Tamsin and Hana and Noah and Javi. They had come this far together and they would go farther still. The night was young, and so were they.

"Good. I was hoping you'd say that." A genuine smile spread across Headmaster Wood's face, full of a dash of pride and a heap of mischief. "Welcome to the revolution."

ACKNOWLEDGMENTS

Every book is its own beast, with its own unique quirks and foibles. *Rated* was no different. It wasn't a book I would have imagined myself writing years ago, but I'm glad I did. But it never would have gotten off the ground without the help of a few lovely and indispensable individuals.

Catherine Drayton: Thank you for having faith in me when my own started to waver. You're the best agent I could have asked for. Seriously.

David Levithan: Thank you for welcoming me to the Scholastic family. I distinctly remember how transformative an experience it was to find *Boy Meets Boy* in my high school's library, and I'm still (and will always be) a little in awe of you.

Zack Clark: Thank you for helping me slap this book into shape. It was a weird, wonderful journey, and I was glad to have you with me on it.

Virginia Boecker: Thank you for listening to me moan and complain about every little thing while I was writing this book. I'd be lost without you.

Amanda, Idil, and Laura: The distance between us may be great (or small), but knowing that there were at least three people in the universe who wanted to read whatever nonsense I wrote was sometimes the only thing that kept me going.

And last but never ever least, my readers: Thank you for sharing a little slice of your time in this vast, unknowable universe with me. There are no words to describe how much that means to any writer, so I won't even try.

ABOUT THE AUTHOR

Melissa Grey is the author of The Girl at Midnight trilogy and *Rated*. She currently works as a freelance writer and lives in New York City.